IF YOUR WORLD SHOULD FALL APART

A novel

Jean Anthony

ALSO BY JEAN ANTHONY

You Were Always On My Mind

You're The One That I Love

AS JS ANTHONY

Charlotte

Sarah Mayfield

© 2023 by Jean Anthony

This is a work of fiction. Names, characters, places, events, organizations and incidents are either products of the author's imagination or are used fictitiously. Any resemblance to actual persons, living or dead, or actual events is purely coincidental.

All rights reserved.

No part of this book may be reproduced, or stored in a retrieval system, or transmitted in any form or by any means, electronic, mechanical, photocopying, recording, or otherwise, without express written permission of the author.

EDISONBOOKS

chapter 1

MILLER WALKED OUT of the house and closed the door. She didn't turn back to look one last time at anything, not even the ocean. The car sat in the driveway packed to the roof. The map was on the dashboard, but she knew where she was going. Into the heart of L.A. traffic, which took every ounce of anyone's courage. Then over the mountains, down into the Central Valley were there were fields as far as the eye could see, cattle, small towns no one ever heard of, dust and heat and glare. After that, it would be north on I-5 forever.

She thought she would finally be forced to slow down coming along the Trinity, thought the adrenaline rush to get far away, an easy *thousand miles* away, would leave her. Instead, the mountains, with their dark pine-covered slopes towering overhead on one side, falling into deep valleys on the other, dictated a relentless pace. The competing road signs launched an assault: *pass, don't pass, construction zone, trucks use lower gears*. Drivers frustrated by a mere two lanes added to the nerve-wracking atmosphere. They roared up behind her: a pickup, a van, something low-slung and rumbling, oh God a logging truck, its huge grill taking up all of the rearview mirror. A fist hit a horn and headlights flashed signaling the universal message: pull over, get out of the way, do it *now*. In her own environment, the 805 and its surroundings in southern California, Miller would at least have thrown the finger. Here in the shaded half-wilderness of what wasn't really yet, but already seemed to be another state, another country, not having one shred of familiarity with the local mindset, she pulled over, too rattled by the rush, the heat, to even look up.

Aware of an unwelcome tremor in her hands, she let her eyes rest on the river. Clear water rippled over rocks and settled in mossy pools. Peaceful was the unaccustomed adjective that flashed through her brain. Then she had to get back on the road.

As the mountains gave way in a steep decline, the temperature dropped and the fog rolled in. The coolness proved welcome, then grew less welcome, bordering on cold, or in the world Miller had come from, freezing. Now there *was* a new state and instantly, it seemed, a new climate. With her right hand she rummaged through the clothing on the floor of the passenger seat, trying to untangle a sweatshirt jacket by yanking on one of its sleeves. The steering wheel jerked, requiring the quickest of reflexes. The tremor resided in her knees as well. She'd been on the road since before dawn on this, the third day of her journey. The mountains had only hindered her progress, though this had been a conscious decision, to cross over that span of green on the map and travel the last of the journey north along the coast. It was all part of the mandated attempt to get a grip on things, the attempt that wasn't working.

The ocean view motel room for which she'd paid extra, meaning still not very much, came with one drawback that Miller hadn't taken into account. There was no ocean view. Here on a cold gray afternoon before Labor Day the thick fog obscured every landmark including the cliff path on which guests walked their dogs. She could hear murmured voices, muted barking, but couldn't see people, dogs or her car in the parking lot, let alone the Pacific Ocean fifty feet away.

In a convenience store she purchased dinner, nachos in a Styrofoam container. She looked over the refrigerated section and decided a Corona suited her mood. Maybe two suited it even more. Back in the room, she pulled the drapes, shutting out the

4

nonexistent view. She typed out only one quick reassuring text and sent it to three people. Then it would be a shower, a book and bed.

In the bathroom, she reluctantly looked in the mirror. Dark hair piled up and anchored with a chopstick. Dark eyes, not as bloodshot as she thought they'd be after three days of road glare. Skin, tan, soon to be faded, a given in a land noted first for torrential rain. Nothing worse than laugh lines, no ripe bloom of youth left but who cared, the bloom of youth was overrated. Too thin, or at least thinner than she had been by a lot, though good bone structure and long legs hopefully still counted for something. The shadow lurking faintly behind even the most innocent expressions, what to do about that? Nothing.

The early morning coastal highway proved no more useful at slowing down the pace, though it should have due to its tough stance on straightaways. There were none. The twists and bends came tight on each other, sometimes cliff on one side and an incongruous elk crossing sign on the other. Miller glanced quickly at the signs, registering only the question of where an elk crossing the road might be going. The sole option was down into the surf.

It should have been the haystack rock formations offshore, the lifting green waves, the dramatic drift from fog to dazzling sunlight that brought her up short, filled with awe. She found appreciation where she could, but awe wasn't in her range these days. Instead, finally, it was the small towns, one after the other, that slowed her down, filled more often than not with back road tourists, the wharf smelling of fish, the shore of rotting timber, the green fields high with the stink of cows.

Stop, she told herself. Try it. Make yourself stop.

The dunes beckoned, huge, monumental, a worthy destination, a natural wonder. The small parking lot held too many posted cautions about theft. Miller climbed one dune and sat on a log on the other side staring at the cold ocean. In her car was approximately everything she now cared about, not all that much of value, but still. She quickly traced her steps back through the soft sand. She'd been warned about criminals, drug addicts, drunken fishermen. She hadn't taken the warnings seriously. There were two RVs in the lot, parked next to each other, one bearing a mural of Mount Rushmore on its side. Her car stood alone, no drug addicts in sight.

The two lanes continued to snake their way alongside the rough waves, with sometimes an abrupt turn inland, sometimes open vistas to miles of gray sand, past tiny strip malls, endless green fields and signs that said only: Rocks. Now and then she caught a glimpse of people on the beach. In the first week of September, they wore coats with hoods, gloves, scarves. The fog had closed in again.

The town names began to be familiar. She was getting close. She clicked a CD into the player, one of the requirements, *The Dreamer: Romances For Alto Flute, Volume 2.* Miller shook her head. Anyone who knew her would think this was a joke, her listening to mood music, holy, haunting, quiet, anything that said New Age on it and involved, or was limited to, a flute. You aren't me, she thought, you haven't been where I've been.

The heavily forested incline appeared first, on the other side of which, she knew, lay the comparatively upscale beach town of Pine Ridge with its chic higher-end clothing stores and gift shops, interesting art galleries, a well-stocked bookstore. Next up the coast, the less upscale town of Oceanview with its bars and restaurants offering steak and fried seafood. It was all coming back to her now.

Lastly, at the traffic light, she turned onto the two-block main street of Winslow. Slowing down became the only option. The much-posted speed limit, strictly enforced, said twenty miles per hour. Slow down or else.

Where the street abruptly ended at the dunes, Miller turned again. Now everything was familiar, each weathered shingle house, vine-covered trellis, graveled drive. She nosed into the driveway several blocks from the pale green condos and windswept golf course that marked the end of the road. She rolled down the window and sat in the car, thankful to the hilt for this place but wondering how it was that she'd landed here where she never expected to be.

Miller dug her purse out of the pile of empty wrappers and containers beside her. She found the key and climbed stiffly out of the car. She could barely remember where she'd been yesterday, or the day before that, though she knew full well where she'd been three months ago. Secure and loved, right up until that moment when there was no security let alone love anymore, no solid ground under her feet, nothing left to hold onto. Lauren Metcalf had got all of it, everything there was to hold onto.

No drama, please, she told herself. No thinking about it right now either, another requirement. Stay in the moment, breathe, listen to your flute music. Seriously? She'd gone to see the woman who had a wall covered with degrees but insisted on being called Janelle, forget the professional terms, without having any faith that such a thing would help. She had to do something, though, that was clear. Falling apart in front of everyone wasn't an enviable response to a life crisis, bringing with it only the added benefits of public embarrassment and humiliation. Therefore, she refused to fall apart. She'd do this and make it work. Damn them all. Not her children, not JC and Sam and Dell, just everyone else.

The outside of her grandparents' house hadn't changed in all the forty-three years she'd known it or likely the fifty years before that. The cedar shake was still a faded silver gray, the front door was still the same shade of deep rose, the massive wall of rhododendrons still bloomed every year without fail.

Miller inserted the key into the lock, turned it and opened the door. Home. Or what would be home for now.

It was too much. Even choosing a route that stretched the journey out over four days didn't alleviate the shock of the transition. She was here. In Oregon. How could that possibly be? Miller needed to get out, take a walk, try that breathing thing again.

Closing the door behind her, turning deliberately away from the car still packed to the roof and coated with road dust, Miller went out into the narrow street and walked along it to where the condo parking lot sat beside a rough, half-paved beach access road. Along the edge of the golf course there had been a newspaper box for the well-known regional paper, *The Oregonian*. When the children were babies and her grandparents still alive, they'd all spent two weeks of the summers here as a family and that had been one of her small pleasures, to walk along the cypress-lined street, coffee in hand, and purchase the morning paper. Maybe it would be of some use, she thought, to perform that familiar errand one more time. Maybe it would be a start to making the journey less entirely surreal.

Surprisingly, the newspaper box was still there, wearing the same salt-pitted and faded mint green coat of paint, accessorized with the same battered, almost opaque plastic door. She fed in coins till the door opened on its tight spring and she could extract the day's news.

At the bottom of the access road, paper in hand, she turned first in one direction and then the other. Was it southern California? Not by any stretch of the imagination, not even close. Given that indisputable truth, this beach still offered up a host of positive attributes. In front of the long, gently rolling dunes, a broad expanse ran unbroken for a mile and a half south to the river. That same unbroken expanse stretched north for another nine miles, or about forever in beach terms, especially on this rough edge of the sea. Low tide created an immense area of solitude, the deepest lows now and then uncovering tide pools. Striking rock formations stood offshore. The horizon was endless. What more could you ask? Where do I start? Miller thought, a transgression immediately taken over by Janelle's calm but forceful voice spelling out the rules one more time, in case she'd missed them the first fifty times. Which Miller would admit, being brain dead back then, was exactly what had happened.

She heard the motorcycle before she saw it. Not a million decibel Harley, not a monster machine screaming through the gears, a bike with a still large but more muted whine, turning over slowly and coming to a quiet stop at the top of the access road. As she watched, the rider, dressed head to toe in black protective leather, shut off the engine. He eased slowly off the bike and lowered the kickstand. Carefully removing his helmet and setting it on the broad seat, he bent over, head down, hands on his knees, groaning in pain.

"Holy shit," he said to no one.

He was young, or younger anyway, and Miller registered him as safe. At least she was sure he wasn't a drunken fisherman.

"Are you okay?" she said.

He stood up and grimaced, pressing both hands into the small of his back. "I will be in about a week. Ouch. I can't tell you how much that hurts."

"I'm sorry," she said. "Seems like it was a long ride." The bike was loaded down with gear.

"So fucking long, from upstate New York by mostly back roads, whose brilliant idea was that? Worth it, don't get me wrong. I just wish somebody had told me what to do when your back goes out. Half a bottle of Advil didn't work and half a bottle of tequila didn't either."

"Maybe heat? Anyway, welcome to the Oregon coast. If this is where you wanted to end up, at least you made it."

"True," he said. "That's a hopeful way to look at it. Thanks." He ran his knuckles hard over the close-cropped dark hair that matched his unshaven jaw. "So you're from here?"

"I just realized what a stupid thing that was to say. Actually, no I'm not. I just got here myself something like twenty minutes ago."

"Then let me welcome you to the Oregon coast," he said, smiling. "Eli Greer." He held out his hand.

Miller stepped in, her handshake strong, she made a point of that, then stepped back again. "Cory Briggs," she said.

He winced. "Ouch again."

"Oh no," she said. "Did I hurt you?"

"No, it wasn't you, seems like it's just when I move a certain way. If it's okay to ask, how far did you come?"

"From north of San Diego, thirteen hundred miles give or take."

"You drove?"

"I did."

"San Diego," he said. "Never been there. Actually, I've never been anywhere out here."

"Out where?"

"West Coast, north to south, border to border, not anywhere."

"That's terrible."

"Seriously. What the hell. But I'm glad to be here." He inhaled. "Smells good," he said.

"I was thinking the same thing," Miller said. "I should go and at least make an attempt at digging all that stuff out of my car. It was nice meeting you."

"Likewise. You're here for a while?"

"Probably. I think so."

"Same here. Are you in the condos?" He nodded at the low gray-green buildings rising in curving rows up from the dunes, backed at the top by an ugly high rise.

"No. My grandmother's house is down the road."

"Well, thanks again for stopping. And if you ever need anything, come knocking. As I understand it, one of those doors over there is mine. No, wait a minute." He searched through several inside pockets and came up with a creased piece of paper. He smoothed it out and looked at it. "Four-fourteen. That would save some time. And if you see me still standing here tomorrow, just shoot me, please."

"Will do," she said. "Hope it doesn't come to that."

"Me, too."

chapter 2

THOUGH THE OUTSIDE of the house had remained the same, over the span of one intense and disturbing period, the interior of the house had changed completely. During her father's last long absence, the case in Singapore that went on for a year, Miller's mother, Jane, had made the summer house her project, coming north constantly to visit with the architect, the contractor, overseeing painters, wallpaper people, cabinet installers, whatever it took. Pouring money into a place that none of them visited any more, that had instead been rented out exclusively to one tenant. The poet. Hugh Donaldson.

Miller flew up with her mother once, browbeaten into the trip, driving out from Portland on the perpetually rain-struck two lanes of Route 26, breathtaking in the rainbow season, full of pines. Her mother chattered. Miller resisted the chatter, driving the rental car staring straight ahead in the gloom. She'd seen only the beginnings of the renovation. A wall removed to open up the living room. The framework for custom floor-to-ceiling bookshelves and three sets of French doors. A new kitchen. Stripped floors and woodwork. All of it was hidden under stepladders, drop cloths, buckets of paint, the aroma of sawdust and toxic chemicals hanging in the air. Nice, she'd said, opening windows, choking on the dust. Apparently, Hugh was in the islands. Islands? What islands? But her mother just waved the question away.

Hugh had seemingly lived well and when he'd died a year ago having no visible heirs, his possessions remained. Someone did something, who knew what, with his clothing and most of his personal effects. Thank God, Miller thought, there wasn't a trench coat hanging in the hall closet or a pair of wingtips underneath the bed, a calfskin address book on the counter. Though there was a large black umbrella in the umbrella stand bearing a tortoise shell handle that could only have been of his choosing and a cabinet full of his monogrammed glassware. Ghosts, Miller noted, she would live with ghosts. Better than what the alternative had come to be.

Though none of it mattered anymore, all of them were gone, still she'd come across reason to wonder about Hugh in other ways than where he'd disappeared to for that week. Fairly widely published for a poet, distinguished in his field, albeit a minor one, why had he chosen to live here? Even the most moody isolationist would surely give out after five or six years, especially as a tenant in someone else's hundred-year-old summer house.

That's when she started watching Jane more closely, the expression on her face that softened with phone calls, the fluttering around flight reservations. Miller couldn't see her mother having an affair with anyone but definitely not with the wallpaper guy, or the architect, who was a woman, so it wasn't that either. In time, it almost seemed as if the renovation was being done not around Hugh but for him, the kitchen to suit his gourmet tastes, the stunning bookshelves expressly for his large and diverse collection.

When Hugh departed, the books remained as well. Since then, the amazing variety of reading material had served only as a literary backdrop for Jane's handiwork, the striped entryway, floral couches, eggshell hues. Gleaming banisters, polished cherry wood cabinets. The shell collections, sea paintings and all those windows and doors giving out onto the dunes, framing the sometimes heart-stopping sunsets and broad ocean view.

Now, stepping into this house that held so much of the past, Miller could hear her mother's voice, nonstop, cheery, affectionate, and her heart sank. She wanted to slide her phone out of her back pocket, punch in the familiar number, say, please for once listen while I talk, and her mother would, except there was no one at that number anymore. And by the way, Mother, what was going on with you and Hugh? Is there a book in here somewhere, or God help us all, a bedroom, dedicated to you?

Miller managed to empty out the car but got no further. Boxes and suitcases remained where she'd dropped them, in the hallway, the kitchen, the bedroom. Now that she was here, slowing down might not even be an issue. She felt as if she'd been run over by a truck.

And she didn't remember what was in the boxes anyway. Once she'd decided she had to take this leap into the unknown, leave, move, get out, the rest came fast and she could only act on instinct, grabbing what came to hand. Precious little time had been wasted on thinking out a strategy, something with a little common sense to it. What did common sense have to do with anything anymore? Or sense of any kind?

She'd packed clothes, she knew that, three suitcases worth and two of those were mostly winter wear, sweaters, coats, items that saw very little use in San Diego. Rain gear, even new Wellingtons from REI, a last minute impulse purchase after considering descriptive accounts of the drenching Oregon winters one more time. Books, the ones she couldn't bear to leave behind or be without. Odd last minute things, a hammer, the pair of scissors from the desk, a metal tape measure, JC's coconut soap that made the bathroom smell wonderful.

She'd stood in the kitchen last, having no idea what to do. The kitchen was hers. Take it all? Leave it? She'd left it. At the last minute, having no idea why, she'd taken down and wrapped four baroque champagne flutes and a set of gold rimmed fruit plates. If she'd ever used them for anything, she couldn't recall it. They were just there, had been for years, taking up space in the cupboard. What attracted her to them, she decided, was that they weren't like anything else she had ever owned, more complicated than her normal tastes yet distinctly feminine. Maybe this was who she'd be now, someone complicated and feminine. On the other hand, maybe not.

One last item along those lines stayed in her mind, more emblematic perhaps than flutes and dessert plates. The little black dress. In the midst of willfully grabbing whatever came first, she'd stopped and moved it from the very back of the closet to the front where she could see it as she threw together a random collection of jeans and shirts. When was the last time she'd worn that dress? To what event? She'd looked good in it. That she understood. At a lithe five-nine, she was made for little black dresses. The thought gave her some small comfort, but she didn't need and couldn't take the dress. She left it.

Her last meal had been consumed somewhere far back down the road and she was hungry, but for what? Cheese and crackers? No, too civilized. The hot dogs? Three packs of Hebrew National in the cooler, what had she been thinking? She hadn't had a hot dog in years. Possibly it was the memory of standing in someone's kitchen with a plate of boiled, sliced up hot dogs, the grease still floating on the water in the pan, spearing each round little disk, running it through pools of ketchup and mustard, biting it off the fork. This must be what they mean by comfort food, she thought. Good. Something to look forward to.

Now, however, with dusk approaching, it was too much trouble to even find a pan and boil water. She was still crashing, coming down, the rush draining away, the frenzy gone, leaving only emptiness. The situation called for immediate sustenance, the more awful the better.

Miller was prepared. She knew herself. She had seen this coming. The bag of potato chips was right there, the onion dip in a container that only needed to be opened. The wine was white, dry, crisp and still cold from the cooler. Perfect. Jane had also rebuilt the deck, once a creaky old affair that leaned alarmingly. Now it was solid as a rock and furnished with thick faded cushions on almost comfortable resin wicker chairs, the real wicker chairs having met their crumbling demise decades ago.

"Here I am, Janelle." Miller sat in one of the chairs, took a long swallow of the wine, tested the dip with a handful of potato chips and pronounced her instincts correct and the experiment successful. She sent three texts again. For the next half hour, she would be okay. Or more than okay, she thought as the sun slipped below the horizon, producing a pink sky reflected in the silver ocean. She only moved to find a sweater as the evening cooled. With some concentration, half the bottle of wine and most of the potato chips, she managed to stay in the chair, watching, not thinking any more than necessary, until the first stars appeared. It was a triumph, one small respectable victory in the long battle over circumstances.

In the morning, Miller found the current week's tide chart online. Here, in theory, or in Janelle's theory at least, was the answer, the way ahead, out of the hole that had been dug for her and into the light. Or maybe somehow, in some way she couldn't yet comprehend, she'd dug that hole for herself. Don't think about it, Janelle had said. All right, I won't, Miller promised, but it was always there, a nagging, lingering doubt, a question mark that made the situation even worse. What if it was her fault somehow? *Did you hear me? Don't think about it.*

This woman. But Miller did as she was told. Don't think about it. Never run, walk. Stop, do not pass mindlessly on by. She put on a jacket with deep pockets. Into the pockets she stuffed tissues, lip balm, a notebook, chocolate, a pen and a small pair of binoculars that she'd paid fifty dollars for, again at REI. Hair pulled back in a ponytail, baseball hat, shades on, let's do it.

A sandy path led through rough beach grass directly to the beach. The day was cool, the sunlight hazy, the tide going out. Miller walked down out of the dunes and crossed the broad stretch of sand. At the water's edge, she turned toward the river. Her assignment was simple: observe, inspect, identify, take notes. Get out of your head is what Janelle would have said if she were in the habit of speaking plain English, which she was not. *Find it for yourself* should have been her motto, worked into some striking piece of expensive abstract art and hung prominently on the wall.

It being what exactly, Miller couldn't say. Here was a start at least, a crab shell of some sort. She'd noticed last night in a cursory pass through the bookshelves that Hugh had owned her same variety of shore guides. Maybe he'd left a notebook, a journal somewhere and she could just copy down what he'd discovered. No, she didn't really mean that. She was sincere about following through with this. In her heart of hearts, she conceded that she desperately needed it to work. She wanted to feel like a human being again, not a stripped down shadow of a person defined only by bitterness and anger.

All right, it was a shell. The crab wasn't in it anymore. That was a good piece of information. Empty shell, no crab. Something had obviously happened to the crab. Did it die? Was it eaten? By what? Fine to have questions, but how was she ever supposed to figure out the answers? She studied the shell then took out the notebook and wrote down a description of it. It was fragile, almost crisp, and pale, the same color as Jane's eggshell walls. That shouldn't be too hard. Then the most obvious inspiration came to her. She took out her phone and snapped a picture of it. If all else failed, she could send the picture to someone, an expert of some sort, those must exist somewhere, and they would send her back the answer.

Ten minutes dwelling on the aspects and provenance of a crab shell, ten minutes totally oblivious to and thoughtless miles away from the realities of her life. Miller considered that Janelle was worth it right there. Ten minutes was gold.

The rest of her walk consisted of the growing awareness that a whole host of objects lay strewn across this huge expanse of beach from the waves to the dunes, creatures and carcasses for all of whom there was no name. A thousand crab shells alone existed in one form or another, obviously an epidemic of dying crabs.

A light rain began to fall. Out at the river, Miller sat on a log. As she watched, a gull dropped down out of the mist and landed ten feet away. He padded around in front of her, pecking at old pieces of dried seaweed. Surprised, Miller studied her hands and watched him out of the corner of her eye. Slowly, like a detective investigating a crime scene, he made a complete circle around the log, worrying tiny chunks of loose driftwood with his beak.

Suddenly he fluttered his wings and lifted up to take a place beside her on the log. Then he was quiet, reflecting on whatever it was that birds reflected on. No more than an arm's length away, he shared her space and a comfortable silence. Miller couldn't imagine what the attraction might be. She had no food, nothing in her pockets that might be construed as food. The chocolate was long gone. The gull seemed content anyway. Here we are, she thought. Just the two of us. How's life for you? Those are weird feet. Do you have parents? What's it like to fly? After a time, the gull uttered two soft, throaty sounds, unfolded his wings and lifted into the sky, flapping slowly off into the distance. She watched until she couldn't see him anymore.

The rain came and went, pushed a little by the breeze. Miller took her time walking back along the flats, listening to the resounding echo as each wave rose, broke in a long line, and hushed into shore. In order to make it a true mile and a half, she went past the dune path by the house and all the way to the access road.

As she stood by the Motor Vehicles Prohibited sign at the beginning of the south beach, two pickups roared down the access road. The first swerved up into the high, sloping dune embankment, carving ruts. The second carried a muscular brown and black pit bull with little slit eyes. The two pickups met in the distance on the north beach, joined by a third pickup and a car. In the middle of the morning, beers were passed around. One of the drivers moved to the back of his truck and unlatched the gate. The pit bull shot out like a bullet, the trajectory aiming him in Miller's direction. She made a mental note to herself: pepper spray. Then she turned and ran.

Halfway up the access road she stopped and looked back. Thank God the pit bull was nowhere in sight. At the same moment, a shrill whistle made her jump. A glance to her left caught the motorcycle rider waving.

His bike and two late model sedans took up only a fraction of the broad condo parking lot, more evidence of a summer-only coast.

"You can do that thing with your fingers," she said as he walked to meet her. She'd never known anybody who actually could. "Eli, right?"

"Rude, I know," he said, "but it's too easy and it works. Yes, Eli, and it's Cory, isn't it? How are you on day two?"

"I'm fine, but call me Miller. Everyone else does. The question is, how are you? How's your back?"

"Hurts like hell, but hot showers do some good, for about five minutes anyway. The thing is, so far I can't get back on the bike."

"Do you have food?"

"People left saltines," he said, "peanut butter, things like that. It's not a problem."

"I've at least got cheese and crackers I can give you." And hot dogs, she thought. And two more bottles of wine.

"No, really, I'm good, but listen, would you like to see the place? I'm only putting it out there because I'm thrilled. It's a whole lot better than I thought it'd be."

"Sure," Miller said. She'd always been curious about the condos. Though they looked modern, local history said they'd been built somewhere in the fifties.

The small fenced-in patio was only a concrete slab with a border of dirt and dead plants, a weathered picnic table and someone's abandoned collection of sand dollars. Inside, a low hallway led past two bedrooms, one locked with a sign that said 'owner' on it and the other open to an unmade king-size bed strewn with clothes. The dark guest bath was plain, accessorized only with a fluffy stack of towels and a basket full of what appeared to be hotel soaps.

Then at the end, the hallway opened dramatically into a broad open space laid out beneath a soaring vaulted ceiling. A wall of glass faced the dunes and the vast expanse of ocean.

"Okay, that's impressive," she said.

Her glance ran over the huge comfortable-looking sectional done in soft beige, the corner fireplace, the wall of shelves filled with a mix of old paperbacks, hand carved seagulls and state of the art media components. A modern dining table by the windows sat eight and the neutral kitchen contained all the necessary appliances. Nothing was sparkling and brand new, but it was all clean and light and airy.

"All those electronics, you're definitely set up as far as entertainment goes. Plus, wow, fairly high-powered binoculars," she said, touching the tripod they sat on.

"With which you can see a bird two miles away. If you're interested in a bird two miles away."

"Do you mind?" Miller gestured in the direction of the kitchen.

"Help yourself. I don't mind at all."

The cabinets held a variety of dishes, cookware and commemorative glasses from far too many golf tournaments. The drawers were filled with one intact set of silverware and then everything from spatulas and skewers to matchbooks and takeout menus. A theme was emerging, small piles of golf tees everywhere. However, nothing edible presented itself beyond condiments and one open box of Pop-Tarts.

"It's got a nice feel to it," Miller said, going to the sliding glass doors. "And the view is spectacular. How did you find it?"

"A friend of a friend. From what I'm told, the owner retired to his other condo on a golf course in Arizona."

"Wise decision. But really, you don't have any food. There's a small grocery store right in town. I can give you a ride, I have to go myself anyway. I'll get my car and be back in a minute."

"Town's just down the road, isn't it?" he said. "I should try and walk it."

"I'll give you my cell number. Call me when you can't make it back."

"Is it that bad?"

"Judging by how you got from there to here?" Miller said, indicating the length of the hallway. "Yes."

"Okay, thanks, you win, but only because I don't have any beer."

"Let me give you my cell number anyway, just in case." She knew she was throwing caution to the wind and didn't care. It was going to be a long solitary time out here and it'd be nice to have someone to talk to now and then. "I just don't ever remember what the number is." She reached in her pocket for the cell phone and pulled out three pale turban-shaped shells that she'd picked up on her walk. "Forgot about these." She set them down momentarily to scroll through her phone.

"I think you've got a freeloader," Eli said. Miller looked up as one of the shells produced a small puddle of water and sand, a set of wavy blue antennae and began to creep along the slick surface of the breakfast bar.

"Oh my God," she said. She grabbed the offending shell gingerly between the tips of a thumb and forefinger. "I'll be right back."

"Wait, where are you going?" he said. "Throw it in the bushes."

"I can't. And there's that pit bull."

"*What* pit bull?"

But she was already running out the door, along the parking lot, down the access road, praying the feelers wouldn't come out again, praying the dog was gone, past the Motor Vehicles Prohibited sign and down to the water. "My fault," she said. "I know this isn't where I found you." She wasn't here to cause anyone's demise. That wasn't part of the plan. "Hope you don't get crushed by a pickup. Hope you're all right."

When Miller pulled into the condo parking lot, she saw the next problem. She'd just have to face it, get through it. These were the small things.

Eli was there waiting. She knew right away from the look on his face. He opened the door and got in.

"Whoa," he said. "What kind of car is this?"

"Don't laugh. It's a Prius."

"Trust me, I'm not laughing. I think I'm not kidding that it's the most badass car I've ever seen. A Prius? That can't be true."

Miller sighed. "Well, it is. See? No place to put a key. It's just the matte black look that hides it."

"Yeah, I'd say that's what it is all right, there isn't a piece of chrome on it anywhere, not even the hubcaps. Is it yours? No wait, maybe that's not a fair question."

"It's entirely fair because no, it's not mine. It's my son's. We traded for a while. Down in southern California a car like this is normal, but I never stopped to consider what it would look like up here."

"It definitely has that drug dealer thing going on, but only till someone tells you it's a Prius. Then that all goes away. Truly, seriously, badass, but I like it. How old's your son?"

Here was another issue. Sam kept getting older all the time. "Twenty-three," she said as she pulled out onto the road.

At least the comeback helped a little. "You're shitting me. You can't have a twenty-three-year-old kid. And I'm not just being polite."

"Thank you," she said, "for not just being polite."

"Where is your son? Is it okay if I ask? What's he do?"

"Remember where I'm from. He's in South Africa on the winter surf tour."

She glanced over in time to see Eli's head hit the back of the seat. "No way," he said. "Who gets to lead a life like that?"

"It's work, too, though," she said. "And stressful, not knowing if you'll make it every time, if there'll be enough money to keep going."

"But I'd bet anything he's doing what he loves."

"He is doing that, every hour of every day since he was old enough to stand on a board."

"It's the kind of life I can't even imagine," he said.

"You've been on some beach somewhere before though, haven't you?"

"Sure, beaches aren't the problem. Actually, I've lived most of the last ten years in New York City, and if you look real hard you can even find beaches there."

"It's just not California."

"If that isn't the truth, I don't know what is. Are we here?"

"This is it," Miller said, pulling up to the curb. "Beer central. Now that I'm thinking about it, we could go to the supermarket in Oceanview if you want. It's got to be cheaper."

"No, this is great."

She left him to his own devices and did some shopping for herself, real food, no more junk. She found him again standing in front of a fairly massive wine selection for such a small place.

"I'll be back," was all she said and he nodded, looking over the racks thoughtfully.

In the car, she handed him a change of address form that she'd retrieved from the post office across the street. "It's all PO boxes," she said. "No mail delivery. Here's the application."

"Small town, here we are."

At the condos, Eli dug in his jeans pocket. "Can't forget to give you back these." He tipped the two shells into her hand. "No visitors. I ran water through them to make sure."

"Blue whatever those things were. The last thing I was expecting, obviously."

"Thanks again for doing this," he said, flinching in pain as he retrieved his two bags of groceries from the back seat. "I've got some things to deal with this weekend, but some night next week let me buy you dinner, okay?"

Was it okay? Yes, she decided, it was. She didn't see herself ever being able to eat in a restaurant alone so this was a welcome delay in facing up to that fact.

"Do you have your phone?" he said. Miller held it up. She watched the screen as he sent her a text. "Now you have my number, too."

He closed the door and shook his head taking in the car again. "You'll hear from me," he said. "But like I said before, if you need anything, here I am."

She watched him walk stiffly through the patio gate. He had to leave one bag of groceries on the picnic table and come back for it, only confirming what she already knew, that youth was overrated.

chapter 3

THE WIND SCREAMED in the night and the rain came in waves. Miller sat bolt upright, listening. The rain continued steady, sheeting down hard. Then the sky split open and a torrent of water hit all at once like a giant spigot on full blast. Finally, the heavens relented and the rain faded to only a thin, syncopated tapping on the roof. She lay back again, thinking, *good lord.*

In the morning, Miller assessed her gear. Green rubber boots and a baseball hat didn't quite do it if the rain kept coming like that. She decided to start at the lower end of the monetary scale. The local directory pointed her north to where Route 1 opened out into shopping sprawl. Fred Meyer was an unfamiliar name, but covering a city block, it would have to produce something useful.

She searched down one aisle after the other through frozen foods, books, shoes, electronics, picture frames, storage, gardening, vacuum cleaners, gift wrap and fifty other sections until she came to outerwear. Forty-nine dollars purchased a vinyl metallic green flannel-lined raincoat with hood. The one good thing to say about it, she considered, was that now the only exposed body part would be her knees.

Out on the damp beach, Miller found herself again with miles of empty space. She checked quickly up along the north beach. No pickups in sight, no pit bulls either. One elderly woman far down on the south beach sent her huge standard poodle into the waves again and again chasing sticks. No harm from that quarter, a little old lady and a big goofy dog.

The rain had left the sand pockmarked and pasty gray. Handfuls of shiny black and blue mussel shells clung together along the tide line. Little gray shorebirds ran and pecked busily along the flats. Miller reluctantly took the binoculars out of her pocket. She'd never quite seen herself as a bird watcher. The birds looked the same up close as they did from a distance, tiny and gray, and they moved so fast that focusing on just one was impossible. Not to mention that the light was all wrong, muting whatever distinguishing features they might have and blending them artfully into the background of gray sand. For now, they would have to stay what they were, just little gray birds.

Then it occurred to her and she went back to the blue and black shells. She bent down, snapped a picture with her phone, took out her notebook and wrote that one word on the first line: *mussels*.

Far out by the river, the tide uncovered an acre of spurting holes. Miller stood watching as two middle-aged women in far more stylish rain gear stomped around on the huge barren flats. One stopped, noting Miller's puzzled expression.

"Razor clams," she said. "Can't dig for them now, there's a ban due to that virus that comes around."

"When the ban's lifted, they'll be even better," the other one said. "Cause they'll have gotten big and fat. What you do is cut that neck part off, it's tough, and chop it up for chowder, then fry the rest. It's a funny taste. First you have to get used to it, then you love it."

Miller hoped her misgivings didn't show. "What do they look like?" she said.

The second woman walked up to the tide line and picked up a shell. She came back and handed it to Miller.

"This is a razor clam?" The oval shell didn't bear any resemblance to a straight razor but was surprisingly beautiful. A symmetrical band of pale violets and blues radiated out from the hinge to cover both sides in a pattern as delicate as a French Impressionist watercolor.

"That's it. Loads of them along here."

After they'd gone, Miller took out her notebook. *Razor clam*, she wrote.

Returning along the access road, her eye caught a sign high in the dunes, almost buried by beach grass. *Stop right there*, Janelle said. All right, all right, I hear you. Miller climbed up into the dunes and parted the tough long strands of grass. She sighed.

There was the answer right in front of her. She'd stacked up all her shore guides on the dining room table and gone through every one of them. Nothing matched what she saw on the beach, but here it was written in official black and white lettering spelling out the restrictions for taking them. She felt like an idiot. The crabs were Dungeness, only the most popular and prolific edible crab on the West Coast, served in season in every restaurant, on ice at every fish counter. The ones washed up on the beach mostly existed as a result of molting then, not death, and were bleached out by sun and weather specifically to trip up someone new to this idea of trying to identify them.

Miller took out the notebook yet again. As an afterthought, she added the date to each line. Yesterday. Today. Who knew what windfall of stunning discoveries might present itself tomorrow?

Another treasure better than gold, a whole afternoon by the ocean with only clams, crabs and birds on her mind.

With the arrival and settling in, the majority of her possessions unpacked and not quite the sense of chaos in the house anymore, the plan allowed for communication. Miller sat down and emailed her children, telling them about the trip, the beach, the house, how things had gone so far, nothing more. Rumination, supposition, recrimination, none of that belonged, nothing with any negative aspect to it had any right to be here. The situation was as it was. All three had their opinions. In JC's case those opinions were virulent and had been made far too well known to anyone within shouting distance. All three had removed themselves to the farthest possible place on the planet, out of reach, out of touch, without the chance at the moment of saying something they might regret forever, which was the point. Not to her, she conceded. Never to her. But still.

She was just glad she could be in touch now, that she could sit down and tap out these small bits and pieces of news and let them know she was fine, she would survive. Then she closed her laptop. No headlines, no outside world and that had nothing to do with Janelle. It was simply that more bad news wouldn't help.

For the evenings, Miller stacked up a fortune's worth of DVDs on the table next to the shore guides, every movie she'd ever wanted to watch, every recommendation anyone had given her and everyone, in the end, had notions of what would be appropriate, what would soothe. Then there were the books, another three stacks, mostly mysteries at one end of the spectrum and at the other, memoirs of women on their own living wild and outrageous lives, hiking a thousand miles, sailing around the world, exploring Antarctica, shooting rapids in the Amazon, sheep herding in Montana, whatever it took. Miller was suddenly overcome with emotion for the friends who had done all this for her. Emotion, however, wasn't one of Janelle's action items either, not right now. And in another way, without wanting to, those friends had let her down.

Miller built a fire in the fireplace, wrote firewood next to pepper spray on the shopping list in the kitchen, picked out a DVD, found the remote, wrapped up in a blanket and settled deep into one of the lilac-flowered couches to spend yet another useful amount of time thinking nothing.

At the weekend, the sun came out and the Labor Day holiday crowd descended. Miller hurried out for an early morning walk along the tide line, picking up shells as she went. She trained the binoculars intently on the flock of little birds, but they were still just small and gray. She'd gone through the bird books and it was hopeless. There were pages of small shorebirds that all looked exactly alike.

In the afternoon, she was glad to sit on Jane's deck reading and enjoying the welcome warmth. After getting deep into a mystery that would provide her with excellent bedtime distraction, Miller surprised herself by picking one of the bird books back up and reading through it carefully, one bird at a time.

As the day progressed, the beach accumulated its fair share of families, teenagers, dog walkers, though still not enough to fill up the whole solitary mile and a half. Once a car, oblivious to the Motor Vehicles Prohibited sign on its concrete pillar, drove slowly down the south beach and back again. Miller frowned. Then something caught her eye. She raised the binoculars, scanning over the slope of the dunes and down to the water. Please tell me I'm not spying, she thought, even though she knew she was. She'd zeroed in on Eli Greer, the athletic build, the dark close-cropped head. With him was a redhead, but not exactly an ordinary one. This was a flaming, screaming redhead, nothing natural going on there, in sprayed-on jeans and a very tight sweater, almost as tall as Miller, with her arm around him, laughing.

Miller checked, watching their progress. He was still moving slowly, still favoring his back. She smiled to herself without meaning to. The redhead looked like the type who might actually put him in traction. And then she wondered, just briefly, where this person had come from. She had to be an import. At least Miller hoped so. She was more hesitant about going to dinner with anyone who could work that fast. Assuming that the dinner invitation still stood. If it didn't, nothing lost.

chapter 4

MILLER HAD BECOME adept at assigning ring tones on her phone, something Dell had taught her. Before she'd used it only for convenience' sake, but now it had a whole different purpose, to help her avoid talking to anyone. For a moment when the phone rang, she stopped in confusion. Then what she'd chosen was so obvious she wondered about herself. It was Eli. None of this was going to work if she couldn't keep her head on straight. It came back to her about the redhead and that she hadn't actually been expecting him to call anyway.

"Hey," he said, jumping right in. "I've checked some things out and I found the perfect place. Well, it's perfect for me anyway. Are we still on for dinner?"

"I'm guessing this is you," Miller said. "I'm fine with it, but are you certain you're free?"

There was a hesitation on the other end of the line. "Why you asked that is an interesting question," he said. "One that'll require some thought on my part. But yes, absolutely. Tonight?"

"Tonight's good," she said. "Run through what perfect means to you so I at least know what to expect."

"For starters, the options go from A to nowhere. And because of my recent past, I want the biggest frigging hamburger on the planet and this place has it. Plus a tall cold beer."

"The important part."

"So I'll pick you up around six?"

"One problem," Miller said. "I don't do motorcycles."

"Neither do I, for the moment anyway. I bought a car."

"You *did*?" Miller said. "You've been busy."

"You know what? The way you said that, I'm going to have to think about that one too. But it's just a Jeep and not a new one. Are you okay with a Jeep?"

Miller took a deep breath. It was possible that her firstborn had been conceived in a Jeep, not an easy feat.
"You still there?" he said.
"I'm still here. Does it have a top?"
"Hey lady, I drive a hard bargain. For the same low price, it even has doors."

Miller stood at the end of the driveway and waited. The Jeep was red and did have doors.
"And the top's even hard." She knocked on it before getting in.
"I heard it rains here, that's why," Eli said. "Is that your house?"
Miller glanced over at the boxy cedar shake with its shutters and rose-colored door. "It is. Or the family's. For a long time."
"You're lucky."
"That's true, I suppose. Give me more about this place. No dress code, right?" She was wearing what she always wore, jeans and running shoes.
"Now that you're committed, I'll tell you. It's a sports bar and I liked it the minute I walked in. I don't know the area, but just a small warning, there are places where a bar like that could get rowdy."
"I don't mind rowdy," Miller said, though she doubted anything here got rowdy, ever. "No fistfights, though." She couldn't remember the last time she'd even been in a bar.
"No fistfights, only loud maybe, depending on what game's on. Do you get rowdy?"
Miller looked at him. "What? You can't be serious. Do you?"
"Hardly ever and not for a long time. A burger'll be about as much excitement as I can take and that's a very sad fact."
At least he was a calm driver and handled a stick shift as if he'd been doing it all his life, which maybe he had. It occurred to her that she didn't actually know anything about him, but she put that thought away.

The bar was roomy but dark, with TV screens everywhere, a pool table at the back, and a blue-lit bar. Many of the tables were already occupied. Eli's face lit up just coming through the door.

"Oh yeah," he said. "And fourteen beers on tap."

Miller considered that if she had to drive him home it wouldn't be a crisis because her own car, her real car, was a stick shift and she had been driving one her whole life. But she found that she wasn't worried. Something about him said he wasn't that kind.

A waiter in a t-shirt and jeans showed them to a table. The large menu that he laid down was specific to a certain type of gourmet. It included seven different sliders, Big Bowls O' Tater Tots and a section called Fry Me A River. Salads came under the heading Health Department.

"Yes? You're still in?" Eli said.

"I'm still in. Love the blue lights."

"That's what sealed the deal for me. The menu first, but then the blue bar. You can't ask for more than that."

"Are you always so happy?" she said.

"That's a joke, right? What'll it be? Are you a salad kind of person? I'm betting not."

"First," Miller said, "we have to get something out of the way."

"Coming from anyone but you that would sound very ominous."

"It's not ominous, it's just the way things have to be and you can't fight me on it, not even for one minute."

"I should be scared," he said, "but I'm not. What?"

"I pay my own way."

"But…"

Miller held up a hand.

"I can't say anything?" he said.

"No, sorry, you can't."

Eli drummed his fingers on the table for a moment. "I'm back," he said. "No thoughts. Nothing. What'll it be?"

Miller smiled and looked at the menu again. "Veggie pizza. It's exactly what I want."

30

"How could you pick the one thing that's not green but still good for you?"

"Instinct. And a Blue Moon on tap. What about you?"

"There, you're a woman after my own heart. Blue Moon plus a burger with everything and onion rings on the side. Done."

The food arrived and it seemed like more than they could possibly have ordered. All the TVs were on, showing four different baseball games and soccer in some other country. Miller thought that she probably hadn't been in a place like this since college. The beer was good and the pizza, outstanding.

"So," Eli said. "Can we talk about why we're here at the end of the known world in faraway Winslow, Oregon?"

"You can," Miller said. "And I'd love to listen. But I can't, and that's just because."

"I'll only say this one thing. I've seen your hand."

Miller covered the pale band across her finger where her wedding rings had been. Why had it taken her forever to give them up? She was silent.

"Are you a runner?" he said out of nowhere.

She could see now that this had been a bad idea. "Why do you ask?"

"You look like you might be. I don't know, it was something to talk about."

"I'm sorry," she said.

"Don't be. I'm sorry for whatever you're going through."

"I was a runner. I'm not supposed to run anymore for a while. I'm supposed to walk. Normally I hate walking, but I'm finding out at least that it's better on the beach. Are you a runner?"

"I am usually. Could I walk with you sometime?"

"If you want to," she said, "of course."

"Do you go to the gym?"

Miller tried to keep a neutral face. "You have a genius for asking all the wrong questions," she said. "Why? Do you go to the gym?"

"In one of my past lives I was a bartender in a very funky bar in New York City where the friendly bartender was also the very

31

unfriendly enforcement officer. And some guys who decide to get throw-down drunk are pretty big mothers that you have to wrestle with a little bit to get cooperation. So for self-defense purposes, yes."

"I've always wondered," she said. "How does someone get into bartending in the first place? I mean where do you even learn how to do it?"

"You learn how to do it best by working with someone good who takes the time to show you. And most of the people I ever knew were on their way to somewhere else anyway."

"Where were you on your way to?"

"Before I answer that, which opens up all kinds of things, would you tell me if you go to the gym?"

Miller hesitated. Janelle hadn't said exactly where to draw the line. How much did she have to not talk about? She decided to jump in but just at the shallow end. If she didn't say something to somebody now and then she'd go crazy, wouldn't she?

"I teach spin," she said. "I taught spin."

"The bike thing? That's insane. People die trying to do that."

"You work hard not to have anybody die. It's very bad for your reputation, not to mention your class schedule, which was busy, five days a week. But I don't do it anymore."

"Jesus, are you freaking out? How do you come down from that?"

"I was freaking out. It was hard, but it's at least a little better now."

"It got too intense?" he said. "Something like that? I've heard of such a thing happening."

"No, it was other stuff. Actually, so much other stuff." Miller realized that if she said one more word her voice would break and she'd come apart. "Your turn," she said. "I'm done. Where were we? Life after bartending."

"Or during," Eli said. "I was starting a graduate degree in architecture, that was supposed to be my future, but I was hating every minute of it. Bartending was a way to flunk out and make a shit load of money doing it. So, you wouldn't go to a gym at all? I was looking for one."

"I don't know," Miller said haltingly. "Slowing down is the goal."

"And for you a treadmill would be slowing way down."

"I think you're maybe a bad influence," she said. "Where have you been that a burger is the key to life?"

"I'll give you one word that says so much, that actually might say it all."

"I can't even imagine. What's the word?"

"Vegan."

"Vegan?" she said. "When? Where?"

"Up until two weeks ago in upstate New York."

"Why do I feel this has to do with a woman?"

"Because it seems like in the end," he said, "everything has to do with a woman."

Miller reflected on what a true statement that was. She turned away from the thought.

"Which brings us to Monica," he said.

Miller held up the last slice of pizza. Strings of cheese dripped off the broccoli and mushrooms. "Monica who might be a redhead," she said, tipping the pizza into her mouth.

"This week she is. But where did you see her? Why didn't you come up and say hello?"

"First, I hardly knew you, and second, I'm being honest here and I expect no less from you…" She hesitated again, not believing she was going to do this. "…it was through binoculars."

"What?" He laughed. "I want to hear how that happened."

"It's just that I'm not interested in being around a lot of people." She glanced around the crowded bar. "Here's fine. On the beach it's different. If I have to be out there I want it all to myself so weekends are out. I was sitting on the deck watching the birds if you really want to know, I kept spotting some kind of hawk, but people were passing by too, and it's just, there you were. Spying wasn't where I was headed. She definitely catches your eye, though, she's gorgeous and…" She searched for the right word.

"…stacked," he said. "You wouldn't be the first person who noticed. And I'm not putting anything out there that she doesn't put out herself. They're not real. Ten thousand dollars' worth of not real to be exact, or so she says."

"I have to ask," Miller said. "How did you find her so fast?"

"If I answer this, you're coming to the gym with me. I dated her for two years in New York. She was a hot shot event planner, I went to a hot shot event, boom. The thing is, we slept over, but we never moved in, never even talked about it, so I assume there were other guys, probably all the time. Then she gave up on New York and moved back to Portland where she was from. We kept in touch, I went through my own shit, she said, wait, I'll come out on weekends, it'll be perfect. So she plans on driving two hours to get here on Saturday and two hours to get back on Sunday. Her thing, not mine."

"Just an observation. She seems, maybe, energetic."

"Energetic is too kind a word for what goes on with her. Strenuous is more like it. Or exhausting is actually the truth. The look on your face is great," he said. "You're thinking something you're not asking. This is just between friends here. I'm not shy."

"I wish you were. Or that I was. With your back? Why aren't you dead?"

"Remember you asked for it. Just this one time, to save me from a very bad fate, she took matters into her own hands, so to speak."

"Oh my God," Miller said. "You're right, I asked for it."

"You're fifteen shades of crimson."

"My fault. Never again."

chapter 5

MILLER WALKED the six blocks into town, her eye traveling along the fronts of the other houses like hers as she passed, and musing over Hugh Donaldson, wondering whether he'd known any of these people, or if they'd known him. Did they care that they had a minor, well, very minor, celebrity in their midst? In most of the houses, the shades were drawn, the windows boarded up, the occupants having taken up residence in more hospitable climates for the winter.

The town itself was only two blocks long and dedicated to the normal small town amenities, gifts, antiques, gardening, real estate, a tiny crowded bakery and café, the Corner Market, the elementary school and out by the two-lane highway, the fire station. What Miller needed was the post office, located across from the market in a handsome converted white clapboard house.

The front door opened onto an entranceway. The room to the left, in what Miller judged would have been the dining room, was taken up with a whole wall of post office boxes. Miller had her own small gold key, but today she only wanted to send postcards.

In the room to the right, two brusque postmistresses, both sporting chopped gray hair, sneakers and reading glasses slipped down their noses, surveyed the incoming patrons with a critical eye. Miller stepped up to the counter and asked for stamps.

"London?" the elder of the two said. "Spain?" She raised her eyebrows as if there was suddenly a highly questionable activity occurring in her domain.

"Yes, please." Janelle's address in San Diego was apparently within reasonable limits and therefore not in need of comment.

The postmistress squinted at her. "You're 2447, aren't you?"

Miller looked around behind her. She couldn't understand to whom this woman was speaking, or to what she was referring. She looked back expectantly, not wanting to seem brainless, but then it came to her. 2447 was her post office box and this sharp-witted old woman had already committed that fact to memory.

"That postal change of address you sent to California? You could have done that online."

Good grief, Miller thought, she knew what mail was sent and now these addresses would add more information to the profile for 2447. Small town didn't begin to convey it. She'd subscribed to several magazines, another required diversion, meaning there'd often be at least something in the box when she opened it, but she could see the two of them quickly perusing the titles, thereby developing yet another set of opinions.

Miller decided it was all too disturbing and she needed to get back to the beach. Ball cap on, collar turned up against the cold breeze, she headed down through the dunes at the end of the street and out to the river.

An entire flock of gulls had settled there, quiet for a change. Individual gulls stretched and preened. They tucked their heads under their wings and napped. They ruffled their feathers and walked a few paces or balanced for long stretches on one leg. She watched one fly off into the distance, disappearing back along the creek while another dropped down out of the sky to settle in companionably among its neighbors. No one hunted or fed or squabbled. Peaceful was a word that surprised her again.

Then she watched over her shoulder as two women in scarves and heavy jackets strode purposefully over the dunes swinging bags of bread. The gulls immediately dropped their reserve and commenced with an ear-splitting screeching and squawking, the shrill noise loud enough to drown out the sound of the waves. The women, delighted with the results, made cooing noises to their captive audience as the gulls fought over the tossed pieces of bread. Miller decided that instead of becoming a calmer, more rational person, she might just extend her embittered outlook to an even larger portion of humanity.

Back at the house, emptying out her pockets, she remembered an identification still to be made. She'd sat eye to eye with one of those gulls and if she couldn't find him in the book, then she ought to give up this whole venture right now. But there was everything she needed, the photos, the arrows pointing to important details, the silvery gray wings, rubbery yellow feet and pale eye, a hard to miss red dot at the end of the beak, a herring gull. Momentarily pleased and even slightly smug, Miller then came back to the reality that she still had miles and miles yet to go.

The weekend turned into camping season, with every variety of vehicle lined up in front of the dunes along the north beach as far as the eye could see. Even from her deck some distance away, Miller couldn't help but notice the pungent aromas of wood smoke and bacon mixed in with the tangy salt air. She also couldn't help but notice, without intention, without the binoculars at all, a handsome couple running along the beach down at the very edge of the waves, his dark head a contrast to her flaming red one. Their long strides matched, steady and at a strong pace, especially given the uneven contours of the damp sand. Something must have cured his back, Miller thought, wishing with all her heart that the mental image from their last conversation would go away.

At the tail end of the weekend, Miller went out to reclaim the beach as her own. Walking along the wide empty stretch with darkness closing in fast, she suddenly took more reassurance than she could ever have imagined from the sight of a car's headlights mindlessly spinning figure eights far off in the distance on the north beach.

chapter 6

ELI CALLED midweek.
"When can I come on your beach walk?"
"Don't you ever say hello?" Miller said.
"Everyone has caller ID or whatever so I just usually skip over that part."
"I've noticed. Tomorrow at ten?" she said. "The tide will be headed out by then."
"I'll be in the parking lot."

"So, what do you do out here?" Eli said. "Just walk and walk and walk?"
"And look at things."
"Like what things?"
Miller pulled the notebook out of her pocket and handed it to him along with a piece of chocolate.
"I can't eat that stuff," he said, "but thank you for offering. Now if it was coffee…"
"Sorry, no coffee."
He went back to the notebook. "So this is a record, keeping track."
"Yes."
"And it's got a purpose."
"It does, somewhat. More or less."
"And you're not going to say what that purpose is."
"Just to be here," she said. "Slow down, stay awake. That's all."
"Got it." He handed her back the notebook. "Someday when you're ready you can tell me about it."
"Believe me, it's nothing anybody'd want to hear. It's just the mess that's someone else's life."
"Try me, okay? How did you know it would be low tide?"

"You can look up tide tables online."

"You're serious about this," he said.

"It's all part of it."

"What are you looking for today?"

"Whatever's out here."

"I know what this is." He bent down and picked up a mangled disc of blue plastic. "This is, or was, some dog's much-loved Frisbee. You can write that down if you want."

"Thanks. Here." Miller handed him the binoculars. "I'll show you what it's like. Tell me what those little birds are."

Eli studied them for a long moment, took down the binoculars and squinted into the light, then studied them again. "I have no idea."

"Welcome to the club."

"But it seems impossible they can run that fast on those tiny little legs and there's a guy in there that only has one."

"One what?"

"One leg."

"Really?" she said.

He gave her back the binoculars. "Scan toward the water. I can't see him right now, but he's in there somewhere."

Miller moved slowly through the flock and found him. "He sort of hops," she said.

"That's a pretty damn fast hop."

"I agree." She lowered the binoculars. "But I still don't know what they are."

"How do you find out?"

"Bird guides, but there're too many little shorebirds that all look like that. I'll just keep watching till I figure it out, which is the point."

"Are we allowed to talk while we're walking and waiting for the next thing to show up?"

"Only two rules. Walk, don't run, and stop, don't ever just pass on by."

"That could probably cover a whole lot of what goes on in anyone's life. But since talking's allowed, I wanted to tell you I got a job."

Miller stopped. "I've managed one change of address and you've bought a car *and* found a job? Doing what?"

"Bartending. Two nights a week at the blue bar."

"They hired you just like that?"

"My résumé might not be much good for anything else, but it's killer for bartending. People see New York City and they fall over."

"Congratulations, I hope. Is that what you had in mind?"

"I didn't have much of anything in mind, just getting away, being in some completely different place. And this is definitely it. But money never hurts and I get to keep my hand in. It's the slow nights, Monday and Tuesday five till close, which is fine with me. And I joined a gym."

"Okay," she said. "You're a crazy person."

"I got you an application, it's not expensive, nothing around here is, but I also have a guest pass that you can use before you decide for sure."

Decide for sure. Janelle would not have good things to say about this. "Don't you need the guest pass for someone else?"

"Someone else, as we'll call her, is never coming to the gym with me. Period. End of story."

"All right then."

Eli bent down to retrieve a soggy chewed up tennis ball. "Dogs leave a lot of their garbage out here." As he stood up, something passed low over their heads.

"Holy crap," Miller said. "That's the hawk."

"I can't believe you just said holy crap. What hawk?"

"The one I've been watching from the deck." The hawk glided down to land at the front of the dunes. "Aaagh. He's eating something."

"Go for it," Eli said. "He's yours."

Miller moved slowly one step at a time toward the bird. With each step she took the hawk looked up, watching her warily.

Suddenly she came to a halt as a second hawk circled overhead. Then a third hawk drifted up over the dunes and landed a short distance away.
"I'm surrounded by hawks," she said.
"Keep going. See what happens."
"Thank you for that brave advice."
As she started to move again, the first hawk lifted into the air, veering sharply to glide down along the tide line. As he turned, a part of the prey clutched in his talons fell to the ground.
"That gave me the chills," Miller said, coming back down. "Where did those other two come from?"
"I don't know, but I think they were more interested in lunch than mounting an attack. Should you check out whatever that piece is?"
"Yes, I should. That doesn't mean I want to." She went over, took out her phone, bent down and snapped a picture, but she'd recognized it already, the head of a solitary shorebird she'd seen in the dunes the day before. "It's a whimbrel," she said.
"That was quick."
"He's been around. I looked him up yesterday in my books. I remember it said his call was a loud whistle."
"Not anymore. Nice, and we've only come half way. But is it always like this?" Eli said. "There's no one here." Low tide had greatly expanded the beach with only one dog walker in sight.
"I know it's different for you on the weekends."
"You saw us again."
"Well, I did, but just by accident. As a matter of fact, I was trying not to look. All I wanted was to figure out that bird back there."
"It's okay," he said. "Because I saw you."
"Then I'll turn the tables. Why didn't you come and say hi?"
"I wouldn't ever do that to you."
"You make her sound more like a nightmare than true love."
"It's hard sometimes to tell which is which, but I don't mean to give that impression. True love? Not quite. I like her, but she's like a tornado, blows through, rearranges all the furniture, then

she's gone again. She's not the type to invest in. Short doses are about all anyone could take."

"How old is she?"

"Twenty-nine," he said. "Same as me. And you can't be thinking that's an age to start settling down. You don't have a dog in that fight."

"A dog in what fight?"

"You can't have an opinion on that subject when you had a child at age twelve. And oh look, there's something else dead."

A small limp body lay at the very edge of the waves, elegantly matte black, with a white front and webbed feet.

"Say holy crap again," he said.

"What is wrong with holy crap?"

"When you've been around people who swear like dock hands, holy crap seems almost, I don't know, sweet or innocent or something."

Miller shook her head. She bent down over the bird. "I don't remember ever seeing this one in the books," she said.

"I wonder how he walks. He's built weird, too much body, not enough leg. Actually hardly any leg at all."

"I'll have to find out."

"There are worse ways for somebody to spend their time. The tide's gone even farther out, so your tide table was right."

"Doesn't it have to be?"

Eli was thoughtful for a minute. "I'm invading your privacy again, feel free to kick me out," he said, "but whose rules are these?"

Though it might be grasping at straws, Janelle had never mentioned keeping her out of the conversation. "I see a therapist," Miller said. "And believe me, I never thought I'd hear myself say those words. But honestly, I was falling apart, so I had to do something."

"Him or her?"

"Her. Janelle, that's what she said to call her anyway, not doctor or anything."

"How long have you been seeing her?"

"Three months."

"That's it? Whatever happened was only that long ago?"

"Don't," Miller said. "Please."

"Sorry. But you must like her and I don't see any way that she's giving you bad advice. Seems like pretty good advice to me."

"I do like her. And I'm grateful to her more than anyone can ever know. But that was also more than I ever wanted to say."

"I hate to tell you this," Eli said, "but guess what's coming up next."

Miller ran her eye down along the damp flats. "That can't even be."

Another black and white bird just like the first one sat huddled at the tide line. Before they could come closer, the bird rose and fumbled his way awkwardly into the waves. Unable to make any headway, he floated slowly back into shore. He looked so small and alone on the huge expanse of beach with no one else around.

"We have to leave him here, don't we?" she said.

"What else are you going to do? I don't think he'll get better in someone's bathtub."

"Seems obvious, but that's the one thing I'm learning. Everything dies."

"I can see where if you stayed out here long enough that's definitely the impression you'd get."

"Now I'm even more curious," Miller said. "I wonder if there's a local guide of some sort. I always walk to the river, but after that do you want to go into town? The path's right there through the dunes."

"This morning my agenda consisted solely of making paper airplanes, so yes, I'd love to."

"Paper airplanes?" she said. "You're kidding."

"I am not."

In the gardening center, Miller found what she was looking for in among the dried wreaths and ceramic birdhouses, a community nature guide. The line drawing perfectly matched the black and white birds on the beach.

"Common murres. I don't even know how to pronounce that," she said. She read down the page. "No wonder they're here. It says that huge rock formation out in the ocean has twenty-eight thousand of them."

"Twenty-seven thousand nine hundred and ninety-eight," Eli said

"You don't think the other one'll make it either?"

"Uh, no."

"And they live on the ocean. They're deep sea divers, that's why they have odd legs. I need this book."

Eli turned to the friendly woman behind the counter. "Do you live here?" he asked. "I feel like I've seen you around."

"I work here," she said. "I do native plant gardens, mostly in this area, a lot in the condos, that's where you might have seen me. But I live inland off Route 53 where there's nothing but forest and it's so peaceful and quiet."

"Seems hard to imagine a place more peaceful and quiet than right here."

"I'll tell you how different it is though. We have thirty elk that bed down at night in the front yard."

"*Thirty*?" Miller said.

"And they're huge," the woman said, grinning.

"Is the rain in the winter as bad as everyone says?" Miller asked.

"Whatever you heard, it's worse. Goes like this." The woman ran her hand back and forth. "Horizontal. I don't think you ever get used to it. But if you'll be here for it, welcome, we're glad to have you. And it rhymes with whir." Miller looked up, puzzled. "The name of the birds."

44

chapter 7

"I'LL DRIVE," Miller said.
"Suit yourself," Eli said. "I'm an enlightened kind of guy."
"Is it a big deal?"
"Never a big deal," he said, getting in the car.
"Then tell me where I'm going."
"North."
"Left?" she said.
He smiled. "Yes, left."
"Just checking." She pulled out onto the highway.
"How come you're called Miller when that's not your name?" he said.

She hesitated, thinking this was all another bad idea. "Miller's my maiden name. It's what everybody called me in high school and then it just stuck. My given name's Corinne, but I was never a Corinne or even a Cory. I was a tomboy my whole life so Miller fits, I guess. If someone yelled out Corinne in a crowded room I wouldn't even turn around."

"Tomboy says sports, does it not? Did you have one?"
"Mr. Question Man. I wonder if that comes from bartending or you're just naturally that way."
"It's not from bartending. You ask one question there and you're dead, you have to listen for an hour."
"Then it's just who you are. I'll take that. Yes, I did have a sport. It was volleyball."
"Wow, I wasn't expecting that," he said. "What kind? Team? Beach?"
"Team. At least in school."
"High school? College?"
"Both." He was getting too close again. She wondered why she didn't learn.
"Scholarship?"

Miller sighed. He was like an attorney. "No, there wasn't a women's volleyball team."

"Then how did you play in college? Intramurals?"

"I would never play intramurals. Don't make me tell you this." She watched his eyes grow wide anticipating what she was going to say.

"Holy shit," he said. "Really?"

"Men's team, really. I was the only one ever, my one claim to fame. Makes me sound totally feminine, doesn't it? But it was their fault. They said I could try out, then when I beat out everybody else they had to let me play."

"And you were good."

"I held my own," she said. "I was just a little intense, a little wired, playing with the boys. I'm stopping now. No more. What about you? What sports did you play?"

"My dad was a high school coach," he said, "so I played every sport he didn't coach."

"It wouldn't have worked? You don't get along?"

"We get along now, just not necessarily then. I wanted to have everything be on my own."

"I can see that. So what sports?"

"He coached basketball and tennis so that left me football and baseball in high school, which was fine with me. College, no sports. Racquetball and running on the side."

"Why not in college?"

"In the middle of New York City, you've got better things to do."

"College in the city? That's crazy. What'd you major in? Look what you started. Now I'm doing it to you."

"Turn left up here and go to the back of the shopping center," he said. "Fine arts with a concentration in metal work."

"I'll shut up now," Miller said. "Mostly because I can't come up with anything to say. I don't think I ever knew anyone who majored in fine arts."

"That's what you get for hanging around with jocks."

The gym was large enough, well lit, clean, not anything like her own but still entirely acceptable. In fact, being so low-key, at the moment it was far more than acceptable. Eli checked them in.

"Do you need the tour?" he said.

"No, I can figure it out on my own." It wasn't hard, free weights here, machines over there, treadmills, ladders, elliptical in the next large room with all the TV monitors. *Forgive me, Janelle, but it's not so bad.* "I just wish I had music."

"Where's yours?" he said. "You must have a ton of set lists."

"I'll have to get new ones. That was all interval training, mostly way too fast for treadmill and I wasn't supposed to keep it anyway."

"I can't help you out with that, but I'll be over this way. Come and find me when you're done."

Miller took a survey down the length of the room. On a weekday morning, it was all just normal gym folk, doing their thing, getting by. She missed her revved-up music, her classes, her hardcore people. Eli was right, it was an adrenaline rush, exciting, challenging every day. Did it become an obsession? She hadn't thought so, at least not until the bad times. Then it was a familiar place to be, a necessary place to be. What was left of the known routine of her life, that was all. It devastated her having to give it up. But she knew it was the right thing to do. With the anxiety and the hard-charging put together, her heart was pounding in her throat and she could barely breathe.

No Lycra today, no tank tops, just an old pair of track pants, a long-sleeved t-shirt and with her hair pulled back in a ponytail she blended in just fine. Miller went past all the talk shows with their headlines scrolling across the bottom of the screen and chose a treadmill in front of old reruns of *Friends*. Without sound only a guess could be made as to what was going on, but what difference did it make?

She started out slow, remembering the feel of it. Walk, don't run, she had to keep telling herself. All right, but let's walk with a purpose. She gradually increased the incline till she liked the amount of effort required. No more checking heart rates, no more sprints and cool downs, just this.

She settled into a comfortable but brisk pace and felt more at home in her own skin than she had in what seemed like a very long time. Then it occurred to her with a small amount of horror that she recognized the *Friends* episode, the one where Monica fell in love with Tom Selleck. Okay, there were worse things than being at a gym in a strange place with nothing else to do but work out on a treadmill and watch Tom Selleck. She was beginning to wonder, if she kept going, would they show the episodes in order and would he be in the next one, when Eli stepped onto the treadmill next to her.

Miller was glad he'd chosen the same type of gym clothes, nothing showing skin or physique.

"You're done?" she said.

"I'll just keep up with you if I can till you're ready."

"I've seen the pace you set. You can keep up. It isn't over yet, that's all."

"What isn't over?" Eli peered up at the screen. "That isn't *Friends*, is it?"

Miller put a finger to her lips. "Shh," she said. "It's more than that. It's Tom Selleck."

"But you can't even hear it."

"Doesn't matter."

"That's way more than I ever wanted to know," he said.

In her driveway, they both got out of the car.

"What did you think?" he said. "Will you join?"

"I have to consult with my conscience since I can't run it by Janelle. But probably. Yes. And so thank you very much for letting me use your guest pass. That was incredibly thoughtful of you."

"If you do join and you get on a schedule and I'm on the same schedule then maybe we can go together."

"Maybe we can," Miller said. "I have a feeling though that going or not would depend on the weather. If it was pouring rain, yes. If not, I need to be out on the beach."

"That works for me. But here," he said, leaning against the car. "I wanted to show you something." He took out his phone and scrolled through a blur of screens. She stood beside him, frowning. When he tapped the last time, a photo of a common murre appeared. He tapped again and held the phone up. She listened and her mouth fell open. The noise was deafening, like a thousand screeching guests at a cocktail party gone very wrong. Actually, it was a community of ten thousand common murres making a whole host of insane bird sounds.

"What *is* that?" she said.

"Bird guide for your phone. I found it after we went to the gardening store. I'd give it to you except I can't put it on your phone for you and you won't let me pay for anything anyway."

"Correct. Now that I know there is such a thing, I'll find it. But it never occurred to me there'd be a way to hear their voice. And you know what it says, all those birds together? He wasn't alone out there."

"Maybe not," Eli said. "Not really."

chapter 8

MILLER BOUGHT a printed tide table in the hardware store. She joined the gym. At the Corner Market, she listened to a heated debate over how to clear salal brush from a neglected piece of property. Ahead of her in line, old Frank mentioned in passing that he'd been flattened between two carts on the golf course but was out of the hospital and doing fine.

After he was gone, the clerk, wrapped in an apron with a pencil stuck in her hair, said, "Those old guys." She clucked a little and shook her head.

In the post office, another crowd had gathered to discuss the best method for repelling deer. Miller worked her way through them to her box, but it was empty. Someone could at least have sent her a magazine. She considered that it was all right, though. Her children stayed in touch, caring about each other, caring about her, and that was everything.

She went out again and up into the dunes to read more carefully the sign about shellfish on the beach.

On the access road next to her, the beach patrol park ranger, his official hat crooked on his head, leaned out the window of his white Cherokee.

"Glad to see somebody's reading our signs."

It wasn't Miller's beach, or her town, or her state, so she didn't feel she should have opinions, but she could ask questions, couldn't she?

"How do people feel about all the driving on the beach?" she said.

"Well," he said, scratching his head. "Some are for it. Some don't like it. Open access, though, that's what it's all about."

"Are there ever problems?"

"You bet. Had a guy broke his foot. Turns out he was out there letting his ten-year-old son drive the Jeep around, no seat belts or anything, and the kid rolled it. They got cited for just about everything in the book." He indicated the notebook on the seat beside him. "Got a lot of complaints right now about camping. Residents are sick of it. Labor Day we had over a hundred campsites. That's a whole lot of waste and garbage and whatnot up there in the dunes."

"Do kids ever get into trouble?" she said, thinking of her own.

"Drinking, partying, the normal kind of thing." He flipped over the notebook page and checked it. "Just gave a warning to a girl in a pickup truck. There she was twenty feet from the sign and she never even saw it. She's moving right now."

Miller glanced up in time to see a huge shiny black truck crossing the beach from south to north.

"Name's Dan, here's my phone number in case there's anything else you ever need to know. Got all kinds of stories, you wouldn't believe the things I see." He let out a long breath. "In the winter, though, I'm pretty happy to just sit in my living room and look out at the rain."

Miller was instantly depressed.

Eli called while she was standing in the kitchen contemplating dinner.

"Hi, this is the guy from the condos, the one with the motorcycle? Is Miller there?" he said.

She smiled. "Thank you for saying hello first. Where are you?"

"It's that job thing, remember? I'm at work and I don't have any bar groupies tonight so I just thought you might want to fill in."

"Bar groupie? Guess what. I didn't even know there was such a thing. But I can't go to a bar on a Tuesday night. And I've never been in a bar by myself ever."

"While that's highly commendable, this isn't just anybody asking. It's me, the one who found a voice for your dead birds."

"That's true, you did, but I was just about to make dinner."

"Didn't somebody I know have only good things to say about the veggie pizza?"

"Okay, you win. They say there's a first time for everything." She tried hard not to think about it.

"It's a brave new world," he said.

"I'll be there in twenty minutes. I'm hanging up now, condo guy."

Many of the tables were occupied and the noise level was high, but there was only one older man seated at the end of the bar. Miller slid onto a stool. It was strange to see Eli on the other side, back-lit in blue, though he seemed perfectly at ease, in his element.

"I'm glad you came," he said. "Good decision."

"I wasn't sure what bar groupies wore." She looked down at her jeans and running shoes.

"Clothes I can guarantee you don't have," he said.

"There's an assumption."

"But close to right, if not dead on. What can I get you? And have you eaten? Do you want dinner?"

"No, yes, dry, white and affordable, the pizza and you know the deal, right?"

"How could I forget the deal? Very dry? Crisp?"

"Yes, please."

She watched as he took a bottle of wine out of the cooler, uncorked it, poured generously and set the glass in front of her.

"This is weird," she said. She tasted the wine. "It's perfect. What is it?"

"Sancerre. Three dollars a glass, plus a dollar tip for the bartender's education fund." He stared her down so that she couldn't say anything. He reached under the counter and arranged a place setting in front of her, mat, flatware, folded napkin.

"You've done this before," she said.

"Only a few thousand times."

Miller glanced up at the screen over the bar. "The Dodgers. I don't know the rules. Are groupies allowed to watch?"

"No. But jocks are. You can't be a Dodgers fan."

"I'm not but the Padres never have a prayer of getting into the playoffs so you have to go somewhere."

"I'll be right back," he said and left to put her order into the kitchen and then take care of the man at the other end of the bar and the woman who'd sat down next to him.

Miller sipped the wine slowly. It was beyond good and she could tell it was expensive. She hoped she didn't get him fired.

"When were you going to tell me about the tattoos?" she said when he came back. He was wearing a black t-shirt that for the first time showed his arms. "That's a lot."

"Only one arm though. I'm finding out that in New York it said one thing, but here it says something else you sort of have to overcome."

"Is that hard?"

"No. I just smile more."

He had a smile that lit up a whole room and would work every time on anyone, but she wasn't about to mention that. She took out her phone, went through the screens and handed it to him.

"You found the bird guide," he said.

"I did. Thank you for that."

"But what is this? The hawk?"

"Yes. Northern harrier. But here, give it back a minute."

She typed in a name, brought up another set of photos and returned it to him.

"The little gray guys," he said. He read the name. "Sanderlings. How did you manage to figure it out?"

"The guide from the gardening store. Maybe it's cheating, but it says they're always here and you can tell them by the dark triangle on their shoulder in the winter. I started over again in the right light, there it was, and once you've seen it you can't understand how you ever missed it."

"I know you're out there all the time and putting everything you've got into this," he said. "It's not cheating."

"I'll be calling you as a character witness."

"But now I want to do it again. When can I go?"

"You can go whenever you want. The beach is free, you know."

"I'm not interested in being out there by myself. Half the fun is seeing what you get into and your Kleenex and chocolate and notebook and everything."

Hello? Janelle? "I've got some things to do tomorrow," she said. "How about Thursday?"

"Wait a minute." He pulled out his phone. "I've got to check when low tide is."

"You have that, too? Unbelievable."

"What do you want to know? I can tell you about mixed and semidiurnal tides, lunar cycles, spring tides, neap tides, I've got it covered."

"Just low tide on Thursday. That's about all I can handle."

"Thursday, winds strong from the south/southwest, high tide at 8:07 AM, low tide at 2:52 PM."

"So let's say one o'clock?"

"I'll be there," he said. "And my faith wasn't misplaced. As far as bar groupies go, you top the charts."

"Thanks," she said. "Words I've been waiting all my life to hear."

chapter 9

THE SAME BANSHEE winds that screamed in the night were still howling in the morning, all trace of gentle breezes gone. Welcome to it, Miller thought, the real world out here.

"I hope you're ready for this," she said. Eli wore a wool pea coat with the collar turned up and a watch cap pulled down to his eyes. She wore a down coat and the same kind of watch cap.

"Chocolate?" she said, holding out a piece.

"One of these days you'll bring coffee."

"You can keep waiting for that to happen if you want."

The wind was in their face from the moment they stepped off the access road, forcing their progress to a snail's pace. Talk was impossible unless they shouted.

The wild conditions brought out the dogs. A very wet and sand-covered Irish setter crashed along in the waves chasing gulls. A Rottweiler loped along in rippling, self-confident strides, master of his own weird universe. As they watched, a woman let her big fluffy chow off the leash and it morphed immediately from a dignified strolling above-it-all presence into an imitation of a pogo stick, bouncing straight up and down all over the beach and then into the waves where it turned and abruptly sank down into the water. Miller didn't think she'd ever seen a dog smile before. This one did.

Farther down the beach, Eli put a hand on her arm to get her attention and pointed. A dead brown pelican lay below the debris of the high tide line, not even wet yet. Eli frowned up at the sky as if the bird might have just dropped out of it. Miller bent down to take a picture. The black and white feathers were still puffed up, blowing in the wind. The dark green gnarly pouch on the underside of the bill glistened like an exotic lizard skin bag in an upscale boutique. The downy yellow face was struck, a mask, the blank eyes no longer searching for fish in endless deep waters.

Miller looked up at Eli and put her hand over her heart. He nodded in agreement. She turned her back to the wind and took out her notebook. He watched over her shoulder as she entered one more bird and date.

"Say that I was with you," he shouted into her ear. "That's important."

She shook her head, then opened the notebook again and wrote + *EG*.

They came across the sanderlings and Miller handed Eli the binoculars. He stared through them for a long time then gave her the thumbs up. She had been scanning the dunes and now she pointed him in that direction. The northern harrier hunted, gliding in a steady line just above the beach grass. He studied the hawk as well then turned to her and mouthed, *Good job*.

Though large black clouds were forming around the headlands to the south, mercifully the wind began to die down.

"This is just the beginning, isn't it?" Eli said. "From now on, it'll only keep getting worse."

"That's what everybody says."

"Pretty amazing though. Feels like some other country out here."

Out at the river, the beach backed around into a large, more sheltered area formed by the dunes. A great blue heron fished in the shallows. Something she could actually identify. She got out her notebook. The entries were accumulating.

Eli took the binoculars. "Something's diving out there," he said. "Stays down for a long time." He kept the binoculars trained on the river then gave them back to her. "I know this one from the lakes in Maine. But see what you think."

Miller waited till the dark silhouette resurfaced then held it in the close-up circle of vision. "Loon," she said. Eli pulled out his phone. When he'd retrieved the information he wanted, he passed it to her. "Great," she said, "but which loon?"

"What's your answer?"

"I have to check in with my consultant," she said. "How big do you think it is?"

"Big. Thirty inches easy."

"Common loon it is. Do I have to put your name next to this one too?"

"No, because now that I'm being called a consultant, I want it at the top, please. Boldface type."

"Ego is not your problem," she said.

"From my perspective, believe me, ego's everyone's problem. So what's next? Now I'm hooked."

"Do you want to try those ducks?" she said. She gestured past the heron out to where the river disappeared around a wide bend.

"What ducks? You've got good eyes."

"Here, take them again." She handed him back the binoculars.

"Do I have to buy a pair of these things?" he said. He adjusted for the distance. "Those are definitely ducks. That's all I've got for you."

She took out her phone. "You describe it and I'll see if I can find anything that fits. What color are they?"

"Brown."

"Are you sure?" she said.

"What other choices are there?"

"Buff? Black? Gray?"

"Throw in buff too, and see what happens."

"Anything else?"

"A funky head."

"I sincerely doubt that the word funky is in here anywhere," she said. "It brings up eleven birds, but they aren't all ducks. Most of them are geese."

Eli checked the photos. "This one," he said. "Maybe."

"Look again. Does it have a blue bill?"

"In this light it could be any color. Blue? I don't know. It's pale."

"This is much easier when someone else is doing all the work," she said.

"I noticed. Guess what, I just got upgraded again from consultant to VP."

"Here's the best part," she said. "We can't miss on this one. It says they have a voice that's a squeak like a bathtub toy."

"What self-respecting duck would want to sound like that?"

Miller pressed the tiny icon that brought up a recording of the voice. They listened. It was a squeak and it did sound like a bathtub toy.

"Go for it?" she said.

"No question."

They moved slowly back along the bank of the river. The heron watched nervously and finally rose up, flapping awkwardly off and issuing a loud raspy squawk.

"We didn't make him happy," Eli said.

They stood in the quiet, the only sound the gusting wind, the muted drumroll of the waves far out at the tide line, and a host of high-pitched squeaks. They looked at each other.

"High five," Eli said.

"American wigeon," Miller said. "Who knew?" She'd never even heard of such a duck and now she had its name in her notebook.

chapter 10

THE POST OFFICE appeared to serve as the center of all the community action. Anyone who stood in the middle of that crowd would surely have access to every piece of gossip in town. Normally Miller paused among them just long enough to clutch the junk mail to her as if it might be meaningful before recycling it when no one was looking.

Today, however, when she inserted the gold key and unlocked the door, there was real mail. Peering through her box, she could see the mail ladies in the sorting room on the other side. Now the two of them had a picture of her that was definitely coming into focus. A thick expensive white envelope from a law firm spoke volumes. But also wedged into the narrow space was a second manila envelope from Janelle. Miller silently thanked her for not including any sort of return address that signaled therapist. The mail ladies would have had a field day with that.

There was no question which she would open first. She sat in the kitchen and came close to tears at Janelle's offering, a Pacific Northwest beachcombing guide. She marveled as she paged through it, so much information, everything from line drawings of the Juan de Fuca plate to a color photo of cast-off Dungeness crab shells, where had *that* been when she needed it? She could call Janelle whenever she wanted and sent a long email once a week, that was the agreed upon arrangement, but nowhere did it mention sending thoughtful books.

The other envelope couldn't wait. She'd known it was coming and she had to face it. She removed everything else from the dining room table, took out the papers and laid them out all the way around the edge. It was the only way she could perform the emotional feat required to absorb so much unwanted information. It was all there in the convoluted and impersonal language of the law profession. She started reading then suddenly turned away. Later would be soon enough.

On the beach, walls of dark cloud covered the horizon in every direction. Briefly the rain let up and the sky broke open to reveal a cathedral of blue framed by brilliant white clouds. Then the sky closed in on itself again and a streak of lightning flashed, arcing from cloud to cloud. Miller tried to remember whether rubber boots grounded someone even if they were standing in water, which she was. While she worked on the idea that the answer was no, a rainbow appeared in the east, shimmering, improbable, breathtakingly beautiful.

She was alone except for a mother and daughter whom she noticed first as small bent figures on a vast surface of slick reflected sky. As Miller came nearer, she smiled at their much more casual approach to rain gear, green garbage bags worn over their winter coats and small plastic produce bags tied around their heads. They were soaked to the skin.

"Are we nuts or what!" the mother said. "We drove three hours to get here, no better sand dollar beach on earth, but it was supposed to be sunny today."

Miller dug in her pocket and gave them the sand dollars she'd picked up. It was the least she could do.

"What do you use them for?" she asked, mystified.

"It's for the holidays. We're decorating the whole tree this year in silver-painted sand dollars."

Miller stared at her in disbelief. "This must be the hard part then," she said. It seemed such an onerous task, all that bending and stooping, combing the miles of tidal flats.

"Actually," the mother said, laughing, "this is the fun part."

Behind them, shots suddenly rang out from the green hills. Miller jumped. "Hunting season, honey," the woman said. "Elk and deer." Miller imagined a deer at that very moment running for its life.

chapter 11

ELI ANSWERED ON the first ring.
"*You're* calling *me*," he said. "What's wrong?"
"Hi," Miller said. "It's your beach friend, the one without the coffee."
"Do you assign ring tones?" he said.
"That's a secret."
"Which means you do. Sometime, we're both going to tell each other at the same time what they are."
"Never."
"Now I really want to know."
"Let's go back to the beginning of this conversation," she said. "And by the way, I have called you. I think. Haven't I?"
"Nope, that's not your style. It's always me who calls you."
"Sorry. Go back again."
"Is there something wrong?" he said. "If there is, what you do is just come out and say it."
"That's not going to be easy."
"This is maddening. If you don't say something soon, I'll be over there at your front door."
"I just need your help, okay?" she said.
"You shouldn't even have to ask. For what?"
"Can you please drive me to get my car?"
There was hesitation on the other end of the line. "Sure," he said. "Where is it? Did it die or something?"
"No, nothing like that. It's at the gym."
"At the gym? Are you all right? You didn't get jumped or anything, did you?"
"No, nothing like that either. It's just embarrassing, that's all. Not over the phone. I'll tell you in the car."

She climbed into the Jeep carefully wearing a heavy sweatshirt jacket with the sleeves pulled down over her hands. Out on the road, heading north, Eli turned to her.

"Okay," he said. "Out with it."

She pulled back the left sleeve. On her arm was a cast with just her thumb and fingers sticking out at the end of it.

"Holy shit. What did you break?"

"My wrist."

"You did that at the gym?"

"Yes."

"No way you're a klutz so there's got to be some other explanation. Just so long as somebody didn't push you around or anything."

"Hopefully that would never happen," she said. "I'm going to be honest with you like I said I always would. It was crowded and there was this guy next to me on the treadmill, older, out of shape, sort of un-gym-like in his Bermuda shorts and Oregon sweatshirt but very sweet. He kept talking to me, just a little, he was pretty out of breath, nice comments like, hey, this looks easy for you and things like that. I didn't exactly mind, but I couldn't concentrate…"

"On Tom Selleck."

"…on *Seinfeld*, for worrying about him. Anyway, I meant to try and say in a polite way that he should slow down, and I turned to him and he thought, I don't know what he thought, but he tried to wink at me and lost his balance and started to go down. I jumped off the treadmill to catch him and at least break his fall, but my wrist came down hard on the railing. They had to call in the paramedics for him. He blew his knee out. They took him away in an ambulance. The guy behind the desk, the short one with the buzz cut, took me to Urgent Care which by the way is right around the corner, good planning, and told me to call him when I was done and he'd take me home, which he did. I feel terrible about all of it. I don't even know the old guy's name."

"That's what he gets for hitting on women he shouldn't be hitting on. But thank God. My worst fear was that you'd left your car because you ended up spending the night somewhere you didn't want to."

"Look at me," Miller said. "I'm a mother with three kids. How would I end up in a situation like that? I wouldn't. Ever. And I know my way around the occasional creep who shows up at a gym. Believe me, this guy wasn't one of those."

"You have three kids?"

"You see? I do. JC's twenty-two, in London with her boyfriend, hopefully in graduate school, that's where she's supposed to be, but I'm having my doubts about that part of it, and Dell's doing her junior year abroad in Spain."

"Your kids came right on top of each other," he said.

"Yes they did."

"And they're all far away."

"Yes they are."

"But why didn't you call me? You know I would have been up there in five seconds. I could have taken you to Urgent Care. I'd have wanted to do that."

"Because," Miller said.

"There's an answer." Eli tapped his fingers on the steering wheel, thinking. "And when did this happen? Today's Monday. Yesterday?"

"No."

"Saturday?"

"Yes."

"It happened almost three days ago and you're just letting me know now?" Eli was thoughtful for another long moment. "Monica was the reason," he said. There was silence. He took a deep annoyed breath and spoke again. "How is your wrist? Does it hurt?"

"Not as much. Now it just throbs. They gave me extra-strength something to take."

"What makes you think you can drive?"

"I'll manage. It's not that far."

"I've got to be at work at five," he said, "but you're coming to my house and I'm making you lunch."

"You don't have to do that."

"I know I don't have to do it, but I am. I'm just warning you, you're from California and I don't have any kale."

"You know what I have? I'd forgotten all about them. Hot dogs."

"Done," he said. "I would kill for a hot dog. Or six."

Eli followed her home and pulled into the driveway behind her.

"What are you doing?" she said.

"You're not carrying anything."

"A package of hot dogs? But since you're here, do you want to see the house?"

"Sure," he said, but as soon as he came in through the front door Miller realized that she'd made a grave mistake. The legal papers were exactly where she'd left them, all around the edge of the dining room table. She closed her eyes and resigned herself. Nothing to be done about it now.

Eli took in everything, the open room, the sofas, the stone fireplace, the French doors and deck and ocean, the bookshelves. The table. It wasn't a difficult conclusion to draw. He stopped and looked at her. It was the right thing, absolutely, but also hard sometimes, she thought, not talking about it, not telling anyone. He went on past the moment as if it hadn't happened, as if all that paperwork didn't exist.

"This is a fine place," he said. "Everything about it. Those bookshelves are a work of art."

"Thank you. My grandparents lived outside Portland so this was only their summer house starting from a long time ago, but it didn't used to look like this at all. My mother took it on as her project. She liked things to be her way and this is definitely her way. Someone rented it. Hugh Donaldson. He was a poet."

Eli was scanning across the rows of books. "Some of his books are right here," he said. "A real poet. A published one."

"He's a little bit famous or so I've heard. I know he got awards and things." She hesitated, standing in the kitchen archway with the hot dogs in her hand. "I think my mother liked him," she said.

"A lot." Eli looked at her again. She met his eyes but let the comment stay where it was.

"Life gets complicated sometimes," he said.

"Yes," she said. "It does."

Since there were no buns, Eli ate his hot dogs folded into toasted bread and smothered with melted cheese, onions, left-behind relish from the refrigerator, mustard, ketchup and half a can of chili.

"That is truly disgusting," Miller said.

"That's a chili cheese dog and it's not disgusting at all. In New York you can pay twelve bucks for that."

"I wouldn't." She ate her hot dogs the way she'd planned to, one slice at a time dragged through pools of ketchup and mustard. "They taste so good it's a crime," she said.

"It's a crime what you're doing to them."

"How did you become a vegan? If I recall correctly, it had to do with a woman."

"Correct," he said. "Her name was Alex. She came in the bar one night with friends and asked for celery juice. Rules number one through five hundred say never date over the bar but the celery juice thing threw me a little and to make a long story short, we ended up together, there was a mistake made and she got pregnant, we rented a farm in upstate New York, she lost the baby. Her dream, besides six kids, was always to be organic, green, postconsumer, carbon neutral, zero waste, off the grid, whatever, and I was driving a pickup that ran on cooking oil, knee deep in shit and compost, living on beans and rice, raising goats to make sweaters and that was all fine, I would have done it, but it wasn't my dream. That's what I found out. You can't live someone else's dream. So to help both of us out, I bought a motorcycle and a very large map and made some phone calls to friends of friends, got the hell out of there and here I am. And I think she lives in a commune now."

"Maybe you don't want to hear this," Miller said, "but I'm sorry about the baby."

"My heart stopped about fifty times on that one. All of it was such a shock." He paused. "But possibly you know about that."

"Possibly I do."

"How old were you? Are we good enough friends yet that I can ask?"

"We're good enough friends. I was twenty. It was..." She started to say 'our' but changed it, "... my senior year."

"And you still graduated?"

"With a month to go. No more volleyball, though, I guess that's obvious. I was a journalism major and lost my place on the editorial staff of the paper, too. That was tough. I loved that job, but I was so exhausted I just couldn't keep up with everything. Not that I regret it or would ever do anything different even if I had the chance. Sam's the best thing that ever happened to me. And then JC and Dell are the other best things."

"Are you able to keep in touch with them?"

"Every day. That's what keeps me sane." Miller pushed another slice of hot dog around with her fork. "And you," she said. "You really have been a good friend and I'm grateful."

"I have your back no matter what," he said. "Trust me on that."

"I do trust you. You and Janelle. The rest of the world, it's a little bit harder right now."

Miller read what she needed to read of the legal documents and made the phone call, watching through the French doors as the wind came up. It shrieked and bellowed out of the southwest, bent on tearing limbs from trees, wires from poles, giving no one any reason to go out. She gladly fought her way down the dune path to the beach.

As she stood with her back turned, the hard drops ricocheting off her vinyl rain gear like small explosions, her eye was caught by a minivan turning onto the north beach. A woman parked, slid open the door, pulled out a blanket and settled it in the flying sand. Her two small daughters stood holding buckets and shovels, their jackets flapping wildly, their hair standing straight out behind them.

Five minutes later, reason having prevailed, the woman packed everything up and was gone.

Miller moved her attention to a crab struggling at the edge of the waves. A gull swooped in, yanked the crab out of the water and began stabbing at it. Miller quickly looked away. Farther along the beach, the body of a mottled brown juvenile gull was ripped violently apart, head and feet torn off, feathers scattered across the wet sand. She turned from the sight again, chastened and subdued.

Far down at the end of the beach, low tide had once again uncovered the acre of razor clams, each burrow marked by a hole surrounded by a wide sand collar. Small spurts of water gurgled up over the collar then percolated quickly back into the sand, making it appear as if the clams were down there in their sandy hiding places exhaling ocean.

Blinking into the rain, Miller pressed hard with her boot against one of the collars. The gurgling immediately stopped. Just to see what would happen, she stomped around in the damp sand. The entire area quieted. A few seconds later, the holes began to sputter again. It was almost, in its own weird way, like having a conversation with a clam, a dialogue of some sort. She'd read enough about them, however, to know that when the tide came back in the razors would have larger problems to deal with. Their predators would swarm in with the ocean waters, flatfish, sea stars, sea snails, carnivorous worms, all of them, like the hawk and the gull, only following the law of survival: eat or be eaten.

Miller closed her eyes and turned back into the wind, letting it tear at her clothes and pulse against her face until her grievances were blown away, drowned in the sting of the rain and crashing sound of the waves.

chapter 12

INSTEAD OF GETTING colder, for a day it grew warmer, a miracle summer passage at the beginning of November. The sun beat down. The wind blew warm and silken from the east, taking the tops off the waves in bridal veil sprays, assembling the breakers into ruler-straight lines of aquarium green. It was a good day for not being alone.

"Hey, it's Miller," she said.

"It's Janis Joplin," Eli said. "That's all I'll say."

"What? Oh no, wait a minute."

"It's true."

"I'll forget I heard that," she said. "What I was calling for was to see if you were interested in a walk on the beach."

"You know I'm always interested in a walk on the beach. And today there's not a hurricane out there. I think I even see the sun."

"But if you don't mind, let's go another way," Eli said in the parking lot. "I want to show you something." He led her up and over the dunes in front of the condos. There on the north beach, tucked into a hilly clump of sand in the middle of the path, was a round silver and black pop-up tent all by itself, no truck or car parked anywhere nearby. They walked quietly past, noting a cooler and quilt piled up against a driftwood log and a pair of huge tennis shoes placed just outside the zipped flap. Ragged snoring issued from the tent's interior.

"What was that?" Miller said down on the beach.

"I don't know. He was there when I went running this morning. Maybe he partied hard all night somewhere, but definitely not here. Whatever happened, he's dead to the world."

"How funny."

Eli touched a large gelatinous circle with his toe. "These are all over the place. What are they?"

"Jellyfish," Miller said.

"That's it?"

"I tried to find out more, but I can't. You look at them and tell me what color all that stuff inside is."

"Blue."

"What kind of blue?"

"Bright blue. Loud blue."

"That's what I see, too. According to my books they should be moon jellyfish, but those have insides that are the opposite of loud blue, like pale yellow and rose."

"We've just discovered a rare new jellyfish then."

"Obviously."

As they walked, the sanderlings skittered ahead of them en masse, swooped around in great arcs behind then flowed on ahead again.

"Maybe this is strange," Eli said, "but I see those guys all the time when I'm running and I like knowing what they are. Why is that?"

"I'll give you Janelle's number."

"Can I borrow the binoculars?"

He raised them to his eyes. "Check it out," he said, handing them back. "I was looking for the one-legged guy. Is that some kind of cosmic joke?"

Miller saw through the binoculars that the entire group had halted in small perfectly still clusters and knots facing into the wind and all of them were standing on one leg.

He glanced up. "Bird alert. Incoming."

A line of black ducks flapped by flashing white wing patches.

"I'm taking your approach," Miller said. "Ducks. Black ducks."

Eli took out his phone. "VP comes to the rescue. Oregon coast, duck, black with white." He held up a photo. "Is it or is it not those ducks?"

Miller took out her notebook. "It is," she said.

"White-winged scoter, whatever that is. What happened to that thing?" The notebook looked as if it had drowned.

"My pockets aren't waterproof. I started copying it all over in another one when I get home."

"But this'll be the one that means something."

The corners were dog-eared and the pages were blurred. "I suppose," she said.

"You're not forgetting to put my name back in when you copy it, are you?"

Miller laughed. "How could I forget?"

"This is what I like," Eli said, bending down to retrieve something from the sand. "That last storm did a number." He picked up a sea-encrusted bottle that had the words *No gasificada* and *Argentina* visible on its side. A few feet away he picked up another. He held it up. "Japanese dishwashing liquid. Do you think it floated all the way here from Japan?"

"Or came from a Japanese ship?"

"Or from somebody here who just thinks the Japanese make a really good dishwashing soap. I wonder what aisle you find that in."

Out at the river, they came across an entirely different type of debris.

"Good grief," Miller said. "What is that?"

"That is, or was, a deer."

"A lady on the beach told me it was hunting season."

"Absolutely. In upstate New York, you didn't dare go five steps past your property at this time of year or someone would be firing at you. Not all hunters are geniuses."

"Like this one?" she said. Only part of the carcass remained and there was no top to the head, no eyes, only half a skull, empty. "They just dumped it in the river?"

"They got what they wanted from it."

"Which is?"

"Look at it. Maybe the haunch for meat. But I'd say the most important part was the antlers to put on their wall."

Miller winced, realizing he was right.

They sat with their backs against a log facing the river. "This is too much," Eli said. "I'd forgotten what sun felt like. And by the way, how are you? How's your wrist?"

"Better. Doesn't hurt nearly as much."

"When do you get the cast off?"

"First week in December."

"Hard to believe all of that's coming up so soon. What is that in the river? It's not a loon, too much white on it."

"I have two thoughts," she said. "One is, if you have a system that works you should stick with it and the other one is the person with top of the page credit should be earning it."

Eli held out his hand for the binoculars. "For starters, it's not duck-shaped, it's that other thing."

"Got it."

"Black and white, big," he said. Miller held up the photos. "None of those. Add gray."

She held up the phone again. "Eleven birds."

"Yes. See, the loon's in there, but it's this one."

"Western grebe," she said. "Another bird I never heard of. And it's got a freaky bright red eye."

"From here I can't tell if it has eyes at all. But the VP scores again."

"What happened to the team part? We're in this together, are we not? I'm the one doing the search, am I not?"

"You're right," he said. "The Briggs-Greer Bird Identifying Team scores again. How's that? To me it sounds more like a law firm."

Crows sailed down out of the sky, creating a nasal ruckus. Behind them, a gull broke into the crow noise with a hoarse guttural voice, honking and scolding like a mad goose.

"Jesus, that's loud," Eli said. "The crows were bad enough. What's his problem?"

"Maybe us," Miller said. "Invading his beach. What is that out there in the sand?" She got up and went to retrieve it. She came back carrying a damp discarded bouquet of long-stemmed yellow chrysanthemums and red carnations.

"You know where I bet this came from?" She sat back down again. "Homecoming."

"Somebody just threw their flowers in the river?"

"Maybe, if the evening was going that way. I think the high school's right up around the bend."

"High school," Eli said. "But who cared about Homecoming? Was there a dance? I don't even remember. The deal breaker was the prom. Did you go?"

"To the prom? Good God, for me it's longer, but even for you that's a long time ago. Yes," she said. "I went."

"With who?"

"I can't believe you're talking about this. Jake Williams."

"Did you sleep with him?"

"Yikes. Just put it right out there. No, I didn't sleep with him. I didn't sleep with anyone in high school."

"Did you have fun at the prom anyway?"

"No. We broke up at two in the morning. I wanted it to be romantic and he wasn't in the mood and I was so tired and wearing a strapless bra that was killing me. When I told him I just wanted to go home, he said I was no fun and he was breaking up with me, which was reasonable at that point, and he made me give back the locket with his picture in it that he'd given me. So actually, it was a terrible night. What about you? Did you go to the prom?"

"I did, with Angela Royer."

"I guess I'm supposed to ask. Did you sleep with her?"

"In the park in the middle of the night, we ditched the schedule, but she hung her dress in a tree so it wouldn't get messed up and some little shit from the school newspaper took a picture of it. The photograph went around the school and then got to her dad."

"Oh my God," Miller said. "That's the best prom story I ever heard. Then what happened?"

"I was never allowed to see her again and as soon as we graduated her grandparents took her to France for the whole summer."

"Where is she now? Do you know?"

"She's a graphic designer in New York and a damned good one," he said. "I've seen some of her stuff. We tried to get together once, but it didn't work out. I forget why. What happened to Jake Williams?"

"I heard he's a doctor and has four kids. Were you and Angela interested in art together?"

"Actually, she's the one who got me into it. I liked her and she was in all those art classes, so I took one with her and then another one and then another one. The thing is, she was different, and a guy taking that much art was different, particularly a guy in sports. She helped me believe in myself and go with what I wanted no matter what anyone else thought."

"I like her and I don't even know her," Miller said. "But why aren't you in it anymore?"

"Just too many things got in the way. I could use a running partner if you want to come out here with me sometimes."

"I thought you had a running partner."

"That's over."

She looked at him. "It is? Why?" She'd been afraid of this.

"Because the next time you break something at the gym, I want to be there."

"Don't," she said. "That's not fair."

"No, that's not it entirely. It was time. And she agreed."

"You'd better be right about that. But about the running, I can't. I shouldn't anyway, but surprising as it might be, I think now I have to walk because I don't want to miss anything."

"Like dead pelicans and Japanese dishwashing liquid."

"Exactly."

"That's a good place to be then," he said.

"You know what?" she said. "It is a good place to be."

On the other hand, she thought, when it hurts so bad you can't stand it, out here in the wind and rain was the only place to be.

chapter 13

IT RAINED FOR twelve hours straight, then twenty-four hours, then twenty-eight hours. Thunder rumbled in the distance and lightning flashed across the sky. Even the word torrential no longer applied to the volume of rain that fell.

On these awful days, there was nothing else to do but go to the gym. Once, Eli simply opened her front door and did a somewhat muted version of his parking lot whistle, scaring Miller half to death.

"Thank heaven I wasn't in the shower," she said. He raised his eyebrows but said nothing.

Miller counted herself lucky. He was easy to be with. They traveled back and forth in the rain and worked out in companionable silence. She knew he watched her from the back of the gym sometimes, checking out who might be her next victim, he assured her later, worried about the cast still on her arm, noticing when she couldn't help it any longer and switched from walking to running. She wasn't pushing hard, the pace was reasonable and it made her feel better, stronger, more like the person she remembered herself to be. He didn't comment, just started now and then running on the treadmill next to hers.

"I can wink and run at the same time," he said.

"So talented, but don't."

Every afternoon Eli texted a photo of whatever he'd found that was of interest and she texted one back. He waited to be asked on beach walks, respecting her privacy, the need for solitude, and for that she was even more grateful.

Even when the rain stopped, rivulets of water still ran like creeks. Miller recognized the dead bird that had been on the access road for days, another Western grebe, his red eye about all that was left to recommend him. At first he'd only been shot, a black bullet hole centered in the back of his head. Now he'd also been flattened by pickup traffic and washed down into the drainage ditch.

Miller watched the northern harrier hunt, soaring low over the dunes. At regular intervals he turned and hung forward in the air, his body taut, staring into the dune grass with seemingly enough intensity to spark a fire. He repeated the pattern all the way down the dunes, working his space, a hunter of genetically honed and bloodlessly efficient skills. She considered that he must be successful, he was still here after all, but the only things she'd seen worth eating in the dunes were wooly bear caterpillars and one long and scary-looking snake.

The storms brought in debris, crab shells, stones, driftwood and dozens of big gaper clam shells that resembled broken crockery after their rough journey into shore. In among the tide wrack was a cache of red rock crab shells and the fragile little gray and pink helmet-shaped carapaces of the mole crab. All of it was already in her notebook. A handful of sea gooseberries decorated the tide line along with a few empty cans of Coors Lite and PBR. A flash of silver caught her eye, a tiny black-striped fish, all iridescent pink and green, something akin to a herring or a smelt. How strange to see a fish here, she thought, and then stopped. It was the ocean. Where else would a fish be?

She didn't usually walk on a rising tide, but Miller was certain she was being careful, staying in a safe zone high up on the beach, surely far enough away from the churning waves. Without warning a sneaker wave bowled in out of nowhere, swirled around her legs and dumped water in over the tops of her rubber boots, soaking her socks and jeans. Standing helplessly in the unexpected rush of surf, she looked down at where her feet had been and experienced a dizziness bordering on vertigo. She was suddenly in the ocean rather than next to it, not at all where she wanted to be. The wave had moved so fast and so far, powering in, suctioning back out, that she could barely hold her footing. She realized in almost a panic that anything with less strength than her own, a child or a dog, could easily have been swept away.

In the kitchen, still shaken, she clicked on her phone and then stared wide-eyed at the screen before she burst out laughing. Every time this happened, she was overwhelmed again with what a simple thing it was and how wonderful it felt, to laugh. "Thank you," she said quietly, running her finger over the screen. The photo, taken from the bartender's perspective was, inconceivably, of the postmistresses grinning lecherously and saluting him with their glasses of whiskey. The text underneath said: *Help!*

chapter 14

A SMALL CROWD on the north beach drew Miller's attention. The shellfish ban was still in place and for the past few weeks, seals had been staggering ashore all along the coast, ill and dying, possibly from eating infected razor clams. Now here was another one. The crowd consisted of a handful of dog walkers, a woman chattily introducing herself to everyone as Marie with her baby from Oceanview, and a young couple from Idaho announcing with awe that they were seeing the ocean for the first time.

The crowd grew to include a local police officer and the general manager of the Oceanview Aquarium who arrived in his rusted-out Datsun station wagon. He wore jeans and a down jacket, carried his scientific gear in a black nylon backpack and wrote his notes out in an old spiral notebook in worse shape than Miller's. She guessed that being the manager of the local aquarium might not be the most sought after job in the world.

The seal, a large one, sleek and brown, swam erratically close into shore then lay still in the water. It appeared to be exhausted. The aquarium manager explained that this was the pattern. The seals came ashore to rest, stayed three or four days and died without ever going back out to sea. What about an autopsy? One of the women asked. Why couldn't anyone say why the seals were dying? The aquarium manager, not paid enough to do the job in the first place, shrugged. His answer seemed to be that sometimes there were no answers.

Where the aquarium manager was reticent, Marie was not. She'd lived here all her life, she told them, and it was obvious she knew a great deal about the beach, the tides, currents, wave patterns, the steelhead runs, the ways of the ocean. Miller walked back up the access road deep in thought, wondering if she would ever know even half that much.

"You can walk right into me if you want. I won't mind."

Miller looked up, startled. Eli was standing in the middle of the road.

"Oh, sorry," she said. "I didn't see you."

"I got that. What's going on down there?"

"A seal's dying. Some of them wanted to try and scare him out into deeper water, but the aquarium manager came and said to leave him alone, it's just what's happening with seals right now."

"Try telling that to the seal. Listen, come with me, I was on my way down to Pine Ridge just to see what's there. Have you ever been?"

"A long time ago," she said. "All I remember is that it's a little upscale, for out here anyway, and there was a good bookstore. I'll go. Just let me get these boots off. I've found out beach weather's different than town weather and people pretty quickly decide that you're strange. Can we stop at the post office, too? I have to mail some things."

"No, we cannot," he said. "Not this post office anyway. We'll find another one somewhere."

Miller stared at him then remembered the photo. "I can't wait to hear how that all went. I laughed so hard I was crying."

"Where are you when I need you?"

"This works out well," Miller said in the car. "I try and send postcards at least a couple times a week, but I was running out of the ones I liked."

"To your kids?"

"To JC and Dell because there's an address. Sam moves around all over the place so I'm obviously glad for email."

"You know you could just post pictures. Where is he now?"

"Thailand, and yes I could post pictures, but don't you like to get things in the mail? That's the fun of it."

"For me there's no discussion. Things that come in the mail are bad. Bills, junk and wedding invitations. Things that come any other way are good. Most of the time anyway. Thailand? That's insane."

"I agree."

He glanced over at her. "Do you worry?"

"I try not to," she said. "Wedding invitations aren't all bad."

"Maybe yours aren't. You haven't asked me to sign your cast yet."

"You're kidding, right? But as soon as it comes off, it's my turn to drive again."

"Of course, it is," he said.

He parked at the end of the one main street in Pine Ridge and they worked their way up one side and down the other. Again, Miller noticed how often they complemented each other. She didn't care much about clothes and he didn't either. They both cared enough about everything else to spend some time browsing in the toy store, antique store, art galleries. Shell shops, surf shops, the kite store. Places that sold handmade jewelry, glassware, pottery, it didn't matter what exactly. She appreciated that although it wasn't always evident, he had a quiet side, and also that they could communicate what was needed with only a look, an expression, a nod.

They spent the most time in the bookstore, seemingly tiny from the front, almost nothing more than an alcove, but opening out to a large room in the back that was stocked to the rafters. Again they went their own ways, directed by whatever caught their eye. Miller wandered through the cooking section, travel, poetry and to her surprise found one of Hugh's volumes. She opened the cover. The book had been signed by the author. She traced the extravagant signature, wondering again. In local history, she paged through three or four beautiful books of photography that transformed the beach into a place she'd never seen before. Another book about the sea held a quotation from John Millington Synge: *He who fears not the sea will soon be drowned.* So it wasn't just her, she thought, and shivered. She settled on Ann Patchett's latest novel in paperback and another by Jess Walter.

She found Eli sitting on the front porch steps already reading his book.

"What is it?" she said. He turned it over and held it up while she read the title. "*American Buffalo.* Is that a history book? Something about Native Americans?"

"It's a guy's book. If you want something to eat go out in the damn wilderness and shoot it yourself."

"Buffalo? I didn't know there were any left to shoot. Or that people still ate them."

"That's why he wrote it. I'll read the good parts to you."

"Honestly," she said, "I just can't wait."

Over sandwiches and beer, he brought up another topic. "Tell me if this is a place you don't want to go," he said, "but Thanksgiving's not so far off. Do you have plans?"

She'd known this would come up, it had to, and she didn't know what to do or even how to talk about it. "I don't," she said quietly.

"I thought this might not be easy. I'm just trying is all. I'm here and if you are too, why don't we do it together? I'll even let you cook."

Miller attempted a smile that wouldn't come. Her eyes filled. "I owe you at least some sort of explanation."

"You don't need to do that. I've seen enough to know what's going on."

"So it's obvious about the divorce," she said. "That's what all those papers were on the table. They keep sending them to me and I keep sending them back."

"It's in court?"

"No, and under the circumstances, it won't be. The only problem is that I'm being asked to keep the house and I won't. I refuse." She took a deep breath. "This is why I'm not supposed to talk about it. It seems like I'm okay, but then I'm not."

She waited. "But Thanksgiving was the one holiday that stayed special through all those years," she said. "The one time when everybody from both families made every effort to be there. It was big, huge, meant so much, to the kids, to all of us." Since that first Thanksgiving, she thought, when after insisting that both families celebrate together, they'd stood up at the table and announced that they were married and watched the horrified looks, both their mothers bursting into tears, and then laid the baby news carefully on top. And now all the impossible and unexpected good that had come from that night was torn apart, broken and thrown away forever.

"Anyway, I get too emotional. That's what happens. I'm warning you, I might not be good company."

"I'm good enough company for both of us. And I didn't mean that about you doing the cooking. I'll do it."

"You cook?"

"Yes, I cook. Do you not remember my hot dogs?" Eli held up the book again. "I'm going out and shoot us a buffalo. I'll be back sometime next year."

"Just a suggestion, but doesn't it make more sense to go out and shoot a turkey?"

"No, you can get those at the Corner Market, free-range, organic, only ever ate hand-raised beetles and grubs and ladybugs and lovingly mashed-up pesticide-free acorns."

"Finish the rest of that sentence," she said.

"And I ordered one already."

"We'll both cook."

"It's good to be consistent," he said. "If you have issues, stay with them, roll with it."

"I totally agree," she said.

chapter 15

THE WIND BLEW at forty knots, gale force. In sixteen-foot seas, a sport fishing boat capsized, killing a man and his thirteen-year-old son. The professional fishermen recognized the ocean's black mood and had not been out. They understood, in their blood, bones and family histories, what came of the deadly mix of wind and waves. Miller began to ignore the weather report and base her beach walking decisions on the presence or absence of the fishing boats. Or the wind trying to separate the house from its roof.

She and Eli planned dinner while running on the treadmills. She'd told him she didn't want the treadmill to distract him from his workout, didn't want him losing his physique and being too weak to throw the mail ladies out of the bar when they got out of line. He assured her he had a great deal of experience with distractions, he could handle women who got out of line and his workouts were just fine, though she doubted it. The subject of Thanksgiving was still difficult, but he never let her stop long enough to dwell on that part of it.

"This will be a first for me, you understand that," she said. "Doing it by myself."

"And what am I again?" he said. "But let's start with the turkey. Brined?"

"Sure. If you're willing."

"Deep fried?"

"My opinion only, but disaster waiting to happen. Also, way too much trouble. Also, the weather."

"True," he said. "Never mind. Sweet potatoes?"

"From scratch," she said. "Mashed with orange juice and spices or fried in real maple syrup and butter, take your pick."

"Jesus. Let me think about it. Stuffing. Do you do oyster?"

"Never," she said.

"Good, then we're doing oyster, you'll like it. Vegetables?"

"Broccoli."

"Mashed potatoes," he said. "With sour cream and cream cheese."

"What? I never heard of such a thing. How to gain five pounds in one meal."

"That's what makes them so good."

"Turnips? Rutabaga? Kohlrabi?" she said. "There's always got to be one vegetable that your grandmother made and everyone hates."

"That all sounds terrible," he said. "None of those. You're also picking up the pace, in case you hadn't noticed."

"Sorry. Cranberries?"

"None of that slippery stuff that comes in a can. The real ones chopped up with oranges and walnuts, yes?"

"Your call, I'd skip the walnuts, but yes. Bread?"

"I don't need bread," he said.

"I don't either. I think at this point we're feeding fifteen people anyway."

"Pie?" he said. "I can take it or leave it."

"Just pumpkin custard then. How do you feel about whipped cream?"

"A bowlful please. And ice cream, too."

"Good grief," she said. "We should incline steeper now."

"What doesn't kill you makes you stronger," he said. "I don't think you've ever heard of that."

They got along well together in the kitchen, even with Miller still awkward in her cast. She decided all of it worked because they were friends. No one had an agenda. Having an argument would be useless, what was the point? They'd split the cost of everything, divided up the labor, the Cowboys and Saints were on the big screen. For a bad day, it wasn't quite so bad. Better to be here than alone staring at the walls or sitting with a box of Kleenex and crying through several movies. All three of her offspring had checked in with early morning phone calls. They were sad, she was sad. Start where you are, do what you can, her mother always said. *Live in the here and now*, Janelle had said enough times that Miller felt like it was written on the inside of her brain. She would do that, live in the here and now, get through, get by.

The sweet potatoes were crisp in the frying pan, the broccoli waiting to be steamed, the custard made, the cream whipped, the cranberry relish cold, tart and chunky. The turkey was covered on a cutting board, a heavenly aroma wafting up from it. Eli stood at the stove making gravy.

"I can't believe you can do that," she said. "Not everybody can. In fact, it scares a lot of people half to death."

"This talent and five bucks will maybe get you a cup of coffee."

"Five bucks? New York City again. Still, it's impressive. And you made the stuffing. You even shucked the oysters."

"There is a world where guys do cook, you know."

"Maybe you're right. It's just that I've never seen it except on TV. Grilling, yes. Gravy? I don't think so."

"The potatoes are done," he said. "Ball's in your court." They'd agreed that evened-up labor required her to do the mashing. She drained the potatoes, tossed them into a bowl, got out the mixer and stared at the ingredients. "Really?" she said. "Everything?"

"Everything. Hold on, Dallas just threw an interception. What's the score? Good, Saints are up." He could make gravy and watch TV from across the room at the same time.

"You're a Saints fan?" she said.

"I'm an anti-Dallas fan. Everybody is."

"I did not know that."

First came the sour cream, then the cream cheese, then the hot milk, then the butter. Miller made a face. "This has to have more calories than a Double Double," she said.

"What's a Double Double?"

"It's a double cheeseburger from In-N-Out. You don't have those?"

"Not that I'm aware of. Are they good?"

"For what they are, yes. Very good."

"I'll have to look it up, see where the nearest one is."

"I hope it's not someplace like Utah."

"That's it. Now you've done it," he said. He took out his phone and made a quick search. "Shit, it is Utah or every town in California. Want to go for a ride?"

Miller lit candles and poured wine as the light faded and the Saints won by a field goal. She surveyed the scene. It was the best family dinner that could possibly be had without a family.

"Don't say anything," Miller said when they sat down to eat. "Okay?"

"No speeches. Just one small prayer. No, two." The infernal wind had come up again. "There go the geraniums," he said as the heavy pots rolled off the deck and into the dunes. "First, please don't let the roof come off and second, please don't let the power go out."

"At least dinner's cooked and we have candles," she said.

"Yes, but now the Jets game is on."

Miller considered that it was a feast, somehow cooked to perfection, one of those lucky moments when everything came together just right. The wind beating against the sliding glass doors created the impression of a snug, safe place protected from the storm. Hopefully anyway, she thought, eyeing how the glass doors bowed inward just slightly in the strongest gusts.

"Now's the time," Miller said. She had decided she wanted to do this. It was important. "You know something at least about my family, but I don't know anything about yours. You said your dad's a coach, but what about your mom? What does she do?"

"Thanksgiving does bring it all up, doesn't it?" he said.

"If it wasn't the right thing to ask, I take it back."

"No, that's okay. We're friends and that's what friends are for, to hear the crap parts of your life."

"Oh no," she said. "Then don't do it, never mind."

"You ever heard of Helen Grace?"

"I don't think so." But she had, the name was somehow familiar.

"Well, way too many people have. For starters, she's whacko." Miller winced. "That's what I call it anyway. You can say creative or original or unique, but that doesn't quite do it for me."

"Who is she?"

"She's a performance artist, fairly well known, for her talent maybe, but also because she can't help but create a big fucking controversy with everything she does. Nothing normal, ever."

"Performance artist," Miller said. "What does that even mean?"

"It means sanctioned craziness that people actually pay to see. She used to change her medium all the time, but she's been in metal for quite a while now, builds things and then has a live onstage completely unpredictable demolition with drills, sledge hammers, blow torches, what have you, and recently I think for political effect she's added reams of newspaper and buckets of blood. And she's naked."

"Oh my God."

"Exactly."

"And your dad's a coach?"

"They aren't married," Eli said. "They weren't ever married. My dad was part of all her madness in the beginning. But then he managed to get out and change his life around, went back to school, married a nice woman, her name's Rebecca, and had three more kids. They live in New Jersey. Two of the kids are in college, one's still in high school. And my mother, who's burned up so many relationships no one can even keep count, is now, so I hear anyway, in Finland or Iceland, one of those countries."

"But she raised you?"

"Sort of. You could call it that. I spent two weeks with her, two weeks with my dad. The two weeks with her, well, when it's all sex, drugs and Metallica, there's not much parenting going on. She tried sometimes, that's all I'll say for her. When I was twelve my dad went to court and I got to live with him permanently."

"And Rebecca? How did that go?"

"Good. I mean, I'd known her for a long time by then. She was like my mom way before she became my mom. And she has her own catering business that I used to work for in the summers, so she's the one who actually taught me how to cook. We get along pretty well."

"I'm glad," Miller said.

"Me, too. But that's then and this is now and I'm sorry, but that's one of the better Thanksgiving dinners I've ever had. You're quiet."

"It was everything anybody could want," she said. "And I mean that."

"What this calls for," he said, "is the best brandy there is, of which I happen to have a bottle, and switching over to my sectional that seats fourteen for better viewing because the Jets are ahead by ten."

"I can't do brandy. I'll help you with the dishes and then it's time for me to go home."

"Have you ever noticed," he said, "that there are two kinds of people in the world, those who for some weird reason believe that cleaning up the kitchen is the perfect ending to a perfect meal and the rest of us who walk away and don't think about it again till morning? Do I have to tell you again? It's the Jets game. And not just any brandy."

"All right," she said. She had never, ever left the dishes. She felt as if Janelle was somewhere writing notes.

The brandy was incredibly smooth and went down with so much warmth she had to close her eyes. "Wow," she said.

"Now if only I had a cigar," Eli said.

"If you had a cigar one of us would be out there getting blown off the balcony and it wouldn't be me. My opinion? For what it's worth? Mark Sanchez is way too good-looking to be a quarterback, to be playing football at all."

"I had the same problem. Too good-looking. Trust me, it was hard. Shouldn't have even been on the field. Killed it for everyone else."

She laughed., not wanting to admit that some of that might be true. "Also incredibly modest," she said.

"That, too."

chapter 16

THE LOCALS SAID big storms were common in winter, just not such a tight string coming one on top of the other, and the wind had never blown that hard for that long. The rain had already set a record, thirteen inches in seven days. In the Oceanview surf shop where Miller went when she was missing Sam, she listened as the woman behind the counter explained to a group of young apprentice riders that there'd be no more surfing lessons for a while due to unprecedented swells, strong currents, chaotic wave patterns and huge logs in the water.

In the post office, everyone agreed that they'd never seen such storms.

At the gym, Miller said, "No incline."
"Why?" Eli said. "Do you think I can't take it?"
"Because I started pushing, and not just myself, but you, too."
"That wasn't pushing at all compared to what you're used to doing."
She glanced quickly at him. There was something in his voice. "And you're saying that because…?"
"I saw your videos."
She went stationary, traveling with the treadmill till she jumped off the back. Eli had to do a double take, she disappeared so fast. "Please tell me that's not true."
He kept running while she stood and watched, arms folded. "I don't know why I didn't think of that sooner," he said. "They're out there, you know. It's not like anyone hid them or anything."
"They were promos for the gym, that's all."
"Hey, come back on the treadmill. I don't like running alone."
"Honestly," Miller said, but she got back on.
"Don't get upset again, this is me your friend talking, but I have to say that you look pretty damn good in Lycra."

"Stop right now or we're going home. Or I'm going home and you can walk."

"I just thought I ought to tell you so it wasn't like I was sneaking around behind your back."

"God forbid. I wonder how I get them to take those things down."

"Judging from the comments, I don't think that's happening."

She got off the treadmill again. Her face was burning. "Okay, we're done," she said.

"No, please," he said, trying hard not to grin. "We've got another three miles to go. And I wanted to tell you something else. Seriously. Stay with me."

"We're doing the incline now, I hope you know that. For all three freaking miles. And it's got nothing to do with my regard for your well-being. In fact, it's the opposite. What?"

"I had the best thing happen," he said. "I got good mail. I got a postcard."

She smiled. The mail ladies wouldn't know her by the name Miller, but it wouldn't be much of a shock if they could recognize her handwriting. Let them talk. She was allowed to send him postcards.

chapter 17

FOR THE FIRST TIME, the tide surged up into the access road, leaving a chaotic pile of logs behind when it receded. On the south beach, the same storm tides were carving three-foot walls out of what had once been soft rolling dunes.

"What is this?" Eli said. He bent down to examine something in the sand. "It's a wooly bear caterpillar. What the hell is he doing out here on the beach?"

"They're not supposed to be here?" Miller said

"It just seems weird. Back home they live in normal caterpillar places with leaves and bushes and things. They're how you predict the winter. If the black band in their middle is wide, it'll be a bad one."

"Does that work?"

"Who knows. But I guess since you don't have winter in California you don't need to worry about it anyway. This one's on a mission to get drowned. Hey, buddy, that's the ocean you're heading for."

"We could turn him around," she said.

"And confuse him completely."

"Given the choice, I think I'd rather be confused than dead, but here's another problem for you to solve, VP." Miller pointed to a flock of gulls at the edge of the waves.

"Seagulls," he said.

"But not like any of the others."

"You couldn't find out what they were?"

"I didn't try. I don't like them."

"I won't ask what that's all about." She handed him the binoculars. "This can't be hard," he said. "How many different kinds of gulls are there?"

Miller held out her phone.

"Eighteen? You're kidding. And they all look alike, give or take a black head here and there." He scrolled through them one at a time then peered through the binoculars again. "Are you ready?"

"Ready and waiting, and I didn't do any work this time."

"The VP is not unaware of that fact. At least you'll have to write it down, that's something. Mew gull." He pressed the sound icon. "I was wrong," he said. "I thought a mew gull would sound like a cat, but that's not a cat, that's just another squawker only not as loud."

"That's what it is," Miller said. "They're too small and meek and quiet. I have no respect for them. If you're going to be a gull, be a gull."

Eli looked at her. "I think you've been out here too long."

Farther down the beach, they came to the body of a loon torn apart, bones broken, innards mangled and flung across the sand.

"What does that?" Miller said. "I keep wondering. It can't be the northern harrier. The books say he doesn't eat big things like that."

"I don't think I want to know." Twenty paces away there was another dead loon, this one intact except for an open wound down to bone on one long scaly leg.

"Get me out to the river," Miller said. "I want to see loons that are alive."

What they found instead was the deer carcass, now mercifully covered by sand. Only pieces of vertebra remained, arcing up like dinosaur bones in a museum.

Coming back along the tide line, Eli picked up a sand dollar and worked it in his hand, rubbing the sand off the pale gritty surface. "I just wanted to let you know something," he said. "I'm going home for Christmas."

Miller glanced at him and then away. She didn't want to be surprised or have an opinion. "That's good, isn't it?"

"I wouldn't go except it's my grandmother's eightieth birthday and you never know when it's going to be the last one."

"You're close to her."

"She took care of me when no one else would. She still does. But you're staying here?" Miller nodded. "And that was planned a long time ago? It's not sudden or anything?" She shook her head no. Another hard subject.

He waited. "Will you be okay?" he said.

"I'll be okay."

"How's your arm?"

It had been strange having him there when the cast came off. Strange and normal at the same time, him sitting patiently while she was taken to x-ray and then worked on with the saw, both of them watching her arm emerge out of the plaster dust wrinkled and dry and shrunken. The doctor told her she had healed well, but now there were instructions to follow. Soak twice a day, rub with lotion, do strengthening exercises and don't attempt anything vigorous.

"Like treadmill?" Eli said.

The doctor was horrified. "Definitely not. How did you break it in the first place?"

"Treadmill," Miller had said, "but…" She narrowed her eyes as Eli stood expectantly waiting for the rest of the explanation.

"My arm's good as new," she said now, "and despite what you keep saying, the treadmill never killed anyone."

"See?" he said. "That's exactly what I mean."

chapter 18

THE HOLIDAY LOOMED. At least here in this smaller, quieter place it came on more slowly, not in a crashing frantic rush of late September merchandising but more as it had somewhere in the dim dark past, occupying a brief and dignified few weeks after the lull of Thanksgiving. It was just now that Christmas trees began appearing for sale at Rite-Aid, elaborate wreaths and sparkling velvety decorations piled up in bins at the garden store, all the essentials for a properly lavish meal took over their prominent section of the Corner Market and the Salvation Army bell started ringing nonstop at the shopping plaza in Oceanview. Miller considered that all of it was still only depressing in the rain.

As always the beach was there, offering nothing in the way of judgment, on some days its finest quality. Two gulls swooped overhead, one engaged in hot pursuit of the other. Whatever they were fighting over dropped to the beach with the clatter of a pair of castanets. Miller picked it up. The object in question was a mussel as long as her hand and shining midnight blue. Attached to the shell were the most outlandish living things she'd ever seen, barnacles three inches high and absolutely lurid, the fat flexible stalks an orange-rose color, the tips composed of many tiny overlapping white plates. The plates opened to reveal, she didn't know what, something wet and bright red. She quickly looked up barnacles, but every description paled in comparison to what was there on the beach. Neither gull, deprived of this stunning item, showed any interest in reclaiming it.

Out at the river, Miller kept her eye on the heron, its posture as motionless as an image in a Japanese silkscreen. She'd gradually become aware of this stillness. Everything that ran or hunted or flew spent an equal, fairly enormous, amount of time not flying or hunting at all. She realized that the stillness so necessary to everyone else was also becoming necessary to her. The heron moved, instantly on the alert, then lifted and flapped gracefully to the other side of the river.

The wind slowed to a slight breeze and mist gathered along the beach, massing quickly into a cold fog that obliterated sun, sky, horizon, dunes. As the fog closed in, Miller was suddenly uncomfortable, alone on an empty beach where the visibility had just dropped to zero.

Other senses immediately came into play. The tang and ferment of the sea grew sharper. She listened for the hush as somewhere nearby a long wave hissed in. The peacefulness of the beach surrounded her, slowing her mind, seamlessly weaving her into its world.

A sound intruded. Before she had time to decode its source she was rushed by a Rottweiler who circled, thumping and spraying sand, then butted his head against the back of her legs. He was old and fat, but that occurred to her only after she assured herself that she wasn't going to die. The dog lumbered on, its owner invisible in the fog. Somehow the peace remained.

"My groupie," Eli said. "It's been a long lonely time without you."

Miller slid into the last seat open at the end of the bar. The room was packed and the conversational hum was high, enhanced by the blaring of seven TVs. "Somehow I doubt that," she said.

"Monday Night Football, never-ending rain and people who got tired of Christmas shopping, that's the mix," he said. "What'll it be? Your preference is Jack and Coke, right?"

"Not if that was the last thing on earth left to drink."

"Whoa, down on Jack. Sancerre?"

"I can't afford Sancerre. Blue Moon, please, at the going rate."

"Everything's three dollars here, didn't I tell you that? Hold that thought."

The seasonal spike in business meant there were now three bartenders who were just barely enough to keep up with the crowd. He came back with her beer.

"I know you're busy," she said. "I won't stay long."

"Are you okay?" he said.
"Yeah, it's just…"
"I know. I'll be right back, but here." He quickly took out his phone, paged through and handed it to her. While he took drink and food orders, she frowned at what he'd pulled up, a restaurant with ocean views, a fireplace and an expensive menu.
"What is this?" she said when he came back.
"Before I leave I wanted to take you out to dinner and everyone here says this place is the best."
She gave back the phone. "You can't take me out. We're friends."
"Then I want us to eat in the same restaurant at the same time, but I'll pay. Hold on."
She enjoyed watching the way he worked, friendly, moving fast but always with a few words and a smile no matter what. He was someone you would want to talk to, sit down and have a drink with, maybe even say things to that couldn't be said to anyone else.
"We have an agreement, remember?" she said.
"How about if my Christmas present to you is that I'll pay your half and your Christmas present to me is that you'll pay my half. And you realize that's the stupidest arrangement there ever was."
"It does look like a lovely place."
"Is it too expensive?" he said. "That's the one thing I was concerned about, given the situation."
"If it's manageable for you, then it is for me, too." There was no way she could ever tell him about the glass house on the bluffs above the ocean.
"I've got to go again," he said. "But you won on your side, so I'm winning on mine. I'm driving."

Miller stood contemplating the meager amount of clothes in her closet. When someone was charging forty-five dollars for a steak did they expect you to show up in a dress? She didn't have a dress. She rummaged through what she did have, good black jeans, black heeled ankle boots, a pale silk blouse, gold hoops, it would have to do. She held out her hand. No French nails. No rings either.

Almost seven months. *Where are you?* She couldn't imagine his life now and had learned the hard way not to try because it only caused a knife-like pain in her heart.

She brushed her hair out hard while she stared at her face in the mirror. Dinner? Really? What had happened to the longing for solitude, quiet, slowing down? Or on the other hand, the desire to crawl into a hole and never come out?

Miller was standing in the driveway when the Jeep pulled up, the headlights shining down the street. She opened the door and climbed in.

"You're out here in the dark," Eli said.

"Why shouldn't I be?" she said. "All the drunken fishermen have gone home for the night."

"What drunken fishermen? I could have come to the door."

"And sat in the living room and made small talk with my parents and given me a corsage. Just like the prom. Well, not your prom."

"That's why guys aren't polite anymore," he said as he turned out onto the highway. "They never get the chance."

"You're polite all the time, but if you'd come to the door I'd have fallen over. You're much more likely to stand out in the street and do that thing where you put your fingers in your mouth and whistle."

"I wouldn't," he said.

"What do you mean you wouldn't? You have."

"That's different. That's for the gym. Then there's the argument over women who do a cross body block to make sure you don't get to the door first. How do you feel when a guy holds a door for you?"

"Special."

"Do you?"

"I'm the one who has to have the babies, so it's the least they can do to show some respect."

"Jesus."

"You asked. But what is it about you tonight? I know. You smell good."

"I took a shower. When I clean up, I do it right," he said, and she laughed.

"But really, what is that scent? I love it."

"Calvin Klein. Something with amber in it, I forget what it's called."

"That a woman sold to you."

"That's the only kind of communicating there is left across the vast divide. Small moments of just trying to reach out and say here, this might help."

"How sad," she said.

"Very sad," he said. "Tragic."

The restaurant sat at the edge of the dunes and was everything Miller had pictured. The holiday accents were light and tasteful, leaving the room in its own glow, the dark outside, the firelight reflected in the huge windows.

"It's beautiful," she said.

"They told me it was."

"What do you do? Go down the bar soliciting recommendations?"

"That's exactly what I do. Makes for instant conversation plus you can learn a lot."

"Apparently."

They were seated at the window, though it didn't matter when the only sight available was the light from the crab boats bobbing out on the cold ocean. Eli wore a look she hadn't expected, a band-collared shirt, a tailored four-button vest, dress pants, dark polished boots.

"You do clean up pretty good," she said.

"Not so bad yourself, lady. What do you want to drink? Feel like a martini?"

"I've had about four martinis in my whole life. I'd probably pass out."

"Not a great idea then. This is a stretch, but were you ever a fan of Campari?"

"You know what? I was," she said. "A whole long time ago. I hadn't thought of that in years."

"Yes, then?"

"Definitely yes."

The room was inviting, warm, and filled to capacity.

"Where did all these people come from?" Miller said.

Eli pulled out his phone, worked it for a minute and passed it across the table. It was the screen for the rooms and rates at the restaurant's oceanfront inn.

"Holy crap," she said. "Not necessarily from here then."

"Don't think so."

They ordered appetizers, salads, a bottle of wine, salmon and filet to share.

"If it wasn't for my grandmother's birthday I wouldn't be doing this, I wouldn't be going home," he said out of nowhere. "I don't want to leave you here."

"Please, you aren't allowed to feel that way," she said. "I told you, I'll be all right. I'm fine. My grandmother meant the world to me so I understand exactly where you are with this."

"Believe it or not, you can't tell someone not to care about you, it doesn't work that way. Now I want to talk about your kids."

Miller went quiet.

"Seriously," he said.

"I don't know," she said. The filet was meltingly tender, the salmon grilled to perfection. She wanted to savor all of it and not have to think about anything else.

"Where are they? Where will they be?"

None of it was ever going to be easy, so she might as well get used to it. And the person sitting across from her was not some stranger. It was Eli.

"Sam's in Australia with friends, Dell's in London with JC. They'll both go to the boyfriend's parents' house for Christmas."

"The boyfriend doesn't get much play here. Not high on your list?"

"This is a bad time in her life and I think he's trying to talk her out of her plans and into his. She's pretty tough though, and Dell will manage in her own quiet way to add fuel to the fire, so I'm not too worried about it. JC will get tired of him one of these days."

"You've met him, though."

"I did," she said. "When he was on a bike tour of the States he stayed with us. Nobody liked him, which was probably why JC did." He'd been arrogant, condescending. Her reaction had been, not with my daughter, though a whole lot of good that had done.

"Is volleyball a thing for your kids?"

"Dell's good, the other two don't care."

"Are they all tall?"

"Dell's same as me, JC not quite, Sam's just an average guy height." Miller had noticed that with only the handful of inches Eli had on her, her heeled boots had brought her close. She knew he'd noticed it, too. She'd always liked that, being able to use her height, confront men by looking them in the eye.

"Would you be willing to show me pictures?"

She hesitated for just a moment then set down her fork and pulled out her phone. Uncertain about which direction to take, she chose. She gave it to him.

"It's all them one way or another. Just don't go back too far." Like seven months' worth.

"They're beautiful kids," he said. He raised his eyes. "They look like you."

She ducked the compliment. "Sometimes," she said.

"The two of them stick pencils and things in their hair like you do. And how many surfboards does he have?"

"Don't ask."

Eli returned the phone. "This is pushing the limits and I know it, so stop me any time. Why don't you want the house?"

"Eli," she said.

"I think your lady doctor's right about the not talking part. Absolutely, I can see that. She just didn't factor in someone like me."

"There's the honest truth." Miller glanced briefly out into the dark night. "It's his house," she said. "He built it, it was his dream."

"He's an architect?"

"Contractor."

"And now he can't go back?"

"If things are still the same, which I'm assuming they are, the kids would never come home again if he was there, or at least not for a long time."

"All three of them feel that way?"

"Yes."

"So it was bad."

"To them it was," she said. "To me it was."

"I didn't mean to lean on you. Thanks for telling me that much. We don't have to talk about it anymore." The tightness in her chest eased. "But I have something for you."

"We're already paying for each other's dinners. There can't be anything else."

"This isn't anything else." He reached into his pants pocket and held up what he'd retrieved. It was a thin patterned rose and lilac string, a friendship bracelet.

"You are crazy," she said. "Where did it come from?"

"So little faith. I made it."

"You didn't. That's not even possible."

"If you watch enough videos, anything's possible. Will you wear it?"

"Yes, I'll wear it. I love it." He had a variety of cords and braided things on his own wrists, but she hadn't ever given them much thought. They were just part of who he was. She held out her wrist, but now she was close to tears. Must be the wine.

They sat in the Jeep outside her house.

"Thank you," she said. "It was an excellent meal in the very best company and I really appreciate that you paid for my half."

"I agree, same to you. Plus you saved me from having to spend the night packing."

"How did I know you'd still have that left to do? I'd drive you to the airport except it's two hours away."

"That's always the problem. You leave the bright lights and big city and then you realize, wow, you're out here in the middle of nowhere."

She had her hand on the door. "Have a good time, okay?" she said. "Be safe."

"Can I call you?" he said.

"No. You can't."

"Why not?"

"Because this is my time. I have to learn to be alone."

"Would you call me? Even once?"

"No. No communication. I'm shutting myself off from everything. Or trying to."

"Texts? Come on. Photos? I can't go for a whole day without sending you a picture of something."

It was true, she thought. He couldn't.

"You won't hear back from me," she said. "The only way I can do this is to stay quiet and see how I can make that be enough."

"There's this then," he said. "On Christmas day at least you need to answer me. Will you do that? Otherwise, I'll be anxious. I'll worry about you."

"Don't say that. That'll make me worry about you worrying."

"I can see where we're both nuts. No one worries about anyone, but will you still send that text?"

"Yes."

"Apart from that, you'll let me know if my house gets blown away, right?"

"Yes."

"Remember, stay away from old men at the gym."

"I wasn't planning on going to the gym."

"Because it's no fun without me," he said.

"No fun at all."

"And don't go in the bar alone. It's a pickup joint."

"Now you tell me."

"Not always, but sometimes. It can be."

"I won't be in bars either, believe me," she said. "Enjoy your family. I'll see you when you get back." She got out of the Jeep.

"Miller," he said, and she held the door. His voice was quieter. "There's a reason even after all our discussion about it that I didn't get out and open the door for you." She had to look away because she knew what that reason was. "I'll miss you," he said.

"I'll miss you, too," she said.

chapter 19

MILLER SHUFFLED ALONG the vast expanse of gray flats at low tide. The boom and crash of the surf was a constant wall of sound. The sun shone for a moment, lighting the dunes in a golden glow. A line of clouds dragged slowly north along the horizon like a caravan of shaggy beasts.

The minus tide had uncovered an acre of tide pools filled with the small turban-shaped shells. She bent down and began to collect them, as usual being careful to check for occupants. Still, a third inspection of her plastic bag held up to the hazy light yielded another pair of antennae, orange this time. Gingerly she picked out the offender and returned him to his watery home. A whole soggy Dungeness crab drifted in one pool. In another were the carcasses of a tiny green crab and a slightly larger sky blue crab, exotic sea life for this barren stretch of beach.

At home, deciding it was a good time for a project, Miller dumped her entire assortment of turban shells onto the kitchen island and began sorting them out in long rows. Seen all in a heap they didn't appear to have much in common, but now patterns emerged.

The smallest shells were only an inch long, wrapped tightly in on themselves and smooth enough to reflect light. There they were in the shell book, the Purple Dwarf Olive. She picked one up again thoughtfully after reading that they'd been collected by women on these shores for thousands of years.

The other shells, the ones that produced antennae, all turned out to be the same shell in different pale shades: channeled basket whelks. It was odd, trying to associate the shells with the slippery creature that had spun each whorl out of its own bodily secretions and was, the books said, a fast-moving and voracious predator. Miller shuddered, thinking of the actual snails she'd seen and imagining them on a plate, with a sauce.

On Christmas Day, the wind pounded against the windows and rain blew in sheets so heavy that it blurred the entire landscape. Through the loneliness Miller sat down and sent three heartfelt messages, then a fourth one to Janelle.

The text requiring an answer arrived at noon. Though it seemed as if he'd just left, Eli had already sent a photo of his father waving at her, clean-cut, dark hair, with that same beautiful smile and then a sweet old lady waving at her, his grandmother. She wondered what on earth he was telling them. This time the picture brought her up short. He was the one smiling at the camera, standing in the snow wearing an Oregon t-shirt and for no obvious reason holding a cat. She looked at the photo for a long time, thinking, then shifted her gaze back to the safety of the rain.

The words, which she'd missed at first with the surprise of seeing his face, said simply, *how are you*? The second text broke through her meditations and made her jump again. It said, *hurry up please, it's freezing out here and I'm allergic to cats*.

She opened one of the French doors, snapped a picture holding the phone up to the onslaught, quickly closing the door again. *I'm fine*, she said underneath. *That cat must be a relative, it has your eyes. You might like to know that it's raining.*

He was as good as his word. There was no more conversation, though she could almost feel his thoughts. And his eyes were like the cat's, the clear gray of the ocean on a quiet day.

She *was* fine, Miller assured herself, except for missing her family so much it hurt, except for the ache in her heart and the gaping hole in her life, except for the anger always right there beneath the surface. She'd never imagined herself being alone, ever, and especially not like this, at Christmas in a place that wasn't even home. *Damn you*, she thought for the thousandth time, but what good did that do? None at all. Her husband, her best friend, the one she'd known since she was nineteen and loved more than life itself, that person was gone. The person he'd become was a stranger.

Even though the house wasn't home, it was oddly comforting to be there among the ghosts. She and Dell both took after her grandmother, tall with all that tumbling dark hair. She was comforted too by her mother's hand in the look of the house, her striving for perfection so opposite to Miller's but lovely and reassuring now in every way, as if she were still here.

Peace, that's what she was experiencing, in the middle of a storm on a rough coast far away from everything and everyone she knew and loved. As she went about making a simple dinner, lighting the candles, listening to the rain, Miller hoped the peace wasn't as fragile as it seemed. She hoped it held.

Instead of raining, it snowed. A thin layer powdered the dunes. The horizon was a sharply drawn edge between icy sea and cold blue sky. With the wind chill hovering in the teens, the air was iron-cold, hard to breathe.

Miller layered long underwear, wool sweaters, a hooded sweatshirt underneath the raincoat, a mistake. She was still cold and the vinyl stiffened till it seemed in danger of cracking. No matter. Better to be out here than trapped inside again.

The beach felt strange, a whole new landscape, bright white over dry gritty sand, unsettling to the eye. Slushy waves rolled in, leaving a mosaic of icy lace when they receded. A small three-person crab boat rocked just outside the breakers, pulling up a long line of traps. Through the binoculars, she could read the name of the boat, the *Fanta Sea*, and see the captain standing spread-legged on the high open bridge. Two men in bulky orange waterproofs quickly cleaned out the traps and set them again while the boat pitched in the waves. As she was trying to imagine just how cold they must be out on the water, she heard the sound of a motor and turned to see a battered turquoise van driving down the beach behind her. She'd noticed the same vehicle days before parked up near the dunes.

Well, this is interesting, Miller thought, watching herself perform an act of supreme idiocy. Was she tired of trucks and people who couldn't read signs? Was she just irritated with the whole world? Was she finally coming unglued? She had no answers, but stepped up and flagged down the van anyway. Instantly she knew she'd made a mistake.

The driver slowed to a stop and rolled down the window. His raffish white hair and moustache set off blue eyes in a weathered face that showed the effects of sun and time but could still be called handsome. He looked at her, amused.

"Did you miss the sign that said Motor Vehicles Prohibited?" she said, her voice not one she recognized.

"I didn't miss it," he said. "See it every day."

"Then...?"

"Got a permit. For collecting firewood." Of course he had a permit. Why was she even out here? She didn't know anything. "Want to see it?" he said, letting his eyes rest on her, still amused. She quickly shook her head no. It was right there in the window, or something that looked like a permit anyway.

"Someone else stopped me the other day," he said. "Said just about the same thing you're saying. Must be that time of year."

"What time of year?"

"When people start getting cranky, like their nerves are shot."

"I am not one of those people," Miller said. "And I apologize. I had no idea."

"I know you didn't. That's what I mean."

"I'm finished here if you are," she said.

"Done," he said. "Thanks for pulling me over to chat." He turned his attention back to the beach and set the truck in gear.

Miller decided to be grateful that he hadn't run her over.

chapter 20

BUNDLED UP ON Jane's couch, Miller watched *The Station Agent*. She watched *Life As A House*. She watched *Kissing Jessica Stein* and wondered who had tossed that into the mix. She watched the Saints play the Falcons, every down, beginning to end, and the Nebraska Cornhuskers play the Washington Huskies in a bowl game even though she didn't know anything about either team. She read a book cover to cover in one day. She went to bed early and slept late, exhausted without being able to say why.

On the last day of the year, reality hit without warning. Janelle hadn't cautioned her about this possibility or told her what to do if it occurred. She'd taken every other measure, walked the beach every day, spent time out at the river with the heron and the gulls, added yet another shell to the notebook, a heart cockle, and one more strange bird, a guillemot. Peace was there for the asking. She knew that now, could feel it when it came. This time it didn't come and it was as if she'd lost everything all over again.

It was only a number, she kept telling herself, on an arbitrary calendar, only a convenience for keeping track of time. If a person's faith was in the moon and stars, then it was just another turn of the planet, the sun came up, the sun went down, get over it. But in truth, her truth anyway, this was the last day of the last year in which she'd been whole, in which she'd been happy. The New Year would bring the end to all of that, marriage, family, everything she'd built her life around, everything she'd trusted and believed in. The end of the Thanksgiving dinners had already come. The first one seemed now like someone else's fantasy, someone else's perfect world. Yes, they'd done some crazy things, but they'd done them together and they had loved each other. She knew that part was real, she'd lived it and he couldn't take it from her. That's where she became hopelessly tangled up. She wanted their life back but hated him with a passion, the two opposites breaking her apart.

Miller was in this state, empty, torn, furious, when the knock came at the door. Fuck Jessica Stein and the Cornhuskers and everyone. There was nobody in town that she knew. Fuck the drug addicts and drunken fishermen. She ignored the knocking even when it got louder.

Then there was somebody on the deck knocking on the French doors. It was Eli.

"Good God," she said, opening the door. "You just scared me shitless." She wondered what she looked like. If it was the same as the way she felt, then total wreck was the answer.

"Wow," he said. "Hello to you, too. Why wouldn't you open the door?"

"How was I supposed to know it was you? When did you get back?"

He was standing there, watching her warily. "Just this minute. I wanted to spend New Year's Eve with you so I was hustling."

"That's not happening, Eli. I can't do that."

"I've got everything," he said. "I took care of it all before I left so it'd be ready when I came back."

"I'm no good to anybody right now. Just leave me alone, let me be by myself."

"I did leave you alone. I didn't call once. Did you get my texts? You said you wouldn't text back and you meant it."

"I answered the one on Christmas." She was being rude and she knew it.

"If you were with me, it wouldn't have to be like this," he said. "We could have a good time and I'd get you through it."

"It's not your job to get me through it. And a good time doesn't solve anything, it isn't enough."

"You won't even try? You won't even think about it?"

"I'm in hell and there's nothing to think about," she said. "Why can't you understand?"

"Do you know how long it is from New York to Chicago and from Chicago to Portland and from Portland to here?" he said.

"Do you know what time I got up this morning? Do you know what time it is for me now? I didn't have to do this. Now I wish I hadn't. I should've spent New Year's Eve in New York City."

"Why didn't you? Anything's better than here."

"Just go is what you're saying."

"I'm not saying anything."

"Yes, you are," he said. "Never mind. I'm going."

She heard the Jeep start up and the tires spin on the gravel. Since there was nothing else to do, no other way to deal with it, she broke down and cried. Then everything washed over her at once and the crying turned into huge wracking sobs.

An hour later she got up from the couch, wiped her face and pulled herself together. She'd made a decision. She went into the kitchen, removed a tray of ice cubes from the freezer, dumped it into the bathroom sink, ran cold water on top and stuck her face in it. When her swollen eyes returned to more than mere slits, she took off the clothes she'd been wearing for the last two days and put on clean ones, jeans, running shoes, a long-sleeved t-shirt, a sweater. She brushed out her hair and twisted it up into a knot anchored with a chopstick.

In the kitchen, she took two bottles of champagne from the refrigerator. Coat on, a bottle in each hand, she headed down the road to the condos. Self-absorption was a terrible side effect of misery, one that drove away the people you needed most and that's what she'd just done. She hoped as a friend he'd forgive, that she could make things right, that he wasn't gone forever.

Miller knocked on Eli's door. When no one answered, she went in. He left his door unlocked and she knew she was always welcome. But she checked in his bedroom where the bed was perpetually unmade, in the bathrooms, the rest of the house was open, simple, hard to hide in, no one was there. Maybe he'd gone out to the beach. It could be breathtaking on a clear night like this, the ink black ocean, a whole universe of stars. She set the bottles of champagne on the counter and decided to wait just a little, give it some time to see if he came back.

109

Then he did come back. What was wrong with her? She hadn't even noticed the Jeep was gone, but she heard it now. For some reason that she couldn't fathom, she braced herself. Suddenly it didn't seem right for her to be here. She had a sick feeling in her stomach, as if she were trespassing, as if this was a stranger coming home, someone she didn't really know at all.

The door opened and it was worse than anything she could possibly have imagined. There was someone with him, a woman, young, pretty, blond, pale, slightly drunk.

"I'm so sorry," Miller said, her voice choked. She'd taken off her coat, but now she grabbed at it.

"Miller?" Eli said, his expression one of shock. "What are you doing here?"

"Nothing," she said. "I had some champagne. It's there. It's yours." She struggled into the coat as she hurried to the door, moving awkwardly past both of them in the deafening silence, sensing the woman's confusion and Eli's as well, feeling his eyes on her. Could there be anything more humiliating? No, there couldn't. If she hadn't wanted to die before, she did now. As she closed the door behind her, she heard the young woman asking what had just happened. She involuntarily put her hands over her ears even though the door was shut. She was running, tears coming again, not wanting to know what his answer might have been.

All Miller wanted was bed, sleep, unconsciousness, to not be aware of anything ever again. Who cared what day it was, what time. She tore off the clothes she'd just put on, got into the sweats that served as nightclothes and crawled deep under the covers. The bed was cold. She moved to one side and wrapped herself in the quilts. Her feet were cold. To take the focus away from the painful scene replaying in her head and her still burning face, she got out of bed and searched in the dark for a pair of socks. She got back into bed. There was a rush in her ears. She shut her eyes tight. Drained, exhausted, she fell gratefully into oblivion.

It wasn't the door opening downstairs that woke her instantly. It was his voice.

"Miller?" Eli said.

"Go away," she yelled.

"What?" he said. "I can't hear you."

"*Go away!*"

"I can't now," he said, standing in the door to her bedroom. "I already took off my shoes. I told you I wanted to spend New Year's Eve with you."

"What are you doing?" she said, alarmed. "If you take off your pants, I swear I'll scream. I've got pepper spray."

"Jesus God, please don't do that to me. I'm taking off my belt, that's all."

"I won't even ask why."

"It's uncomfortable, that's why. Move over. We need to talk. You're dressed aren't you? That's a dumb question. I know you well enough to know you've got seven different layers on."

"You're not in any place to have an opinion on that," she said.

"Actually, I am." She'd unfortunately already moved over enough that there was room. He climbed in under what was left of the covers, shifted the pillows and lay down on his back. Miller huddled at the far edge with the quilts pulled completely up to her neck and wrapped tightly around her.

"You smell like limes," she said.

"Too many tequila shots. I owe you an explanation."

"You owe me nothing. I shouldn't have been there."

"I was hurt," he said. "Do you understand that?"

"Yes. I was being a bitch."

"Then we're clear on that point. So listen and take me at my word. I went to the bar and had some drinks and the people there on New Year's Eve are not necessarily having the good time you'd think they'd be having."

"Eli, forget this. You can do what you want whenever you want."

"That's not the truth."

"Who was she, for God's sake?" Miller said, even though she'd sworn to herself that she wouldn't ask.

"I don't know. Just someone."

"That's how it works? Just someone?"

"Sometimes, yes, that's how it works."

"Is she local?"

"Visiting," he said.

"What happened to her?"

"I took her home. She was staying with a friend. I gave her the champagne, hope you don't mind, I've got two more bottles. You don't have to like this, I'm sure you won't, but what that would have been was a one-time deal, a mercy fuck, that's all, nothing more ever."

Miller was suddenly far down under the quilts with a pillow over her head to mute the screaming. When she came back up for air, she was still livid. "You can't say those kinds of things to me," she said. "I hate the word fuck when it's used like that. I *hate* it."

"Okay, but you're missing the point. It was supposed to be a mercy…hookup, but for me, not her. She took pity on me because I looked like I'd just had my heart cut out."

"Heart cut out? Oh my God."

"The thing is," he said, "there's this elephant in the room that we're not talking about."

"There's not an elephant in the room. There's just this tequila-swilling bartender in my bed."

"I'll say it again. I wanted to be with you, Miller. I'm not your enemy. If you were having it rough, I wish I'd been here. I wish I'd never gone away. Wait," he said. "Where's your remote?"

"What does that have to do with anything?"

He felt around on the bedside table till he found it and clicked on the TV, creating a white glare that blinded them both. The West Coast count down was coming and then there it was, the New Year whether anybody wanted it or not.

"See?" he said. "Over. Done and gone. Give me some credit. There are things I do understand. Maybe this year's been crap, but some of the days haven't been so bad, at least not for me, and that's because of you."

Miller was completely lost. He turned the TV off, plunging them back into darkness.

"I should go," he said. "I'm so tired. I just want you to know from the bottom of my heart how sorry I am."

"Eli," she said. "Stop apologizing. There's nothing to be sorry for. I presumed on our friendship and I feel horrible that I did that. Talk about invading someone's privacy. It won't happen again."

"Are you aware of where I am right now? Presume away all you want, but I'll always be way ahead of you on that score. It's me who has things that won't ever happen again and that's a promise. If you stop speaking to me, I'll miss you even more than I did this past week and that would not be a good thing. Or if you keep your distance or anything. I mean it."

He waited. "Silence on the other side of the bed is never a hopeful sign," he said. He turned back the covers and got up. "I'm leaving now." Still nothing. "No matter what else was going on," he said, "I was wrong and I will forever regret it."

And then he was gone, leaving Miller with the covers over her head doing even more thinking.

chapter 21

SHE DIDN'T WAIT long, not even one whole day.
    Her text said: *Beach?*
    His answer: *Yes.*
Two o'clock?
Yes.
    And Eli was there on the access road, waiting. Nothing was said. Nothing needed to be said. He motioned for her hand. She held it out and he pushed up the sleeve till the friendship bracelet showed on her wrist. She jumped at his touch. His eyes were steady on her.
    "Just checking," he said, still holding her with his eyes. He gave back her hand. "Anything new while I was gone?"
    She quickly composed herself. "Yes," she said, and pulled out her phone to show him.
    "Pigeon guillemot? Something else unpronounceable. Looks like the smaller cousin to that other guy. Alive or dead?"
    "Dead."
    "Stupid question."
    The tide had ebbed out as far as Miller had ever seen it go, leaving such a huge expanse that all the holiday people still visiting had no trouble finding room to wander. The vacationers did what everyone did at the beach. Small children built messy sand castles in the cold and decorated driftwood logs with rows of shells. Several dog owners had brought ball launchers especially useful for Labrador retrievers. The dogs bounded after the high lobs again and again, running their hearts out, quivering with anticipation and pure joy. A bearded man appearing far too old and professorial for such activities set off bottle rockets in the dunes.
    "Did you have dogs?" Eli said, following a setter racing along the waves.

"Yellow labs. Three of them. The last one was Lucy. She was a great dog. They all were." There was an idea that hadn't occurred to her. Get a dog. It was something to think about, not now, but some day. "Did you?"

"Not growing up and not in New York, which personally I think is cruel though a million dog lovers don't agree with me. At the farm, we had a black lab puppy who was the cutest thing on earth but dumb as a post. For the rest, Rebecca's a cat person and I seriously am allergic to them. The one in the photo was only for effect."

"Even if you didn't like him, he seemed to like you. Thanks by the way, that was very sweet of you."

"I'm glad something was." He picked up another piece of debris from the tide. "A Japanese sports drink. Aquarius. What do they do, just pitch it over the side of the boat when they're done with it? There aren't a whole lot of Japanese tourists sitting on the beach with their sports drinks."

"Probably that's what everyone does, pitches it over the side. Who'll ever know?"

"I'll know," Eli said, holding up the bottle for everyone to see and pointing at it.

It seemed as if all the birds had disappeared, no squawking gulls or massed flocks of sanderlings, no loons diving or herons hunting out at the river. Something floated in the current, though. Eli took the binoculars. "It's a seal," he said. "Just his head's showing."

"Is he sick?"

"I don't know. Let me go ask him." Please, she thought, don't let anything else get in the way of whatever this is.

At the back of the river in the quiet cove, she expected the flock of ducks to be the American wigeons they'd already identified, but these birds were something else entirely.

"You have to see this," Eli said, looking through the binoculars again. "That is the wildest thing ever. Who makes up these birds?" He put down the binoculars for a minute. "I just asked a very heavy question."

"Call Janelle. But first let's figure out what it is." She took out her phone.

"Duck," he said. "Obvious. Medium-sized. But they're not just one main color."

"What are they?"

"Black and white."

"There's a choice for that. Here." She handed him the phone. Only one duck had come up.

"Yes!" he said. "Bufflehead? That's terrible. I agree with the look. I don't agree with the name at all."

Miller took the binoculars. What she saw made her think more of geometric modern art than ducks.

As the afternoon light began to fade, casting long shadows and turning the tidal flats silver, Eli put a hand on her arm. "Is that really happening?" he said.

A large family had gathered around the now familiar sight of a common murre sitting stubbornly at the edge of the waves, head twisting, beak held high, tuxedo-fronted and desperate-looking in the sand.

"It's hurt," one of them announced. As they closed in, the bird panicked, flapping its wings and flopping around on legs that were out of control and useless. One of the men in the group walked quietly around the murre and picked it up very carefully, very gently from behind, wrapping its body in his gloved hands. "What are you going to do with it now?" someone in the group asked.

Another family member chimed in. "That's dinner," she said. Whatever their intentions, the family moved companionably up the access road, their beach bird still in hand.

"Good grief," Miller said. "I suppose it's a natural reaction to try and help." She was remembering her own instincts in that direction.

"Yeah, but how many people actually follow up on it?"

At the condo parking lot, there was a decision to be made. Eli turned to her.

"I ate the French bread and spinach dip for breakfast, sorry, but the lobster and champagne's still there," he said. "And it is New

Year's Day. They haven't stopped celebrating up in the high rise. Could I talk you into dinner?"

Miller hadn't been sure she'd ever be able to walk through that door again. She took a deep breath. If he could put it behind him, all of it, then she could, too.

"What can I do?" Miller said.

"Pull up a stool and sit on it and don't touch anything."

"I could set the table."

"No you couldn't. That takes five seconds." He had briefly stored two champagne glasses in the freezer. Now he took them out and popped the cork on the champagne, expertly, she noticed, without any of the contortions she sometimes needed. Setting a glass down in front of her, he retrieved a bottle of limoncello from a cabinet and poured, then added the champagne.

"Just be a little careful," he said.

"Your drinks come with a warning?"

"Some of them do."

She sat at the breakfast bar remembering the shell creeping along with its blue antennae waving. That seemed like a lifetime ago. She had no trouble keeping her eyes on him as he moved around the small space, lighting the broiler, opening and closing the refrigerator.

"Now that I think about it, you weren't here, how did you come by all those lobster tails?" she said.

"I had them FedExed to the bar." He was serious about the celebration he'd been planning.

"And wow, you're a butter addict."

"Lobster requires it. Someday I'll have a gut and then it'll be off the list. Beer, too."

Some day when you're older, she thought, and it was a reminder. She got up and walked around the room. The night had already faded to black and the rain had come up again, throwing itself against the sliding glass.

"You're still making paper airplanes?" she said. The living room floor was littered with them.

"It concentrates my mind and I need that for a project I'm working on."

"A project? Is it all right if I ask what it is? I'd really like to know."

He wiped his hands on a dishtowel then went to the media shelves, pulled a large sketchbook out of a drawer and brought it to the dining table. He flipped open the cover to reveal a very clean and detailed drawing of something that resembled a meticulously rendered bird's wing made up of several different parallel sections and attached to a stand of some sort.

She looked at him. "That's amazing. What is it?"

He turned over the page to the next sketch that showed exactly the same object, only now the sections had begun to separate. With each following page, the sculpture opened more and more until it was something incredibly lovely, she couldn't say exactly what, the sections all flying out at angles from the center. Eli took out his phone and scrolled through to photos of this very same object, only in real life, a shiny metal piece standing on a worktable in a cluttered garage.

"Eli, oh my gosh, this is who you are."

"Maybe. I hope so. It's just a beginning." He scrolled through to photographs of several others in various stages of production, each unique, all along the same lines. "Later, when I have better working conditions, they'll look more finished."

"Better working conditions? Where are you now?"

"In an auto body shop in Oceanview," he said. "The guy's nice, I rent out part of his space and some of his tools."

Miller paged back through the drawings. "But how does it open like that?"

"They're kinetic. They turn and spin and open and close all at the same time. They're balanced so that a touch will do it, but also the wind. Just not this wind. I'd have to go find them ten miles up the road."

Miller studied him. "Is this what you came out here for?" she said.

"Partly, to find the space and quiet where I could at least think about it."

"I'm completely in awe."

"In awe. Miller, I could so easily have ignored everything, picked up more shifts at the bar, hung out, passed the time and all of that would have stayed right where it was, only ideas in my head. But when I saw how much effort you put into the hard stuff going on in your life, working at it day after day after day, I realized if you could do that, I could make this happen, everything's possible. And if I couldn't make it happen, I at least had to try."

"That can't have anything to do with me," she said, embarrassed.

"Yes, it can. It does. And now I've got to get back to my real job, which is grilling lobster."

She was glad to have the conversation go in another direction. "I see what you mean about this," she said, holding up her glass. "It's so good you want more before you've even finished what you have."

"A very old trick that bartenders use to keep bars in business."

"You did everything," Miller said at the table. She noticed that the sketchbook was gone, carefully put away again.

"And you managed to not do anything. We're making progress. Cheers."

"Cheers," she said, and meant it. She couldn't even remember when she'd last had lobster. She forked a luscious morsel out of one of the shells arranged on her plate and dipped it in lemony butter. Pure heaven.

"Now for even more revelations. Do you want to tell me about the ring?" She'd noticed it immediately on his left hand, nothing she'd ever seen him wear before, though some instinct for preservation had made her cautious about it. The ring was a thin cobalt blue band edged in silver.

Eli glanced at his hand. "I used to wear it at work when things got awkward," he said. "It puts people on pause, encourages them to reconsider what they might've been thinking."

"Women, you mean." It could be a wedding band, especially the way he was wearing it, although not like any other wedding band she'd ever seen.

"Remember I'm talking New York City. Guys too."

"Guys hit on you?"

"In New York, all the time. The ring was my dad's, though. He made it, actually. When he was with my mom, he was a pretty good silversmith. Hard to believe, seeing who he is now. But do you want to know why I'm wearing it?"

"No," Miller said suddenly.

He ignored her. "It's because I made a promise to someone who's important to me and this is my way of showing that no matter what, I won't go back on that promise."

Miller was silent for a moment. "I didn't ask for promises," she said. "I told you, it's your life and you can do what you want with it."

"That's what you don't understand. I am doing what I want with it. The other part of why I came out here was to be alone, take stock of a pretty sorry situation, ask some hard questions, and instead I'm out there finding dead birds and Japanese sports drinks and thinking there must be a God because there are so many crazy-looking ducks in the river."

"But you've also got to remember the reason that I'm here," she said. "A therapist and a whole other completely messed up life that's not going away."

"Do you think I'm not aware of that? I just told you, I watch you go through that every day."

"What I'm trying to say then is this," she said. "You have to get rid of the elephant in the room. It's not okay."

"Ah, the elephant..." Miller had nothing but empty shells and a pool of butter left on her plate. She was draining the last of her second glass of champagne. "I've been thinking about that," he said. "A lot."

She cursed the flush creeping up her neck. "That was get rid of it, not think about it." She put down her glass and pushed back her chair. "Thank you, this was unbelievable, all of it. You're great and you're my friend and I love you, but I'm going."

"You're sure?"

"Yes."

"Then I'm driving you home."

Miller gritted her teeth. She had no experience with this kind of thing. What was she supposed to do now? "It's two blocks. No you aren't."

"Here's what. You're the one who keeps saying I can do what I want."

"Let me take that back."

"Too late."

Reluctantly, Miller got in the Jeep. The rain was still coming down hard. She would have been soaked to the skin.

Instead of pulling up out front, Eli turned into the driveway behind the Prius and parked, turning off the lights. The rain drummed incessantly on the roof and ran in a river down the windshield.

"What you do with the elephant in the room is not ignore it," he said. "You acknowledge it, admit that it's there. You deal with it."

Miller was marshalling an argument but to no useful purpose. The Jeep was narrow, the seats too close. Before she could find something to offer, he reached over and traced his fingers down her cheek, then leaned in and kissed her. He was gentle, his kiss long, slow, thoughtful. Miller felt as if she'd gone to another place, somewhere far outside her recognizable world. She knew someone else who could kiss like that, someone she'd spent a lot of time kissing, they used to laugh about burning the house down, from early on right up until when that other name entered the conversation, right up until the day she found out about Lauren Metcalf.

But this wasn't Lauren Metcalf, this was Eli and she had to wake up and see the huge line she was crossing. Then it got too confusing and she didn't care about the huge line because she needed to focus all of her attention on kissing him back. Done with coherent thought, stunned by the wonderful feel of him, she responded with a wanting so strong it frightened her. She gripped the front of his coat, his hands went into her hair and the kisses kept coming, deeper and faster, generating heat.

"The gearshift gets in the way," he said, his voice rough with emotion.

"I know," she said. Struggling, all in a rush, they climbed over the seats and into the back, Eli sliding down and pulling her on top of him, bulky in their coats, nowhere for their feet to go. He hit his head on the window frame, she rammed her knee into the seat belt holder, but still they were hungry, mouth on mouth, not able to get enough, steam from their exertions completely fogging up the windows.

Miller couldn't say how it happened, but they were crawling out of the Jeep, they were out of their minds, she knew it now, wild frantic kisses in the rain, stumbling through the front door, falling onto the couch, never even pausing to catch their breath.

"I won't let anything happen," Eli said. His words were only a whisper. "I don't have any protection."

"What?" she said. Protection? Why was he telling her he was defenseless, what was he talking about? She died a thousand deaths in the flash of the next instant when she realized what he meant, for her all of that was hundreds of years ago, how embarrassing, they were light years apart, from different planets. But then they were wrapped up again, devouring each other.

The pace had to slow. Eyes closed, they lingered over one last long kiss then reluctantly came up for air. Miller groaned, slowly pulling herself away from him. What were they *doing*? She wasn't nineteen anymore and he wasn't either. She worked her way to a sitting position, her legs across him, and sank back into the cushions. Eli shifted underneath her until his head was propped up against the sofa arm.

"Holy shit," he said.

Though Miller's hair was everywhere and her face was on fire, at least her pulse was slowing.

He rested a hand on her thigh, suddenly such an intimate gesture, and her heart rate went back up.

"You all right?" he said.

She nodded. She could feel him watching her.

"Miller, seriously, that's the best thing that's happened to me in a very long time." She turned to look at him, aware of the conflicting emotions showing in her face. "I see where you're going," he said. "Stay with me, right here, right now. Don't think about it."

She couldn't tell him that she didn't have to think about it. Right here, right now didn't ever last. This was the end. She wouldn't let it go any further. She couldn't. He belonged with pale blondes and energetic redheads, younger women without the complications of lawyers and therapists in their life, women who understood what protection meant and probably brought their own.

Miller let her eyes stay on him anyway. She wanted to keep just that much, the memory of how good it felt to be with him.

"Say you care about me," he said. "That's all I ask."

"I do," she said. "You know I do."

"And I care about you, more than you'll ever know, so that's everything."

"You make it all sound so simple."

"That's because it is."

"What happens now?" Great question, she thought, just a little late.

"Kick me out tonight, but let me back in tomorrow."

"Or put a lock on the door."

"We're not done, Miller. Anything like that between two people? It's only the beginning."

Her cheeks were burning. "No more," she said.

"No more what?" he said. "I love it when you blush."

chapter 22

MILLER SENT the text early.

It said: *Goodbye. Going into the convent. Taking my vows this afternoon. I mean it.*

His answer: *I am now on record as wanting to sleep with a nun. Where is it, I'll be right there, wear something...black?*

She stared at her phone, trying hard to ignore the way electricity ran from her scalp down to her toes. She had an approach, though, the only one possible, and resigned herself to the process. It wouldn't be fun, but that couldn't be helped. There were too many other women who needed to be kissed like that. This time she'd be prepared, she'd be expecting them and not walk in unannounced. She would never walk in unannounced again.

The body of a small seabird lay alone in the sand, black with white cheeks and tiny gray webbed feet. Miller looked it up. It was an ancient murrelet. She snapped a photo then hesitated. Acting on instincts that were obviously not trustworthy anymore, she sent the photo.

Eli texted back: *Murrelets are an important part of the peregrine falcon's diet. Just what every species hopes for itself.*

His second text: *Spend the night with me.*

She quickly closed her phone. This wasn't anything she had ever bargained for or even seen coming because she hadn't allowed herself to see it. She had tried to keep her thoughts steadfastly elsewhere, dwelling on the safety and well-being of her children, on living with the pain, on not having any thoughts at all.

The heron monitored low tide at the river, exactly the color of the water he stared into. He turned in annoyance at her presence, his dagger-like beak flashing in the light. She almost stepped on the northern harrier perched low on a small chunk of driftwood. He rose and flapped slowly past her on creaky-sounding wings.

She considered that sometimes maybe it was even hard being a hawk.

Coming around the bend from the river, Miller was suddenly faced with the turquoise van again, parked where she'd first seen it, high up on the beach by the dunes. Still stinging from the last encounter, she tried to move quickly on by, but the owner was standing in front of his van watching her. Dignity gone again.

"I think we've met," he said. He was still attractive in that disheveled kind of way even though his clothes were grimy and his lined face was streaked with sweat and sawdust.

"I was hoping you wouldn't remember," she said.

He wiped his forehead with a sleeve. "Not likely. In case you hadn't noticed, there's not much goes on out here."

"I had noticed, that's why I like it."

"Do you?" he said.

She felt it was odd, the way he asked the question.

"Yes, I do, which is also why I reacted the way I did. I'm sorry, I was being a jerk."

"I doubt you could be a jerk if you tried. I am, though. Hear about it all the time."

"That's nicer than I deserve." She held out her hand. "Miller," she said.

His hand was cold but strong. "That's really your name?" he said, and she wondered again.

"It's what people call me."

"What people call me is Luca."

"And that's really your name?" she said. He smiled.

"I'm just curious," she said. "Where I come from..."

"Which is?"

"Southern California." She noted the deep breath he took. "...I don't think you're allowed to take things like this from the beach."

"I told you I had a permit, but it's also salvage rights, oldest law on the books. Finders, keepers."

"Maybe it's only growing things. Beach plants. Is this firewood?" A chainsaw lay on the ground with chunks and pieces scattered all around. The van already sagged under the weight of its load.

"Today it is, but that's unfortunate. Damned shame when cedar gets cut up like this, there's way more money in shakes. Log needs to be hauled out whole though and this van couldn't haul a dead cat."

"I didn't know you sold it. Is it a good living?" Everything she said seemed to amuse him.

"I don't know," he said. "It's not how I make my living."

"You do it for fun?"

"There's a question. Fun? No, I don't think so."

"I didn't mean to ask. You don't have to tell me," she said. He was maddening.

"Mostly, it keeps me out of trouble. I'm better being out here than somewhere else."

"You can recognize all these kinds of wood when they're just logs washed up on the beach," she said. "I envy that."

"Just a word of wisdom from your elders, there are probably more useful things to envy."

Irritating was the other word that came to mind, though maybe he should be the one feeling that way about her. "Have you been doing this for a long time?"

"About forever, give or take, and right at the moment I've got to get back to it," he said, squinting out at the ocean. "Tide's coming in." He moved slowly as he bent down and picked up the saw.

Miller watched as the chainsaw bit and chips flew, the perfume of cedar filling the air. She picked up a discarded block that showed a golden-hued grain like fine furniture and counted the rings.

"One hundred and fourteen," she said.

"Sounds about right. Take that and anything else you want. Just don't spend it all in one place."

Miller agreed that they could still go to the gym together, but she would drive.

"How about if it was your car, but I drove?" Eli said. "I've never driven a Prius before."

Although she watched him closely, he only appeared to be marveling at the weirdness of a car that had no key and went silent at stop signs and traffic lights. Then he came back around.

"And who would ever think of making out in a Prius anyway?" he said.

"Your days are numbered."

"I know," he said. He smiled and she had to look away.

On the treadmill, she put in her earphones for the music and watched *Seinfeld* reruns without the sound. *Friends* had somehow disappeared. When Eli joined her, he settled into her pace and was quiet. He had earphones in, too. Miller turned as he motioned something to her. He was asking for her cell phone. She pulled out the cord and gave it to him, frowning. He scrolled his to play and handed it to her. She gave him a questioning look, then attached it and listened as she ran.

Her face flushed instantly. Kings of Leon. "I Could Use Somebody." She stayed with it till the end, that raw heartache voice, then handed it back to him, still flushed.

"Good workout music," he said.

"Nice try. Give me back my Jack Johnson."

chapter 23

SEVERAL DAYS OF huge high tides piled up a mountain of debris that blocked the access road until the yellow county front loader could come and scrape everything up into the dunes again, a never-ending project. Only the most high-set, intrepid four-wheel drive vehicles could negotiate such barriers and they did, even at the risk of a broken axle. One tide ferried in a heavy, ten-foot piece of tarred planking with massive rusted bolts. With the next tide it was gone, lifted and floated back out to sea with alarming ease. Miller prayed that Sam was surfing in any other kind of ocean.

She tried to walk on the beach, but on an ebbing tide that had always been safe, a wave came barreling in out of nowhere, hitting the apparent high tide line and roaring far beyond it. She was totally unprepared for the energy and violence of the incoming crest and ran, scrambling up over the dune wall on her hands and knees, pulling her feet up just as the wave exploded beneath her. Covered with sand, her heart pounding, she considered that fear was becoming too much of a companion in this ocean world.

On the treadmills, Eli motioned for her phone.
"We can't keep doing this," she said.
"That's what I've been telling you." He scrolled to the song and exchanged with her. It was Snow Patrol, "You're All I Have."
Miller ran, hardly able to listen. The song was on her top ten working playlist, ride the hard beat, sprint through the chorus. And unfortunately she knew every word. In one way, it was unfair, so much heartfelt effort wasted, though she didn't for a minute believe he hadn't worked this before. It was too easy for him. At least it definitely took her mind off everything else in her life.

Now she was ready, however. She took a minute to breathe.

"Be careful what you start," she said, holding out her hand. They switched phones, she scrolled through hers, grateful that they both could keep up a pace and not fall on their face even while fooling around so much, and handed it back to him.

"What's this?" he said.

"Did I ask you what's this? But I'll tell you. It's the other side of the elephant."

"I wasn't aware that the elephant had sides. I thought it was more of a concept kind of thing."

"You were wrong," she said. "It's big and gray and real and it stomps all over everything."

"All right then. Score one for the home team. I have a feeling the VP's going down."

Eli listened. It was the Raveonettes, "Forget That You're Young," haunting Danish indie rock that she doubted was on anyone's playlist, but it fit the moment.

When the song was finished, he handed back her phone, took his own, got off the treadmill and lay down on the floor behind it.

"I'd hate to know what people think of us at this point," she said over her shoulder.

"Hopefully they're all more interested in Tom Selleck. But really, that's what this is?"

"What what is?"

"Why you won't sleep with me?"

"Oh lord," Miller said. She stopped and got off herself. She stood looking down at him. "Eli, get up." People were casting sideways glances now, likely wondering if the resuscitation team was necessary.

"It's not the bartending or the motorcycle or the tattoos or the mercy…hookup that never happened?" he said, staring at the ceiling.

"No more," she said. "Not here." She reached down for his hand and pulled him up.

They drove home in silence. In her driveway, he turned off the car.

"I'm twenty-nine," he said. "That's next door to thirty which is not young, it's halfway to being dead."

"What you just said, how you feel about that? That's exactly what I'm trying to tell you. We're not even Mars and Venus, we're giraffes and cement trucks."

"What? Okay, but you are so wrong. Everybody's halfway to being dead."

"I'm more halfway than you are. Done. End of story."

"Miller, believe me, there is no done, no end of story. But before you jump on that too, there's a playoff game coming up on Sunday and you have to watch it with me, Jets versus the Patriots, best game of the year. Will you just say yes?" She didn't answer. "We made out in the Jeep, not my house," he said.

"I'd really appreciate if you'd stop reminding me of that."

"I want to keep reminding you because it's good between us. You know it and I know it."

"Eli, you said you wouldn't let anything happen and you meant it in your way, but I won't let anything happen either."

"I meant it in my way, yes, but that was only for right then. Forever wasn't exactly what I had in mind."

"It is what I have in mind."

"You're serious, aren't you?" he said.

"I have to be."

Eli stared out the side window for a long moment before he spoke again. "I don't know where you get this," he said. "There's nobody out here who cares who we are or what we do and that shouldn't matter anyway. It's just you and me. I've made it pretty clear where I am with this and I understand if it's not where you are, but I'm not convinced that's the truth."

"You're too good at this," Miller said. "I don't know how to deal with it at all."

"Too good at what?"

"The woman thing."

"The woman thing? You mean coming on to someone? I'm making it up as I go along. Miller, we've said all along we'd be honest, so that's what I'm being even if it sounds bad. I've never had to do this before, would never have even considered it. But my life in the last five years or so has been exactly two women anyway. Beyond that, well, if we're going to get into it, do you want to trade numbers?"

"Numbers? You're aware that a whole lot of the time I don't even know what you're talking about."

"Numbers. How many people you've slept with. If everyone's upfront about their numbers, then all the cards are right there on the table."

"I don't have a number."

"I hate to tell you this but if you have children, you have a number, that number can be just one and not to get too personal, but I'm betting it isn't. Oh my God, you're crimson again."

"Why won't you believe me?" she said. "I can't do this."

"Here's my number so my cards are on the table at least. It's seventeen and it's almost all high school and college. After that, in New York, I didn't want to be that person anymore."

Miller blew out a long breath, sitting in the passenger seat of her own car. "I don't know what to say."

"Here's what. We have to approach this from a whole other direction because I can't take things the way they are anymore. I'm getting out of the car and walking down that road and that'll be it for now. No more beach walks, no more gym, no Jets game, no Mark Sanchez, no phone calls, no texting or sexting or anything."

Sexting, she thought. God. "What I will do is send you a picture of my hand with this ring on it every damn day. And there's nothing to agree to in all of this because you don't get a say."

He opened the door, got out, closed it and was gone. It occurred to her that at least he hadn't slammed it. She watched him walk away then stayed for a long time where she was. It couldn't be like this for everyone. She wanted to hug JC and Dell if this in any way resembled the life they led. She wanted to hug them anyway, and Sam, too.

chapter 24

MILLER FELT AS IF she now had just that many more things not to think about. Eli had disappeared from the face of the earth. He sent the promised photo every day, but that was all. She knew where to find him, it wouldn't take much. Just walk into the blue bar on one of his nights. That was something she wasn't going to do.

She went to the gym alone. On the treadmill, she listened to her own music. *Seinfeld* had been replaced by *Cheers*. She found herself pressing again, picking up the pace, raising the incline. She stopped and slowed down.

An entire collection of movies remained. Miller doubled down on those when the nights began to seem even longer, one for early evening which came at four o'clock, one for later, after a dinner of whatever she threw together or got from takeout. There were older ones, Alfred Hitchcock, Cary Grant, Paul Newman, Jane Fonda. Slightly newer ones, the Coen brothers, Steven Spielberg. Seemingly every movie Kevin Costner and Robert Redford ever made. The same for Julia Roberts. She had to stop watching George Clooney and Jennifer Lopez together, there was too much heat, taking her mind where she didn't want it to go.

Still the photo came every day.

Miller stood out in the dunes under a lowering sky of sullen gray, with the wind pushing against her, staring out at an impossible sight. At high tide, there was no beach, only a vast and ominous expanse of dark water churning against the now five-foot high wall of the dunes. Incoming waves hit the wall and broke right in front of her, shooting up curtains of spray before falling heavily backward in great slapping crests of yellow foam. The backwash ferried branches and tree trunks along in a deadly logjam heading swiftly north. She stepped farther and farther back, blinking as she put her arm up, trying to shield her face from the spray and stinging sand.

From her high perch, she squinted in disbelief as a chrome-laden pickup truck roared down the access road, ready for the challenge of the storm. Immediately the heavy vehicle was caught sideways in the surf with logs floating all around and waves washing up over the tires. As soon as the next wave collapsed and receded, the driver beat a hasty retreat. A teenager in a baseball hat and heavy jacket took his place, maneuvering his open Jeep back and forth to dodge huge chunks of wood, veering sharply up into the still sloping north dunes as the tumultuous surf pushed forward. Miller kept her eye on him until he disappeared in the mists, careening down the beach in the backwash, his dog running alongside. When she returned to her house, she anxiously watched the news, but there was no report of a missing teenager.

Miller opened her post office box and felt her stomach turn. More legal documents. Revisions, amendments, she'd been told in her weekly phone call that they were coming. If you were here, her lawyer kept saying, we could mediate this far more quickly. If I were there, Miller thought, I'd have killed someone by now.

Closer to her heart were postcards from Dell, the museum at Bilbao, how amazing that her baby was there, and Sam, of the turquoise blue waters in Bali. She loved their handwriting, so familiar, loved what they had to say. They were doing well, or so it seemed, holding up, getting everything they could out of these incredible opportunities. If this had to happen, at least there was some good coming out of it. JC emailed, called, but was not ever likely to take the time to find a postcard, write it, buy a stamp, locate a mailbox.

Miller quickly stuffed all the mail in the inside pocket of her raincoat, making it even bulkier, and went up over the dunes and out to the river. On an unusually quiet ocean day, fear banished for the moment, here was solace. Here was peace. There had been a pair of loons in residence for the last week or so and she followed them with fascination. They dove continually, snaking abruptly down into the water then popping up a minute later twenty yards away. As opposed to the obscure feeding patterns of other birds, these two appeared to consume their weight in slippery marine life. As she held them in the binocular sights, one dragged up something from the bottom that he struggled with, shaking it like a dog, biting it in pieces and tossing back his head so that, telescoped, she could see the shape of the thing sliding down his long throat.

The unending storms had pushed the dunes back even farther, creating what were suddenly steep eight- and nine-foot cliffs. Fortunately, the tide was very low or she wouldn't be here. The dunes were a fortress, no scrambling up over them now, and she didn't trust the ocean at all anymore.

Two old men passed her in their white pickup, making her sigh again at the vehicle traffic, but she had learned her lesson. They stopped, got out of the truck with an ax and chainsaw and set about splitting a large log that had caught their eye. One of the men was small and ropey, sweat dripping down his grizzled face and darkening the brim of his ball cap. The other wore pants that hung on his bony frame and an old flannel shirt that was already covered in sawdust. She laughed as their dog jumped out of the truck to join them, a tiny pug wearing pearls and a leopard coat.

Miller watched the game alone. She couldn't bear to be asking that same question now of someone else. *Where are you?* She knew only one thing for certain, that wherever Eli was, he was also watching the game. He couldn't possibly stand to miss it, his team, his GQ quarterback. No, she knew one other thing. He still sent the photo faithfully every day and she found that, despite all her fervent wishes to the contrary, the gesture moved her.

She picked up her phone after all three Mark Sanchez touchdowns. Would it hurt to just send a picture of the TV screen? It would hurt. Dammit, she thought. Tom Brady, the other GQ quarterback, got sacked five times. The Jets were on the verge of winning. Their coach was hysterical on the sidelines. It was too much. She put her head in her hands. Just say no and keep on saying it. The voice in her head wasn't saying it quite loudly enough though. Another interfering voice had begun insisting it was not the big deal she was making it out to be. And a third voice she could barely acknowledge had somehow gotten into far more problematic territory than that.

chapter 25

THE DAY STARTED OUT calm and cold, with alternating cloud and sun. The fierce southwest winds revived at midafternoon. An hour later they were screaming. Since the tides were still very high, attempting a beach walk was out of the question. Restless, Miller got in the car and drove to the small bookstore she'd found in Oceanview with a local interest section and a whole shelf of books about surfing. For Sam's sake, she picked up every new book she found, always wanting another window into the world he loved.

The road to the store was blocked with sawhorses and police tape. Waves crested the nearby embankment and surged over the sidewalks and into the flooded parking lot of the hotel next door.

Heading quickly home, she pulled on her boots and fought her way out to the dunes to find a frightening sight. The world had gone berserk. The wind shrieked and the lethal ocean waters once more covered the entire beach. One set of waves built to a staggering height, exploded, then fell back and collided with the next set in towering walls of water. The combined roar of the surf and wind was deafening.

Miller focused on keeping her wits about her, staying alert, stepping back farther and farther into the beach grass. When the first waves unthinkably breached the dunes, she turned and ran.

It was almost dark. Blasts of wind were still pounding the house. In the fading light, she could see the waves now from the deck, spreading far up into the dunes in chaotic lines of surf, the spray glowing white. She checked frantically around her mother's living room. She didn't know what to do, where to start. Would the French doors hold? She tested them. They were sound, the locks and bolts strong. The problem was all that glass. Maybe the deck would break the power of the waves. *What was she thinking*? If waves came anywhere near the deck, a complete disaster was at hand. She imagined seawater soaking into the pale blue rugs, pooling around the legs of the dining table, creeping up through the lavender-flowered pattern of the sofas.

Then the power went out. She looked over at her laptop as the screen shut down. Shit. There were some useful things she'd remembered at least, not one but three flashlights, all with good batteries. One was in the kitchen. She felt around till she found it in the drawer and with light then pulled out the boxes of candles and matches. She weighed her options, trying to decide whether it was safe to ride it out or if that was foolish to even think about and she should be packing right now for a hotel, and not one on the beachfront.

She was caught, still uncertain, when the front door opened.

"Hey, stranger. Thought you'd still be here," Eli said. He pushed back the hood of his sweatshirt. He had brought his own flashlight. Training it out toward the deck, he gave a low whistle of appreciation. "This isn't good, you know. Time to go. Evacuation plan being put in place. Turns out you are spending the night with me after all. I'll sleep on the couch." His condo was two rows back from the dunes and high enough on the rise to be far out of harm's way.

She stood staring at him. He was the same, she was the same. Nothing had changed. She found herself incredibly grateful.

"What?" he said.

"Nothing," she said. "I'll sleep on the couch."

"There's the Miller I've come to know and love. Jesus, have I missed her. Get your things. Depending on how this goes, you might be staying for a while. Don't forget your phone, but crap, the chargers won't work. And the warmest coat you have. If the power stays off, it'll be pretty fricking cold, and that's inside."

Miller already had her phone in her back pocket. Upstairs using a flashlight, she grabbed some clothes, ran into the bathroom for her toothbrush and jammed it into her pocket then went back for the hairbrush. In the kitchen, she filled a bag with the candles and matches. Eli was at the French doors, still watching. It was such an eerie, unnerving sight. Where there should have been grass and sand there was only water throwing back the flashlight's beam in sickening waves.

"I refuse to believe it'll come this far," she said. "It just can't."

"I know it's hard, but in the end, this is all just nothing. Replaceable. You? Not so much. Let's get out of here."

"Just let me get some firewood from the garage," she said. She loaded Luca's cedar pieces onto the floor on the passenger side of the Jeep with the wind raging all around her.

"Were you a Girl Scout?' he said as she got in.

"Good God, no. Were you?"

"I tried, but they wouldn't let me in."

The headlights of the Jeep picked out surf breaking halfway up the access road, swamping the pile of logs and debris.

Inside the condo, Eli put down the flashlight. Before he could locate any candles, Miller had set out hers and lit them, a sea of ivory pillars that cast the high open room in a soft glow.

"You *were* a Girl Scout," he said.

"There are some things I know how to do, that's all."

They stood looking at each other. Eli spoke first. "This is interesting. Now what? Food, maybe. Have you eaten?"

"I should have thought of that," she said. "I could have brought cheese and crackers at least."

"I can do that one better, I've got cheese, crackers and salami. I'd say what's needed most here, though, is a bottle of wine. Could you do a red?"

"You know what? You're good at that and I'll like whatever you choose."

"There's a Miller I don't recognize at all."

It was strange with everything dark and the candlelight creating odd shadows. Miller lit more candles and set them on the breakfast bar as Eli moved around the kitchen. "I forgot, I have three kinds of cheese and I even have grapes," he said. "It's a feast." He brought out plates, napkins, a breadboard. "I might not have mentioned that when the bar in New York was slow, I filled in as a waiter."

"Well rounded."

"That's me."

Miller curled up at one end of the sectional facing a large blacked out TV. The wine was mellow and smooth, a well-chosen distraction.

"What is it with this place?" she said. "Whoever Mother Nature is, you start wanting to hate her."

"I'd never thought of it quite so personally as that. I've got this urge to put on music at least, forget about the TV. What the hell did those pioneers do? Sit in the dark listening to the coyotes eat their chickens? What kind of life was that?"

"I think you're supposed to get out your banjo or your violin or something."

"That'll be the day. No musical talent here."

"None here either. Or you could mend the fishing nets, since we live on the coast, and I could knit, if only I knew how."

"Basically," he said, "we'd be dead of either starvation or boredom in about three days."

"No takeout."

"And the peanut butter's almost gone. I'd let you have the last spoonful, though."

"Thank you."

They ate what there was to eat in comfortable silence, neither wanting to know what the other was thinking, enjoying the quiet strangeness of the evening but aware that there was still time to fill.

"So this is a challenge, but we should rise above it," Eli said. "What do you want to talk about? How about movies we've watched in the last two weeks?"

While we weren't texting or sexting, she thought. "You did that, too? I wonder if we've ever in our lives watched the same movie, never mind in the last two weeks."

"Try me."

"I'll throw out four," she said. "*Mystic Pizza, Sleeping With The Enemy, Runaway Bride* and *The Mexican*."

"I give up already. What are they? I've never heard of any of them."

139

"Julia Roberts. Your list? I hate to think."

"*Fast and Furious One, Two, Three* and *Four*. All on cable, it was a marathon."

"Since there's obviously no hope for this, I'll concede a little," she said. "*Forgetting Sarah Marshall*."

Eli fell back against the cushions. "Thank you, lord. Judd Apatow. Which means…"

"Here's a test," Miller said. "And I can tell you right now who's going to flunk it."

"I should be cautious then, but screw that. *40 Year Old Virgin*."

"*Knocked Up. 40 Year Old Virgin*, ugh."

"Ugh? What kind of comment is that? It's a hilarious movie. I could have said *Superbad*, you know, but I didn't."

"Unfortunately," Miller said, "I'm familiar with *Superbad*. Michael Sera, *Juno*."

"*Juno*, no way. I couldn't even watch the trailer. But you've taken us to a very fine place."

"And that would be?"

"Michael Sera," he said. "*Arrested Development*."

"First of all, you're now in TV shows instead of movies. Second, I concede again. I did watch *Arrested Development*, some of it anyway."

"And you thought it was funny, right?"

"Sometimes. Insane is more like it. They lost me though when the dad became two guys and one of them was living in the attic."

"Doesn't matter, we both watched it. And from there you can get through Jason Bateman to *Up In The Air*. George Clooney. Good job."

"And from there to *Michael Clayton*," Miller said quickly. "And what's her name with the red hair. Tilda Swinton."

"Or from there to *Out of Sight*. George Clooney and Jennifer Lopez? Tell me you haven't seen that movie."

"I haven't." Not quite true, but only till the scene in the trunk before she had to turn it off. He didn't need to know that.

"George Clooney's too easy, though. *Ocean's Eleve*n alone could take you anywhere."

"Back to *The Mexican*," she said.
"What?"
"*Ocean's Eleven*. Brad Pitt and Julia Roberts in *The Mexican*. Brad Pitt in *Thelma & Louise*."
"I believe that's Susan Sarandon in *Thelma & Louise*."
"Susan Sarandon in *Bull Durham*," she said, "which takes us to Kevin Costner and you don't want to go there."
"Though *Bull Durham*, Tim Robbins, takes us to *Shawshank Redemption*."
"Best movie ever."
"See?" he said. "Agreed. Totally. We could go Morgan Freeman, but that's too easy, too. Let's start over. Frances McDormand. You know I'm saying *Fargo*."
"*Laurel Canyon*."
"Whoa, points for the lady."
"*Almost Famous*."
"Win, win and win. Great movie. We don't have such a bad track record. There's hope for us, Miller."
"Eli," she said. "You're great at this, but I'm done. Maybe could we call it a night?" She wanted to get past the couch and the candlelight and into the dark and the quiet.
"One more glass of wine."
"Just one."
Eli poured the wine and then stretched his feet out on the coffee table. The candlelight flickered.
"Best dead bird you've seen," he said.
"The pelican. You were with me, remember? Best, most beautiful, saddest. They're all beautiful in their own way. But hold on, I forgot." She slid her phone out of her pocket and pulled up the photo. "I found a banded bird last week, dead as usual. You go online and report the band number and they tell you what it is, where it was banded and even who banded it. I took a screen shot of it to send you, but then I didn't." She handed it to him.
"A juvenile white-fronted goose from Alaska? That's crazy. Good job. Too bad it wasn't a good job for him." He paused for just a moment. "Why didn't you send it?"

"Because you said not to."

"How many other photos did you take and not send?"

"Only three or four, some birds. Scroll back. They're in there."

"This is more than three or four. You watched the Jets game? Okay, Miller. We're at a moment here."

"What moment?" she said, scarcely daring to breathe.

"Watch me." To her relief, he took out his own phone and called her number, still holding her phone.

He laughed as the beginning 'ooh wahs' made clear what it was, The Ad Libs, 1965, "The Boy From New York City."

"What did you think it'd be?" she said. "There was no choice."

He hung up and called his number from her phone. Then she was laughing too, but also wide-eyed. Loud emphatic chords sounded and then Janis Joplin's ear-splitting wail from "Cry, Baby."

"I always know it's you," he said.

"You'd definitely know it was somebody." And this was from the beginning. They were both crazy.

"Finished," he said. "What do I have to do to get you to take the bed and let me sleep on the couch?"

"Just be nice when I tell you forget it."

"Right, I hear you. No fighting. The hall bathroom's yours."

"I always seem to be saying it, but thank you, for everything."

"You're welcome for everything." He stood up, taking the plates and wine glasses with him.

Before she could rearrange herself on the cushions, he was back with a quilt. She was already wearing her down coat. "And here are pillows." He had three. "Anything else?" She shook her head no. "Good night, then. Sleep tight. Don't let the bed bugs bite."

The room was cold. Miller blew out the candles. Then it was cold and dark. She opened the sliding glass just a fraction. The wind had died down. She could hear the surf, still roaring, but impossible to tell from this distance how close it was. The whole world was black, no lights anywhere.

She'd brought another pair of socks and pulled them on over the pair she was already wearing, then wrapped up in the heavy quilt and curled into a ball in the middle of the sectional. She considered how odd it was without power, no little red lights glowing, no digital clock faces, no hum of appliances, only silence. And the acute awareness of Eli somewhere in that silence.

The fetal position didn't work. Neither did lying on her back. Or on her side. Or at the end of the couch instead of in the middle. Put all those thoughts away, she kept telling herself. Just hold on, get past it. But something in her didn't want to get past it.

She waited, agitated and not close to sleep. According to her phone, an hour had gone by. Waking him up would be a mistake. Maybe he'd had second thoughts anyway, changed his mind, given up, though she knew none of that was true. *Open your eyes*, Janelle had said. *Pay attention to what's right in front of you.* Someone else in that blind advice-giving period had said live like you'll die tomorrow. She wondered if those were the same things. Probably not. But it wasn't hard to see what was right in front of her. All she could manage in the way of doing something about it was to take both pairs of socks back off.

"The Boy From New York City" sounded in her pocket, muffled but still jolting in the stillness. Miller closed her eyes and answered the call.

"How are you doing?" Eli said.

"I'm okay."

"Really?"

"No."

"I've never heard anybody make so much noise with a couch and a quilt."

"I didn't mean to keep you awake."

"You didn't. But I've got an offer to make. What if I meet you halfway?"

"What if you're wrong in what you're thinking?" she said, but her voice was shaky.

"Am I wrong?"

"No."

"Offer accepted?"

"No. I'll figure something out, but it has to be on my own. Eli, this is ridiculous," she said. "Hang up the phone."

She walked over to the sliding doors and pressed her face against the cold glass.

When she turned around, he was there.

He reached out, gently brushing back her hair. "Listen," he said. "This is all my doing, my fault, and it's too hard on you. Let's go back to the way things were and just forget about it for a while."

"I don't want to forget about it," she said. He was standing close. "I'm ready." She could barely see his expression.

"Ready for what? An execution? It's like you're going through torture. I'm better than that."

"I agree. Don't pay any attention to me. I have so little idea of what I'm doing it's pathetic."

"No, you took what I said wrong. I'm *better* than that. I'm good."

"What? Have you ever heard of humility? Or how about managed expectations?"

"Humility, no, but I am managing expectations," he said. "I haven't said yet how good."

"And you know this how?"

"I'll text you a survey."

"One to ten?"

"One to ten with room if you absolutely need it to go for twelve."

"You'd better be careful," she said. "You're way out there on a limb."

"I'm realizing that. And I've got the one person most willing to run and find a saw."

"You know I'm going to want that text."

He was quiet for a moment. "Does that mean yes?"

"I've been trying to tell you. I just don't know how."

"Are you sure?"

"I am. I'm sure."

He reached out again in the dark and traced his fingers gently over her mouth, then kissed her in a tender, quiet way that made her even more sure. She moved into him, her bare feet on his, and kissed him back, willingly losing herself in the pleasures of his mouth.

In the bedroom, he undid the front of the bulky coat. He helped her out of it and it slid to the floor. He felt for the zipper of the sweatshirt jacket and that also fell to the floor. He worked the t-shirt up and over her head and then both of them together fumbled with her jeans as they fell backward onto the bed. She kicked the jeans off and they turned and locked into each other, kissing again, exploring, tasting.

He shifted away from her just long enough to wrestle out of his own layers then fitted her close down the length of him. When she kissed him more urgently, he pulled all the bedding on top of them and did what she wanted him to do, his hands touching her everywhere, what was left of her clothing pitched outside the blankets into the darkness.

"Miller," he said, his mouth sliding slowly down over her body. She waited, suspended and breathless, all her nerve endings alive, then gasped as he effortlessly took her away. She brought him back up, embracing him hard and kissing him with everything she had. He reached out, fumbling in the drawer of the nightstand, and she suddenly entered unfamiliar territory, a stranger in a strange land.

"You don't have to do that," she said, her voice hoarse.

"We'll talk," he said, his voice gone, too.

Miller shut her eyes tight, her fingers pressing deep into his back, not knowing what to expect. Her eyes suddenly flew open even though it didn't matter in the dark. They had to be honest with each other, she thought. On some level at least, they both knew what they were doing, and in theory neither one had any reason to be shy.

"Oh my God, what is that?" she whispered. She put her fingers on his mouth. "Are you smiling?"

"Shh," he said.

And then she was gone, surrendering to him, aware only of his strength, his passion, willing to follow him anywhere, crying out as they went over the edge together and down into mindless oblivion.

Afterwards, they held each other, both trembling. He wrapped the blankets tight around them and they lay quietly for a long time, only stroking, touching.

"Miller, I need to know," Eli said into the quiet. "Do you still have misgivings? I don't want this beautiful ship to sink before it even sails."

"Only the ones that'll always be there, they come with the territory. But no more than that. Honestly."

"That shouldn't make me feel better, but it does. Next up is we freeze our asses off."

After they had found their clothes and decided by Braille what belonged to whom, they buried themselves under the covers again, their bare feet still touching. The room was pitch black.

"I can't help it," Miller said. "I have to know. What was that?"

"I'll show you in the morning if you want, but essentially they come that way, more than a little, uh, slippery."

"Aaaagh," she said.

"You asked. It works, doesn't it?"

"Yes. It does." It was a complete surprise, beyond anything she'd ever been aware of.

"But why don't you think they're needed?" he said. "Since we're talking about it."

"I take strong pills. I have to. Not for that, for something else, but it covers all the bases, doesn't it?"

"Well, if it's okay, let me ask you some things."

Miller clapped her hands over her ears. It was so much freaking easier to just be married. "Go ahead."

"What's your real number?"

"Three and a half."

"I don't think that's possible, but we'll skip that part. Here's my point. I have a number, you have a number. You can really cover your ears for this one. Monica has a number, and I can guarantee you it's not seventeen."

She removed her hands. "I do have kids who were teenagers and I am aware that you sleep with everybody the person you sleep with has slept with."

"That's it, more or less. Miller, I don't want to take you down any more hard roads, but there's another side to this. Think about it."

She did think about it and wondered why she hadn't before. "Shit."

"That's what I thought. Do you want to tell me about it?"

"Lauren Metcalf."

"For how long? Do you have any idea?"

"I don't at all. It was such a shock I could barely deal with the fact of it, let alone dates and times and places."

"Who is she? Did you know her?"

"Eli," Miller said and then advised herself to just get it over with. "It's a small town where we lived, on the coast up from San Diego. And everybody knows her, she's the fucking mayor. Add on to that, she's the mother of JC's best friend. Add on to that, we went to school together. Add on to that, even though she's a raging conservative and my husband's a screaming liberal, he was her biggest campaign contributor. Add on to that, when some wiseass with an ax to grind caught them coming out of a hotel in Palm Springs, the photo he took was, I swear, on every phone in town within five minutes. Add on to that, people had heard rumors, but no one could find the courage to tell me. Add on to that, her husband called me up and unbelievably suggested we go out for a drink. First I had to find Janelle and have her explain to me how I was ever going to survive. Then I only wanted one thing, to get the hell out of there."

"Jesus Christ. That explains a whole lot. I'm sorry, Miller."

"I'm sorry, too. I just don't understand how I never saw it coming. There wasn't anything different, no fights, no long silences, no…abstinence. How did he pull that off? And the kicker is that she's everything I'm not, and that he never ever went for, perfect hair, perfect makeup, expensive jewelry, all the labels, she was born wearing Louboutin four-inch heels. What the hell is that?" She took a deep breath. "I'm done. I wish it would all just go away. And now because of me, you're sleeping with Lauren Metcalf. And her husband who's an idiot. Nice."

"We're good," he said. "It's okay."

"Where did you come from?"

"Mars by way of cement trucks apparently. Do you think you could sleep now?"

"Yes. Even if my living room's part of the beach."

"Maybe there'll be new dead birds."

"Something to look forward to," she said.

chapter 26

MILLER WOKE TO A more familiar place than she'd been in what felt like a very long time, a cold bed, yes, but not alone. That aspect of the night took no getting used to at all, arms touching, backs, knees, feet, however the positions unconsciously worked out, a hand resting on a hip, a person's quick intake of breath in dreams. The rest of it, however, was another matter entirely.

It seemed late even though the light was still dim along the wall. Eli was sleeping soundly. She crept out of bed, picked her coat up from the floor, took her green boots out onto the patio and closed the door softly behind her. She didn't know how any of this worked, but for the moment all of her attention had to be on the house.

A glance down the access road revealed that the logjam was still there, but the tide had receded far out into the distance. Thank God. It was cold. If Eli hadn't stayed so close, she would have been frozen even under all that down. Eli. She had no idea what to do, how to act, what to say. Was there etiquette involved? Were there rules? Likely she would find out one way or the other when she did everything wrong.

He reached her, running.

"Why didn't you wake me up?" he said.

"Because you looked so peaceful."

"I was, till you weren't there."

"I have to find out, that's all."

"I know."

She cautiously opened the door and went in, down the hall past the study and the kitchen. It could have been worse, much worse. Only one pane of the middle set of French doors was smashed. Glass littered the rug, but there was hardly any dampness.

"What did that?" Eli said, frowning. He peered out onto the deck in the gray light then turned and swept his eyes over the living room. "Something." He gauged the trajectory again then bent down, reached under one of the sofas and came up with a fist-sized rock.

Miller stared at it. "How did that happen?" She thought of the logs pitching around in the surf.

"Maybe you can tell from outside." He unlocked the door and the cold sea air rushed in. Fifteen feet into the dunes, the answer became clear. The sand was suddenly hollow, crusted, breaking easily as a boot sank down into it. This had been, for whatever brief moment, the tide line. Miller felt sick.

"Jesus," she said. "It came that close."

Stepping carefully, Eli went into the beach grass and came back with a sizeable sturdy glass jar with a red lid that had also been thrown up by the waves. "Here. Now you've got something to put your rock in."

In the house, she contemplated the shattered glass. "I should vacuum this up."

"Show me how you're going to turn the vacuum cleaner on. I can board it up if you have something to do that with."

"Forgot, no power. Like what?"

"Anything that size, cardboard, a magazine? Do you have duct tape?"

No duct tape. "I have a hammer."

"That's not exactly duct tape but...do you have nails?"

Note to self. "Never mind," she said. "I'll deal with it later." She realized that it would be easy to let him do it when in fact she needed to do it herself. She rolled up a towel from the guest bathroom and jammed it into the opening. "Done. For now."

"Then could I suggest coffee?" he said. "And maybe breakfast to go with it?"

"Eggs, bacon, hash browns, toast." She was suddenly starving.

"As long as it's some place with heat."

"Let me just run upstairs and change," she said. "I'm not a fan of staying in the same clothes I slept in."

"I hardly ever do that."

She hesitated. "And my toothbrush is at your house."

"Oh yeah, it is," he said, smiling.

Miller insisted on going to Pine Ridge. She didn't want to take the chance of anyone seeing them together and having thoughts about it. This was what she didn't understand. Who *were* they now? Was everything different? She didn't know anything.

Eli was watching her as she drove. "I know what you're thinking. But you're wrong," he said. "No one can tell."

"Women can always tell." She considered the postmistresses, the garden lady, the clerk at the Corner Market.

"Guys just make up shit. And most of the time they're a hundred percent wrong."

"I don't want anybody making up anything."

"They couldn't come close anyway."

She brought her eyes quickly back from him to the road.

"Miller," he said, "you are a gorgeous piece of work."

They ate in a pancake house that offered strong coffee and every item that could possibly be construed as breakfast. She scrolled quickly through the local news and passed her phone to him. Seas hit thirty feet before high tide. No one could remember an ocean so huge. A pickup was rolled and crushed, but the driver escaped. Beachgoers reported seeing a woman and her dog swept away, but that had not been confirmed. A restaurant manager in Pine Ridge said she put the Closed sign on the door when a wave washed over a car in the parking lot. A rock pitched up by the surf broke her window and dumped seaweed onto the restaurant floor. She reported that the bartender immediately invented a new drink named after the rock.

"As bartenders always do with rocks thrown through windows," Eli said.

Thirty-five-foot swells had even kept the Coast Guard in port.

When Miller asked, the waitress told them the power was only out from Oceanview north along the coast, including the entire town of Winslow.

"Heard it might be a day or two yet till they get it back on. You're not from around here? This'll make you feel better." She put down a laminated article on the Pine Ridge tsunami alert system, billed as the most sophisticated in the world.

"Good grief," Miller said. "I think we're supposed to feel lucky that it wasn't a tidal wave."

"We could check into a hotel."

Miller had been in the process of adding more ketchup to her hash browns but froze with the bottle in midair.

"Am I freaking you out?" he said.

"No." She had to work on breathing again. "Yes."

"Then here's another plan. If the gym has power we could go there, work out and catch some of the Vikings playoff game, shower, drive around in the car till our phones are charged…" He reached out to take her hand. "…stay with me, and end up at the bar to watch the Jets game. This is the big one."

"Didn't we just talk about this? Not the bar, not for me anyway."

"We can sit in a corner in the dark."

"It'll be packed. You know it will."

"Even better. Nobody'll even notice."

"Eli, you *work* there."

He held her with his eyes. "I'm not letting go of you," he said. "Just the gym for now?"

"Yes." She wanted to run for an hour. Hard.

On the way back up to Winslow, Eli suddenly put out his hand.

"Wait, wait, wait. Pull over."

Fifty feet back from the road was a field full of cow elk, scruffy and mottled, like giant gangly horses with big heads and knobby knees.

"They're huge," Miller said. "I've never seen one before."

"I never have either, not in real life and definitely not that close."

They were clumsy-looking and moon-eyed, staring out into space while they munched peaceably on the damp grass.

"What's to stop them from just wandering out into the road?" she said.

"Nothing, seems like. Do you ever get the feeling we're on some other planet far, far away?"

All the time, she thought, for so many reasons.

Miller did run hard and it felt good. Unforeseen circumstances, Janelle. Seriously unforeseen. After Eli finished his workout, he chose a treadmill five over so that he wouldn't get caught up in her pace. That way he could watch the Vikings game without going into cardiac arrest. Returning to her house, they found the lights on just as she'd left them before the storm.

"Electricity," she said. "We're saved."

Eli stood waiting in the hallway.

"If you ask me just one dumb question, I swear I'll scream."

"I don't want to assume anything," he said. "That's all."

"I don't know where your head is. Come in, stay, and don't ever do that again. You don't understand. I'm depending on you to not be confused, because I'm totally confused."

There was the smile again. "Where's your remote?" he said in the living room.

"Somewhere in all that junk on the coffee table. I'm going to make dinner. It'll take some time."

"You are?"

"I wanted to before, but things got in the way."

"I won't ask which things you're referring to." He was still digging for the remote. "What are you making?"

"Spinach lasagna."

"Sounds good. Where did you get all these DVDs? I'll bet even Roger Ebert didn't have this many."

"From friends, for purposes of distraction."

He picked one up. "*Tin Cup*. Love it. Rene Russo."

"That would be Kevin Costner."

"Hold on, I forgot Cheech Marin is in it, that's all anyone needs to know. Plus, best ending to a sports movie ever, even if it is about golf." He hesitated. "Want to watch it tonight?"

His gaze stayed on her. She nodded, meeting his eyes.

"On second thought," he said, "I don't really care about the Vikings and the Jets game doesn't start for another half hour. I'm going out and get some things."

"Like what? I have everything here."

"Duct tape so you can put something better over that window because I know you're dying to do it. The firewood you left in my Jeep since the wind isn't howling anymore. More of the wine from last night if you thought it was good."

"It was very good."

"I'll be back then."

"Wait. Is it expensive?"

"It's incredibly expensive and that's why this time I'm buying two bottles."

When he returned, he set items on the kitchen counter, the tape, the wine. "For you," he said and held out his offering, another toothbrush. She took it without being able to say anything.

"The expression on your face is worth it right there," he said. "Where's the vacuum cleaner?"

"In the hall closet."

And then he was kneeling on the pale blue carpet to pick up the shards, vacuuming up the rest, coiling up the cord, putting the vacuum cleaner away, moving past her to wrap the glass in paper towels and toss it in the trash. This isn't happening, she thought. Then he built a roaring fire in the fireplace. Then he turned to the towel stuck in the French doors.

"Just let me do it. It'll take two minutes. You can fix the next one."

"Fine. Do it. Thank you." Ten more minutes and they'd be talking about how to spend their fiftieth anniversary.

He found the remote, clicked on the game and turned the TV so that the screen was visible from the kitchen.

"I don't want you to miss anything," he said. He studied the recipe on the open page of the cookbook. "Complicated."

"Therapy. Of the regular ordinary kitchen variety, not the Janelle disaster avoidance kind."

"I can make the bechamel if you want, I'm good at it."
"You are?"
"Gravy, bechamel, it's all the same thing."
"To you, maybe. Go ahead, but you can't see the screen from over there."
"I'll live. They're terrible today anyway and Roethlisberger's a Mack truck when he gets going. Damn Steelers. Another touchdown. My point exactly."

It took most of the first half for all the layers of the lasagna to come together, assembled in a large glass baking dish, enough for an army.

"That's quite a project," he said.
"But we can wait till the end."
"You don't mind?"
"Of course, I don't mind."
"They're coming back."
"I can see that. Mark Sanchez, the chosen one."
"Maybe, maybe not."

Miller set the lasagna in the oven at the beginning of the fourth quarter. They both watched the Jets come heartbreakingly close and lose in the last two minutes.

"Not his fault, though," Eli said. "The defense crapped it up. Too bad."

They ate in front of the darkened windows accompanied by wine and candlelight. They sat together on the sofa watching Kevin Costner and Rene Russo with more wine, Eli's hand absently on her thigh through the last half, then not so absently for the final hilarious showdown at the U.S. Open.

"My house, my dishes," she said.

"I can help with that, too." But the only help seemed to be reaching around her to turn the water off. The lasagna should have been put away, but then she was trapped against the refrigerator, the dishes and lasagna forgotten.

Kissing heatedly on the stairs, they tripped and fell, both trying to work their way out of t-shirts and sweaters. Reaching the bed, they struggled frantically with what was left of their clothing then pulled each other close, seeking, exploring, causing soft sounds of pleasure in the dark. He thrilled her with his hands until she was full of longing and tenderness, dying for him, the wanting overwhelming both of them. Her breath caught as he produced the surprise out of nowhere.

"Not actually duct tape," she said.

"Other things," he said softly.

He found her again, burying his face in her hair as she wrapped him into her arms, focusing all of her being on him, journeying with him gladly to the urgent place where their hunger wanted them to go.

When it was over, neither of them had any need to disturb the electricity still running between them. In the quiet, the touching continued. Miller trailed her fingers over the gym-built front of him. Eli ran his hand along her throat, over her shoulder, slowly all the way down the curve of her back. And then it wasn't over at all.

chapter 27

THEY SPENT THE MORNING with leftovers and the paper Miller had retrieved from the salt-encrusted box.
"What's this?" Eli said.
"It's called a newspaper. You can fold it, roll it, cut it up, make paper dolls, confetti, tape it to the walls or even start a fire with it if you want."
"Crazy. What will they think of next?"
They added coffee from Hugh's espresso machine.
"I'm addicted already. I have to get one of these things. But now I'm going home."
"You are?" Miller was taken aback, confused again.
"I don't want to ruin a good thing. You need time to yourself. I don't, but you do."
"That sounds like I should start seeing you instead of Janelle," she said.
"I always respected how Dr. Melfi stayed professional and didn't sleep with Tony Soprano," he said, "and I feel the same way. For that reason, regretfully, I can't be your therapist."
"I'm having trouble imagining you as Lorraine Bracco, but I guess that's your problem, not mine."
"So it's my night at the bar," he said.
"I've already lost track of this conversation."
"Last call's midnight, usually clears out on Mondays by twelve-thirty."
What had happened to the shallow end of the pool? This was off the diving board into fifteen feet. At least she hoped it was fifteen feet.
"You just throw that out and leave it there?" she said. "Why won't you help me with these things? Okay, the door's open, but you don't have to be here if you don't want to."
"You're out of your mind," he said.

Miller walked for restless hours on the beach. She watched a movie. Dell called. JC emailed. She ate dinner. She read in bed then turned out the light.

She heard the front door open, heard him take the stairs two at a time.

"Miller?" he said. "What are you hiding from?"

She was deep down in the bed with the blankets pulled over her head. "Myself," she said.

"At least you're honest. This time I am taking off my pants. No pepper spray, we're agreed on that, right?"

She lowered the blankets. "No pepper spray. Scout's honor." She heard him pause. And then he was beside her in the dark.

"Sorry, I know I smell like the bar," he said. "Occupational hazard."

"Maraschino cherries."

"Seriously? Great. But I found something out." He laced his fingers into hers and slid his bare foot up and down her leg. She wondered at how naturally these things came to him and whether he knew exactly the effect they had. Likely, though she still didn't understand whether seventeen was a whole lot or not so many and there was no one she could possibly ask. "We're in trouble," he said. "Or I am anyway."

"Why is that?"

"You're all I thought about. I couldn't even remember how to make a Missouri Mule, in part because it's the most godawful drink on earth, but some guy orders it every night, and in part because I just couldn't get you out of my head. You do things to me, Miller."

"That scares me," she said.

"It scares me, too."

"Here's what you know my answer is to everything. Don't think about it."

"I'll go with that," he said, unlacing their fingers.

She closed her eyes and let it happen, loving the way he kissed, the way he touched, how well he knew her already. Everything else was allowed to fade away. They gave their attention over solely to pleasing each other, trading secrets, taking turns. When the time was right, they shifted together, mouth on warm mouth, body seamless on body, giving everything, moving soundlessly, smiling in the dark.

The morning light was soft and gentle and matched Miller's mood.

"The beach is calling," she said.

"Is it calling both of us?"

"Yes, it is."

"Let me get the weather report," he said. He opened one of the French doors and held out his hand. "Rain, but not much. No sound of hissing and shrieking and sheets being torn apart. For here, what constitutes a perfect day. Let's do it."

Eli stopped as the swooping flock of sanderlings came to a sudden halt on the damp flats in front of them. Miller handed him the binoculars. "I gave up on this," she said. "See what you can do."

"I thought you had them."

"No, go ahead and look. There's someone else in there."

He spent a long time staring at the flock. "I see them. They're a little bigger, a little darker. Try it and see what comes up."

Miller took out her phone. She held it up. "None of those, I don't think," he said. "How about using the bill? It's different, curved down some." She added the bill shape and only one bird came up.

"I don't know. Scroll through the photos. Wait, there it is, winter, not summer. Dunlin."

Miller took out her notebook. She had to flip through many pages before coming to a new line.

"Unfair," he said. "You've been out here without me."

"Remember there is a purpose to this."

A flock of mousy shorebirds had taken up residence on the island that was exposed when the tide was low in the river.

"These too," Miller said. "I just don't know."

Eli looked through the binoculars again. "Being a VP is exhausting," he said. "They blend in so well with those wet rocks that it's hard to tell exactly where they are let alone what they are."

Miller scrolled through the bird guide. "This is what I came up with but it doesn't work."

He took her phone. "Those birds have black legs, but the ones I'm seeing have orange legs. What do you do about that? Hold on. Check it out. Black turnstones have, uh, black legs, but ruddy turnstones have orange legs. That's what they are."

"It's hopeless, I can't upgrade you any more." Miller glanced up in time to see the turquoise van coming down the beach.

"Not what I needed right now," she said. It wasn't what she ever needed, not with Eli there.

"Who is it?" he said. "Wait, that's Luca."

Miller stared at him. "You know him?"

"Yes, I know him. He's one of the regulars."

"Wonderful," she said and then the van was pulling up alongside them, the window down.

"Nice ride," Eli said.

"Don't make them like this anymore, there's a reason for that."

"What's out here today?" Miller said. Luca's eyes rested on her for a beat too long, studying, amused again.

"Nothing of interest," he said.

"I'm doubting that."

"Half a harbor porpoise."

"I'll never learn," Miller said.

"Who got the other half?" Eli said.

"Probably a shark. Don't go swimming. Also found two sofa cushions and a feather from a turkey vulture."

Miller frowned. He was impossible.

"Have to get going," he said. "Got a busy day." He put the truck in gear.

"See you later," Eli said.

"Seems likely."

"Okay, I give up," Eli said when he was gone. "Where did you ever meet up with him?"

"Don't ask."

"Now I really want to know."

"I was just standing out here one day, minding my own business, watching a crab boat, when he drove up behind me in the van. For some reason all of a sudden the whole cars on the beach thing got to me, so I flagged him down and asked if he'd seen the sign that said Motor Vehicles Prohibited. Stop smiling."

"I'm trying not to. So then what?"

"He said he had a permit to gather firewood and asked me if I wanted to see it and I said no and had to apologize. Wasn't the highlight of my day."

"He's a good guy, though."

"Good guy? He's maddening."

"What is that interest he's got in you, Miller? I mean, I like looking at you, too, but something's going on with him."

When Eli's two days of work were finished, although it seemed that another important decision awaited them, they both simply ignored it.

"What do you want for dinner?" he said.

"Are you cooking?" she said, walking right past any last shred of caution she might have left.

"Yes, I am, at my house. Your kitchen's better, but I've got more cable. And my jigsaw puzzle."

"I can't believe you're doing that. It'll take up the whole dining room table. And it's of the ocean. You'll be eighty-two and it won't be finished."

"If you help me, maybe I'll only be sixty-three. That's what the pioneers did. I'm sure of it."

"I want Ina Garten to cook shrimp scampi like I saw her do on the Food Network," Miller said.

"What?"

"You asked what I wanted for dinner."

"The downside of cable. I'll get Ina on the phone except isn't she in the Hamptons or somewhere? Dinner might not be ready right away."

"I think I've just learned that you watch more than a little of the Food Network," she said.

"Don't forget, bartenders work at night, so they've got all those days to fill up. Food Network, Discovery Channel and *The Great British Bake Off*. That's all I'll admit to. And books and an art gallery now and then. I do have some culture in me somewhere."

They weren't moving in. It wasn't like that at all, she told herself.

chapter 28

WHEN ELI'S BAR NIGHTS came around again and for the first time in a week Miller walked back into her own house, she felt like the shape shifter in a Navajo detective novel, unable to recognize her face in the mirror, the life she was living, the person she'd become. What was this called? Shacking up? The sleepover that never ends? It was all beyond any conceivable notion of herself that she'd ever had.

She was curled up on the couch in the evening trying to read when Eli called. She stared at her phone as she picked it up. It wasn't like him to call from work.

"I'm sending you a text," he said. "That's all I can do."

"What's wrong? You don't sound like yourself at all."

"You'll see. Please don't bail on me."

"I'm no good with surprises," she said, hating the sudden cold edge to her voice that said she trusted no one.

"Hey," he said gently, "it's nothing like that. But in its own screwed up way, it's worse."

"For God's sake," she said. "Hang up and send me the text."

"Here goes nothing."

She sat on the sofa, frozen. No more sudden news, she didn't need it. Everything about Lauren Metcalf came flooding back to her. Then the text was there. She stared at her phone again, not understanding.

It was a photo of a woman sitting at the bar. She was older, maybe mid-fifties, and striking, dressed in black, with silver hair pulled severely back from her face into a long braid that fell down over one shoulder. At her ears were large silver hoops. The hand that held a wine glass showed rings on every finger. Miller was totally in the dark. She texted a line of question marks.

The answer that came back was simple and so horrifying that Miller almost fell off the couch.

My mother, it said.

"Oh shit," Miller said. "No, no, no, this cannot be happening." The last thing she ever wanted in all of her life was to be in even the most remote proximity to Eli's mother. It was her worst nightmare come true. *See?* she yelled at herself. This is why this was such a bad idea. This is what you get for being with someone you shouldn't be with. Bail? He didn't know the half of it.

Where is she staying? she texted quickly so that they wouldn't end up in the same hotel.

My house. Miller?

I am out of here, she wrote. Her fingers were flying over the keys.

Goddammit, he answered.

And then she was gone, moving fast. Packing only took opening a few drawers, a run through the bathroom, throw it all in a backpack, grab the book from the couch, her coat, turn out the lights, get in the car and head south. He'd see when he came past that she meant it. She wasn't there. The door was unlocked if he wanted to be sure.

It quickly occurred to her that if he got in his car, hers stood out like a black shadow on a white wall. She swerved onto the side roads in Winslow, all two of them, which got her off the main street. She had to go out on the two-lane highway heading south, there was no choice, but jumped back off immediately after the ten seconds it took on the bridge to cross the river. Then, though it seemed impossible in such a small place, she was lost in Oceanview. Thinking fast, she kept making right-hand turns until she came to the beach. This would have to do. She hoped she wasn't mistaken in believing that he'd assume she went north, to stay in the familiar area around the gym, or south to Pine Ridge where they'd had dinner and actually talked about the inn there. In minutes, she found the esplanade with its multitude of hotels.

And then there was nothing to it. She chose one, it was early, still the dinner hour, found the desk clerk, obtained an oceanfront room on a winter weeknight for almost nothing and put down her credit card. But it was only when she was in the room, turning on the shaded lights, setting the backpack on the bed, that she could breathe again.

Miller peered out but couldn't see the ocean, only the floodlit dunes. Another storm was coming, there was always another storm coming, but here if a rock pitched through the window it was someone else's problem, not hers.

It took a while before she got up the courage to check her phone. Her impulse for back roads had been a sound one. He couldn't keep driving around on his break, he'd have to get back to work fairly quickly.

Where the fuck did you go? he wrote.

Just somewhere. Let me stay there.

Whatever they'd gotten themselves into, he kept it honest. She admired that about him. He didn't hold back. He never hid what he was feeling or thinking. He'd forgive her, she knew that in her heart, but his other life was something he had to deal with on his own. She couldn't and wouldn't be a part of it. And because he knew her, he'd already been aware of exactly how she would react.

Now all she could do was wait.

On the first day Miller stayed close, eating in nearby restaurants, enjoying the feeling of being on vacation, even a cold gray one with rain threatening every minute. She walked this oddly unfamiliar beach where she actually encountered people, backed as it was by so many low-rise hotels. She read and slept and sent messages to Spain, London, Tavarua.

In the afternoon, the next text came.

You can run, lady, but you can't hide. Are these possibly yours?

She put her face in her hands. The photo was of bikini underwear and yes, it was hers. The next photo showed hair bands in the open palm of his hand.

Or these?

The last one, taken in his bathroom, focused on a jar of rose-scented moisturizer.

Or this? And none of these were found by me so you can imagine there are some questions.

Mercifully the message ended there. Please just let her leave. Didn't this woman have something, anything else pressing that she needed to get to right now?

Thank you for sending me pictures of my underwear, she answered then turned off her phone. She could feel him smiling. Round one to the boy from New York City.

By the second day, Miller was beginning to feel like a prisoner. The car was a problem, but Eli couldn't be everywhere at once. If terrible odds were going to put her out on the highway at the same time he was going by, then so be it. And what he was doing with his mother at this point, she couldn't even imagine. This wasn't exactly the entertainment mecca of the western world. She decided to risk everything and go where she wanted, to her own beach.

She saw on the local map in the lobby that she could hop out quickly on the highway and then back into Winslow on the same roads that had brought her here. She remembered the women who'd come down out of the dunes that day to feed the seagulls. They'd had access somewhere from this southern end, which suited her perfectly.

The one place on the beach to which she'd never ventured was the small rough island in the middle of the quiet cove, back by the river where the heron hunted. There was always the possibility of crossing over to it and then getting caught by the tide, but the water in the cove was very low and she decided to chance it.

She stepped carefully one foot at a time over the slippery rocks, scattering the flock of turnstones she hadn't even seen, pulling her baseball cap lower as rain began to fall. In the sandy depression in the middle of the island, she stopped, puzzled at what she'd found. Hidden among the sheltered dune grass and beach plants stood a tall thin driftwood cross fastened at its junctures with cast-off fishing line and artfully decorated with dangling holdfasts of bull kelp. Whatever its reason for being here, it lent the island a quiet grace. Miller sat at the outer edge of the island for a long time, watching the chopped surface of the river as it flowed to the ocean, feeling the rain on her face.

Retracing her steps back onto the beach, she went down to the waves. All the storms proved deadly now and concern had recently been expressed for the feeding patterns of the seabirds. She came upon a dead common murre, one tiny auklet after another, and then what was definitely a common loon, as large as a goose, with a thick beak and limp webbed feet. The storms hadn't killed him though. He'd been shot like the grebe, a small hole blasted deep into his breast. A stunning inch long fish, shining turquoise and silver, as exquisite as a handcrafted piece of jewelry, lay in the tide wrack.

The last birds she found were all the same and yet again unfamiliar. Should she? Yes, she should. Look at what he was texting her. She sent Eli a photo.

He replied almost immediately.

You're killing me, the text said. She waited. It didn't take long before the second text came.

Kittiwake, damn you. Get in out of the rain.

All at once an ominous greenish darkness rolled out of the north and converged with mist and black clouds moving from the south. Quickly, an entire bank of foul weather overtook the river. Miller ran as hail pelted down in a freezing curtain, skittering and bouncing on the hard sand.

"Good God," she said to no one. How did a car survive in this place, let alone a person?

Back in the hotel, she soaked in the tub then ate takeout and read her book. When the text came, she could only shake her head in disbelief. What to do with him? There were no words to the text, only an image of her car in the parking lot outside the hotel, taken in daylight, which gave her notice that he wasn't still out there lurking in the dark.

Thank you for the picture of my car, she typed.

You're welcome, he answered.

Stalker, she wrote without any hesitation.

CSI, he texted back.

CSI my ass.

Sad guy.

Sad guy my ass.
Yeeeowww.

The call came the next morning. Miller glanced at the clock, grateful that it was before checkout time and she wouldn't be charged for another day.

"How are you doing?" she said.

"I've been better. You bailed on me."

"You knew I would. We talked about it. Those misgivings? Right there, that's a whole lot of them."

"Okay, whatever, she's gone. What are you doing with your day?"

"Some things."

"Dinner here?"

"I'll bring Chinese. Text me what you want."

"Goddamn, you are stubborn. Come here and we'll decide then and have it delivered. That way it's a whole lot easier to fight over who pays for it."

"Done," she said. "And you'll tell me what happened, right? You're willing to do that?"

"It would take years to tell you what happened, I mean in a generic sense, but yes, if that's what you want, we can talk about it."

chapter 29

MILLER CONSIDERED THE hotel room one last time. It was less than spectacular, but perfect actually for a getaway if you hadn't already gotten very far away. Maybe storm watching was a popular winter sport here, sun worshipping activities certainly weren't, and there were two deep comfortable chairs in a bay window that provided the right view. Anyone could see exactly when the black clouds met the greenish ones and the birds started flying backwards.

She ran errands and headed home. The house gave no evidence of his having been there. She put down the backpack, unloaded bags onto the dining room table, was about to go upstairs, turned and stopped in her tracks. She squinted to make sure of what she was seeing. There was a silver-haired woman in a long black coat sitting on her deck. Miller cursed. Naturally this would happen. She suddenly had some very specific questions, none of which would likely have answers right now. She steadied herself and opened the French doors. And then they just stared at each other as two women might who'd discovered a very unlikely connection.

"Forgive me," Miller said. "Eli told me your name, but I don't remember it."

"You didn't do a search?" The voice was throaty, a smoker's voice. The question was merely curious, as if everyone else in the world had done a search, why not you?

"I didn't," Miller said. "My experience of Eli is that he's a pretty private person when he wants to be."

"Helen Grace," the woman said. "I didn't pry, but he wasn't forthcoming about you, either."

Thank God, even though Helen Grace now knew what her underwear looked like.

"Cory Briggs," Miller said. "But everyone calls me Miller. It's cold out here. Would you like to come in?"

"Yes, but aren't you going to ask me how I came to be sitting on your deck?"

"Not yet. But how did you get here? Where's your car?" They were still taking the measure of each other.

"A friend dropped me off," Helen said.

"Oh. You had someone with you." She wondered now exactly what Eli had gotten himself into.

"I kept him out of sight. He stayed in a hotel somewhere."

Probably right next door.

As Miller reconciled herself to the situation, she was more able to take in this person obviously so far outside the boundaries of life as Miller knew it. The coat might have been a man's, voluminous, with a large collar turned up. Underneath was a long black sweater over army pants and heavy black boots. The rings were still there along with broad silver cuffs on each wrist. But no makeup, Miller noted. And good skin, stunning hair. Just nothing that corresponded to Eli except the color of her eyes.

"I can tell your house has been done, as they say," Helen said. "It's perfect, exactly what'd you'd expect."

Was that a compliment? Miller didn't know. She said thank you anyway. "It was my grandparents' house," she said, "and then my mother's. Actually, it's exactly who she is. Can I offer you something to drink? Coffee? I have espresso, water, tea, there might be a Coke somewhere."

"Wine?" Helen said.

They were down to it already. Hopefully it was past noon. "All I have is white, but it's a good white, dry, crisp."

"Excellent. You don't mind if I look around?"

"Help yourself. As I said, nothing here is mine. Or very little anyway." Please let nothing of Eli's be here, Miller thought.

She poured the wine, came back out from the kitchen and handed Helen the glass. She'd poured large, for herself, too.

"Great collection of books," Helen said.

"A poet, Hugh Donaldson, used to live here. Those are his books, or were. He's dead now."

"Hugh Donaldson," Helen said. "So that's who it is. The house was only described to me as the poet's house."

"It was?" Miller said, startled. Who would call it that? "And you've heard of him?"

"In the circles where I travel, he's very well known. I like his darker work, it's so clean and fierce, rips everything apart. If I'm not mistaken, I actually met him at a reading somewhere once." She pulled out a volume and turned it over to the jacket photo of a man with a handsome profile and wavy white hair. "Yes, that's him. I hate to trouble you, but could we go back outside? I'm a smoker."

Miller noticed that there was no question as to whether smoking was permissible. She felt for Eli again.

"Not a problem." Miller got her coat and a relic ashtray from the kitchen. She'd long ago surrendered the chairs to the protection of the garage. Instead, they sat on the built-in bench surrounding the deck. Helen was the type of smoker who inhaled and never exhaled, better for those around her, not so great for herself.

"Do you have children?" Helen said out of nowhere and Miller straightened. She had no need for shared confessions and would give as little as possible without being rude. It was all bad enough already.

"Three," she said.

"Are they here?"

"No."

"Far away?" That was an interesting question.

"Very far away, at the moment anyway."

"Would you tell me where?" Helen said, "and then you have my word, I won't ask any more about them."

"One daughter's in London, the other's in Spain, both in school, and my son's traveling. Right now he's in Tavarua."

Helen sipped the wine, studying her. The intensity of the look reminded Miller of Luca. They could stare all they wanted, but it wouldn't do them any good. She glanced down at her hands, at everything said by the absence of wedding rings. So what, she told herself.

"I'm aware of what an imposition this is," Helen said after a long moment. "Certainly not anything you were expecting." Now and then, despite the cigarettes, her voice sounded like Eli's. "I wouldn't have come if I hadn't grown so curious. Anything to do with you makes him smile."

Miller wanted to crawl under the bench and disappear. She couldn't be having this conversation.

"I hope you understand," she said, "but there's nothing I can say on that subject. Seriously. Nothing."

"I understand," Helen said. "I've been a fairly unconventional person all my life, lovers coming and going, and not ever enough room or time for Eli, though I think he came to welcome that fact. His father's a much better parent, which was fortunate for everyone. But I'm glad just this once to meet someone in his life, to see what makes him happy. And he is, you know."

Miller drank her early afternoon wine. She was having none of this. Helen took a long drag on her cigarette and coughed up her lungs into the cold sea air.

"He's talented," Helen said, veering off again, and Miller was instantly on the alert. "Very. The work he did in college was already so finished. His senior thesis was flawless, artistically, intellectually. And then he stopped. Do you know why?" Miller realized with a jolt that Helen had no idea about Eli's sculptures. He hadn't told her anything. She just shook her head no. "Because what he loves most is what I love most and he can't stand it, that we could be so alike, even in just that one way. So he refused, because he refuses me."

Miller considered how delusional that was, and how sad.

"You aren't going to talk about him at all, are you?" Helen said.

"I'm not," Miller said. "I told you, I can't. But now I do want to ask that question. How did you find out who I was or where I lived?"

"It's actually amusing," Helen said. "I learned everything completely by accident from this man at the bar."

172

"Man at the bar?" What was she talking about?

"Intriguing as far as older men go." Miller closed her eyes. Older men? It had to be him. "Since I'd taken Eli by surprise and he was somewhat in a state, he introduced me to this person so that he could take care of his customers and this person could take care of me."

"And he knew where I lived?" Miller said, incredulous.

"I just wondered out loud, the way even a bad parent might, if Eli was alone. I couldn't understand at all why he was out here in the middle of nowhere in the first place. He said you and Eli were friends and being a woman whose mind always goes there anyway, I made the leap. Then, what was his name...?"

"Luca?"

"...yes, told me you were from California, you were staying in the poet's house out here along the road, the one with the rose-colored door. Thank God he was right, or I'd have been sitting on some complete stranger's deck." She laughed at the thought and coughed again.

Luca? What on earth.

Helen stubbed out her cigarette in the ashtray. She'd almost finished the wine. So had Miller. "Would you like another glass?" Miller offered, gritting her teeth.

"No, I have to go. We're flying out of Portland later on today, headed for New York and then Bhutan, the happiest country on earth, you know. We're going to make a short film there."

Miller had no words. She could only stare at this very striking woman who in her own unusual way would stop traffic anywhere.

Helen stood up. "Thank you for your hospitality," she said. "You didn't have to invite me in."

Well, I did, Miller thought, you were sitting out here in the cold. Was I supposed to leave you there?

"I'm glad to have met you," Helen said. "And now I have one more request, which may seem strange. I couldn't help but see that interesting thing you and Eli do with your phones. Would you take a picture of me and send it to him? I don't want to hide anything from him, not have him know that I've been here."

Miller considered the possibility of his having a heart attack. "Of course," she said. She pulled her phone out of her back pocket. Helen didn't pose, only leveled those cool gray eyes at the camera. Miller shivered and snapped the picture. "Do you want me to send it right now?"

"No, wait till I've gone. I probably wouldn't want to see what he said."

Miller thought they'd likely hear it from here.

They walked out to the street together. "Can I give you a ride anywhere?" Miller said, still confused about exactly where this friend might be.

"No, I'll walk into town. Walking is one of my passions. Is this your car?"

"Yes, it is." Let Helen Grace think what she wanted about drug dealer vehicles.

They shook hands, what else was there to do? Two strong grips, all those rings pressing, one last long look.

"Travel safe," Miller said.

"Or possibly not," Helen said.

Whatever that meant. Miller took a deep breath and went back in the house.

chapter 30

WHEN SHE LET HERSELF into Eli's house, which even now continued to give her that one fraction of a second's pause, he was in the shower.

"I'm here," she shouted from the hallway.

"Want to come join me?"

"No."

"I don't know why not. You always did before."

"That's not me. You're thinking of someone else," she said and couldn't hear his response, which was probably just as well. She closed the bedroom door.

"Why did you decide to take a shower at this time of day?" she asked when he appeared, fully clothed.

"So I'd smell good for you." He was wearing his Calvin amber. Don't ask questions if you don't want to know the answer. "And here." He held up something pink. "I washed your underwear."

"Damn you," she said.

"Hey, it wasn't me who left them in the bed."

"Give me a minute to get over that." She had to compose herself again, still seeing the woman on her porch. "I'm back. Are you ready for what's apparently the major chore of ordering food together?"

"I am. I even took a nap this afternoon so I'm completely calm, nerves of steel, an endless reservoir of patience. Ready, steady, go."

"It's not that bad," she said.

When they had decided on enough food for six, he made the phone call. At the end, he held his hand over the phone. "Too bad, they'll only take one credit card." He held his out.

"Go ahead," she said.

"Wait a minute, that was way too easy." While he was giving the address, she took cash out of the pocket of her jeans and laid the bills down on the table.

"You think you're so smart," he said when he hung up. "There are a million ways to get around that."

"Or you could actually keep it. But since you're calm, I've got something to show you."

"How could I not want to know what that's all about?"

She turned on her phone and prepared herself, then handed it to him.

"Fucking hell no," he said. "How did you get this?"

"When I came back from the hotel she was sitting on my deck."

"Jesus Christ. And then what?"

"She came into the house, we talked a little, went back out on the deck so she could smoke, had a glass of wine, that was it."

"I apologize, Miller. I'm so sorry, especially when you went to a hotel to avoid that very same thing. Goddammit, she is just maddening. Always has been. A total flake, out of control, lives in some parallel universe."

"She's not your average housewife, I'll give you that. But I have to tell you, she was there on my deck because of you."

"But only out of curiosity. Not anything to do with my welfare or yours either."

"She asked about my kids. She didn't have to do that."

"Again, question the motivation, always. But hold on a minute. I didn't say a thing so how did she know where to find you? Or even who you were?"

"My thoughts exactly. She talked to Luca. That's what she said anyway."

"Luca? When she was with him at the bar? How can that even be? And where does Luca get his information?"

"Here's what she told me. She said she was sitting with him because you were in a state…"

"In a state doesn't even begin to cover it."

"…and he put the two of us together, told her where I was from and that I lived in what he called the poet's house."

"Do you have any idea what's going on?"

"I imagine at some point when I get up the courage, I'll have to ask him. But why did your mother come all the way out here in the first place?"

"Here's where you see what I mean," he said. "She thinks she's going to die."

"Soon? Is she sick?"

"No. She's whacko. She's having visions, which are way more likely from all the weed she smokes than anything astral or metaphysical. She came out to say goodbye. She did coincidentally however have a speaking engagement in Portland, though who lets her speak to anyone is beyond me."

"She said she's on her way to Bhutan...to film something?"

"Yes. That's in preparation for the dying. It's a wonder she didn't kill herself a long time ago what with the fire and blowtorches and explosions and everything. Maybe that's what she's thinking of. Could we talk about something else now?"

The food arrived and they spread it out across the entire table. Miller had learned from experience that anything left over would show up at breakfast. When dinner was finished, they sat down for one more episode of *The Wire*.

"Eli," Miller said when he started running his thumb slowly over the palm of her hand, again in that seemingly absent way that wasn't.

"I knew it," he said, keeping his eyes on the screen. "It's why I was more pissed off at my mother showing up than any other reason there could possibly be. Give you two days on your own to think about it and we're right back where we started."

"We're practically living together."

"And your point is? Personally, I don't have a problem with that. At all."

She steeled herself. This was something she had to do. "I do have a problem with it," she said. "Because of who I am, because this is me. You tell me how it ends. If one of us gets hurt, either one, you or me, I couldn't take it. Believe me, I think I'd go crazy."

Eli found the remote and clicked off the TV. "Do you know how much time I spend thinking about Lauren Metcalf?" Her voice was breaking. "Do you know how much time I spend thinking about what went wrong, how something you were so sure of could shatter into a thousand pieces just like that? I promise you, I can't go through that again. You and I are moving in different directions and that's just life, just the way it is. Today we're here, tomorrow we're gone, it's over. If you can do that, more power to you, but I can't."

Eli took a long look at the ceiling, then his gaze came back to her. "Here's the thing, Miller," he said. "I know we've perfected the art of avoidance, but I don't want to think about any of this. First, the possibility exists that you're wrong. Maybe it doesn't have to end. Who knows what will happen? And if you're right and we only have so much time, which way do you go then? Do you hold back or do you decide to give it everything you've got?" He shifted so that he was facing her. "Here's how I look at it," he said. "I'm in this private and very special place that we're making together, two maybe not so random people who run into each other and for whatever reason like what happens when they do. Maybe they make each other laugh. Maybe they see something. Maybe there's heat and joy and comfort and a thousand other things that make it worth fighting for. And that's what I'm doing."

"Even if it ends."

"If that time comes, we'll deal with it. And by then I think we'd have a way to deal with it, we'd have talked it through and figured it out."

"What if we get sick of each other?"

"Only you could come up with that. That's a chance you take, I guess, the same with anything you get involved in. Me, I'm not planning on it."

"What if we fight?"

"Where have you been? We do that already and we do it really well. It's one of the things I love most about being with you. You know, maybe, with not all the time in the world, you put a whole lot more effort into making it better instead of worse, into being kind and taking care of each other. How amazing would that be?"

Always seeing things from a better angle, Miller thought. "Help me out, then," she said.

"Let me try this," he said. "I'm asking you, right now, to have dinner with me every night for as far into the future as you can see. You can put a date on that if you want, but I'm not going to."

"Dinner and bring a toothbrush," she said. Never mind that there was already a toothbrush at his house. And hers. Never mind that they were, in fact, living together.

"No one says there has to be a toothbrush. Or where dinner would be or anything. Okay, let's add this in. As an experiment, I'm excluding Monday and Tuesdays. Who knows if you'll want those days to yourself, or we'll appreciate each other more for it, or if nobody wants that at all. So now I've asked you and we'll just see what happens. Are you with me?"

She waited, listening to the voices in her head. They told her what she already knew. For her sanity, the back and forth had to end. She had to make a very clear decision one way or the other. Yes or no. In or out. They also told her something else she already knew. She didn't want out. She didn't want to say no to any of it.

She let out a long breath. "Here's the truth I have to admit," she said. "My efforts to sabotage this thing have been sincere and heartfelt and to my mind anyway valid and reasonable, but I'm tired of it. I can't do that anymore. If I survived meeting your mother, then I'm pretty sure I can survive anything."

"Never did I think I'd have a reason to be glad about that woman."

"I agree with Mondays and Tuesdays."

"All right, but that isn't what I'm waiting for."

"I never imagined a situation like this, ever, not in my wildest dreams," she said. "I'm still afraid of bad things happening. I have to be. But somehow you make me believe that, despite everything, it could be okay."

"It'll be so much more than okay, trust me," he said. "So we're good, right?"

"We're good," she said, hoping fervently that was true.

"Do you want to keep watching?" he said, gesturing at the TV. She shook her head no. "Not just *The Wire*, not anything?"

Miller stood up and reached out her hand. "Now you have to trust me," she said.

In the bedroom while he held his breath she put her hands on his shoulders and pressed him gently down onto the bed. She undressed him slowly, easing off his shoes, bringing the sweater up over his head and then the t-shirt, undoing the belt, unzipping his jeans and then he made a sound and had to close his eyes. She paused only long enough to remove most of her own clothes. Leaning over him, she took his face in her hands and kissed his mouth, tasting him, exploring. Her mouth traveled softly over his face, his eyes, still kissing, along his jaw, down over his throat, moving deliciously along the length of his workout body, farther down to his runner's thighs, his knees, the soles of his feet, coming back up, spending time, attentive, thoughtful, as generous as he had always been. When she knew from the tension in every muscle of his body that he was near, she was the one who reached in the drawer, who accomplished that unfamiliar task using only what was left of her common sense. And then she was over him, bracing herself, moving, using her thighs, bringing him with her in a strong steadily escalating rhythm. If she was going to be all in, then be all in, take the place of the blondes and redheads at least for a little while, do this for the one with the heart and the smile, her VP, her dinner date, the bartender in her bed, the boy from New York City. Here's what she had and she would give it to him. He was beautiful and the pleasure was all hers. And then there were no more thoughts.

chapter 31

THE WEATHER TURNED monotonously violent. The winds were extraordinary, beyond belief. "Blame this round of storms on a giant low pressure system centered over British Columbia that sucked air from Washington and Oregon," reported the Oregonian. "We call that *wind*," said a meteorologist in Portland. Miller wondered who would call it anything else.

A second front bringing gusts in excess of sixty miles per hour was expected within hours. The next storm with gusty wind and showers was slated to move in right behind it. The sky was dark and filled with clouds. The first fat drops began pelting the windows.

There was one place in the house Miller hadn't ever felt the need to explore. The study seemed to be just more of Hugh Donaldson. Nothing in particular signaled that ownership. A comfortable upholstered chair at a mahogany desk, more built-in shelves, more books, they could have been anyone's. The room was sheltered, cozy, cocoon-like. The throw draped over the small loveseat was in the pale violet-blue shade that Jane had loved. With nothing else in mind, Miller decided to spend her morning here.

As she ran her fingers over the titles on the shelves, an awareness slowly dawned on her. They all in one way or another touched on the sea, the coast, the state of Oregon in every facet. What did this have to do with poetry? she wondered. Particularly dark poetry. These books were far more concerned with natural, political, military, ancient, local, off the beaten track history. Suddenly her thoughts flew back to her grandfather. He had been a professor of history at a small college in Portland. She realized with a start that these weren't Hugh's at all. They were her grandfather's. What was her mother thinking, leaving everything here just as it was, no one to even be aware of its existence unless they randomly decided to walk in and take a look around?

She went through the titles more slowly. Some of the books were so old it seemed they might fall apart at any minute. Again, she wondered what they could possibly be doing here. Gently she pulled out one of the oldest-looking, the leather binding dry and cracked, the pages beyond yellowed. The gold stamped lettering on the spine read: *The People Touched By The River* by Ada McPherson.

Miller frowned, concentrating. Something was coming back to her, family stories her grandmother had told her in those long ago childhood summers in this house. Hardly daring to touch the pages, she opened the cover and turned to the dedication. This was what she had remembered, the original brave pioneer woman who came over the mountains to settle in Oregon Territory. Emma, her young daughter. And here on this crackling page it said: *To Emma White Flower.*

The voice in her head urged her on. She slid the book with extreme care back into its place on the shelf. There were deep drawers at the bottom of the bookshelves. She opened them and found the rest of it. Her grandfather must have pursued this topic for many years, his wife's ancestry, his children's legacy, a subject already dear to his heart. There were several worn cardboard boxes. Miller lifted the first one out and set it on the desk. Inside was a treasure of faded old clippings, photographs, tintypes, papers from historical societies, plus pages and pages of handwritten notes and on the very bottom, bound sections of a manuscript. Being book-minded, Hugh must have come across all of this and Miller considered for the first time that she would have liked very much to talk to him, not about her mother but about everything else.

Miller's grandmother was named Emma. She began to read slowly through the notes, about the People and all the others to whom she might belong.

After a long while, she stretched and got up. The rain was never going to end. She returned everything to the box, knowing that she would come back and read all of it. At the bookshelf, she scanned through some of the other titles, pulled out *The Journals Of Lewis And Clark* and opened to a bookmarked page. She laughed, reading William Clark's entry from his own long winter on the Oregon coast. "Those squalls were suckceeded by rain O! how Tremendious is the day. This dredfull wind and rain..." Two hundred years and nothing had changed.

These were the Mondays and Tuesdays, Eli's working days, the absent days. Not enough beach, too much time. Miller decided to run errands, to the library, the hardware store and then the Corner Market where something appealing might announce itself as dinner. She browsed for an hour in the bookstore. It was such a pleasant small place. She bought a book, *The Girl With The Dragon Tattoo*. Here in the land of torrential downpours, a riveting yet complicated novel that took many days to get through, in a series of riveting and complicated novels, might solve several problems all at once.

In the hardware store, though Eli had already crossed duct tape off her list, she meant to finally purchase nails to go with the hammer and maybe in addition even a screwdriver, or possibly, now she considered herself a genius, *two* screwdrivers, one regular and one Phillips. If Hugh had tools, or had fixed anything ever in his life, that was nowhere apparent. Pliers, she thought, going down the aisles, a wrench and wait, they sold birdfeeders, would one of those be interesting to have? She came to her senses. Not in winter, not in these winds. And with the hawk nearby it wouldn't be interesting at all, watching songbirds snatched from their little perches one by one.

Realizing she was in danger of running completely amok in the hardware store, she rounded the last aisle headed for the checkout counter, but halted where she was. Luca stood directly in her path, contemplating fishhooks. As he glanced up, she saw again that look, something in his eyes when they met hers.

"It's me again," she said.

"So I see," he said.

"I had a surprise a while back that might have something to do with you."

He nodded, seemingly aware of what she was talking about. He put the package of fishhooks back on the rack.

"I'll be honest," he said, "and everybody knows this about me, it's no big revelation, but I don't do much talking without a drink in my hand. So maybe, if you want to talk, and we could do that, the bar would be my choice. If you're lucky, I might even buy. Nothing forward, just talk."

Nothing forward. He had decades on her. Then it occurred to her not to go down that road.

"I don't know," she said. She was still having enough difficulty dealing with the public idea of Eli, let alone showing up at the bar when he was there.

"Your call. Let it be then."

Let *what* be? Dammit to hell.

"All right," she said. "One beer, or whatever."

"My preference is for the whatever."

Eli had just started his shift behind the bar. He held her with his eyes for just the fraction of a second that she needed.

"If you don't mind, I'd rather be at a table," Miller said.

"I was done minding things a long time ago."

Luca sat opposite her and they ordered from the waitress. He shrugged off his coat. "Might as well try and be comfortable."

She intended to keep hers on, this wouldn't take very long, but the room was too hot and she relented. For a few moments, they just stared at each other. She was conscious of Eli keeping watch.

Their drinks came, her Blue Moon and his bourbon.

"I don't want to get too much into my personal life," Miller said, which was ridiculous, that's exactly where she had to be headed, "but for reasons we won't go into, I ended up, as I said, a while back, having a conversation with a woman named Helen Grace who just appeared out of nowhere on my back deck."

"That's her name?" Luca said.

"You didn't know her name?"

"She said it, I guess, but it didn't register. Obviously." He took a long swallow of his drink.

"I need something to eat," Miller said. She wanted something that would sit well, keep the beer from going to her head. "And thanks for the offer, but it's me with the questions, so it's me who's paying."

What was it about those blue eyes? Miller felt as if they were going right through her.

"Are women your age all like this? I'm just asking."

"I'm getting the flatbread and spinach dip," Miller said, ignoring the question. "What do you want?"

"I'm good. I don't like to mix booze and food."

"I don't think that's a good sign." What was she, his mother?

"Nope. Never is, never was."

"Where was I?" Miller said, completely flustered.

"With whatever her name was on your back deck."

"Yes, that. First, you presumed a couple things. And then you told her where I lived."

"I try not to do too much presuming, don't think that was the case. She might have done some on her own. But you're right about the house. I remember. I did tell her."

"How did you know such a thing?"

"You have the car. It has California plates. This is a small town. There aren't many out-of-state plates here ever, let alone in the winter. And I drive past there all the time, it's the only way to the beach."

Miller broke off a piece of flatbread and ran it through the dip. "You described it as the poet's house."

"I probably did that, too."

"But you wouldn't say what poet."

"If this lady told you all this, she has a way better memory than I do. Poets are poets. Just happens that a poet lived there. Maybe that's how I referred to it."

"And why would you do that?"

"Why are you called Miller?" he said. "That's not a name."

"What does that have to do with anything?"

"Everything has to do with something."

What the *hell*. "It's my maiden name." Which told him that she'd been married. "It's from back in high school. It just stuck."

For some reason, the blue eyes zeroed in on her more intently. "Remember who started this," he said.

"You did."

"My involvement was purely by accident, she showed up, I took her off Eli's hands. Believe me, no one should ever attempt any kind of meaningful conversation in a bar, especially when one of them has been there a while."

"Great. However, there you were and so now here we are."

"The poet's Hugh Donaldson."

"Something we agree on," Miller said. "You'd met him?"

He took another long sip and the eyes were on her again. "Hugh Donaldson was my brother."

Miller stared at him in disbelief. But now that she knew, she could see it. The resemblance to those book jacket photos was striking. She put her head in her hands. "I can't even deal with this. But if that's true, then I have a thousand questions."

"It is true. Ask away."

She didn't even know where to begin. "I can't do this unless you eat something."

"Christ," he said. He smiled though, completely what she hadn't expected, and called over the waitress to order rib eye egg rolls. He also ordered another drink. "You're not exactly a cheap bar buddy."

"I said I was paying."

"I heard you."

"Question number one," she said, but then that question, concerning her mother, was exactly the one she couldn't possibly ask. "Actually, never mind about the questions." He waited, not helpful. She tried to collect her thoughts then started over. "Tell me about him."

"Not much to tell. We grew up here. He was older than me and he had a rough time of it, got in fights, got kicked out of school, then kicked out of the house, ran away and joined the army and got kicked out of there, too, found himself a friend, an education, a new life and for all that time he never came back home."

"Why didn't he?"

"One good reason, our old man at the door with a shotgun."

"You're serious."

"I am serious."

Miller frowned, trying to take it all in. "Mothers love their sons."

"Not always."

"He did come back, though."

"Sure, forty-some years later."

"Why then, after all that time?"

"We're in the confessional now," Luca said. "And that's okay, I've been there too many times, it's nothing. He came back because he thought I was totally fucked up and he decided maybe he could help, do something about it."

"Were you? Fucked up I mean?"

"Still am. By choice."

"By choice? That's terrible. Was he right? Could he help?"

"I was glad to have him back, but I didn't want help. He did me a favor, though, so I'll always remember him for that."

"Could I ask what it was?"

"You could, but you won't get an answer."

"I understand," Miller said. There were so many questions for which she herself didn't hand out answers. "Have you read his poetry?"

"Haven't. I heard some of it's good, but I wouldn't know for sure even if I did read it. Heard some of it's angry which wouldn't surprise me, considering, but I wouldn't know about that either."

Miller thought for a moment, wondering if there was another way to get at what she needed to know. "Was he ever married? Did he have children?"

Luca looked at her. "You're way far down on the food chain if you have to be asking that. He was gay. You didn't know that?"

"*Gay?*" Miller said. She was shocked, but then suddenly her family's ship righted, came off the rocks. "No, I had no idea." A poet with exquisite taste. Why hadn't it ever occurred to her? Because in her mind she was always too busy looking for other signs, the ones that said he'd been much more than a tenant.

"That house is filled with things that belonged to him," she said. "Were you ever in there?"

She sensed calculation in Luca's answer. "I didn't need to be. I've been some places, but somehow I ended up right back where I started, back on the old homestead. So Hugh came to me. We sat around, drank his expensive booze and reminisced about the good old days."

"He had so many books. They have to belong to you. Don't you want them?"

"No. I don't." He took a last long swallow of his drink.

"All right, but there's this. I don't know whether you're aware or not but that house was my grandmother's, so now it's mine. I can't live with the thought that you'll never change your mind." She pulled out a pen and wrote her cell number on a drink napkin.

"You shouldn't be doing this," he said.

"There are so many things I shouldn't be doing. And I am paying."

"That's nice, but it's already paid." Luca pushed the check in front of her.

Eli. She sighed. But no matter, the heavy weight had been lifted. Her mother was her mother again.

"Got to go," Luca said, getting up.

"Me, too, but thanks. You don't know how grateful I am for what you've told me."

She watched him walk out the door before she detoured briefly to the bar.

"Everything good in your world?" Eli said.

"Every minute of the day. Thank you for taking care of that despite our deal."

"That's what I'm here for despite our deal. How are you doing with the Monday/Tuesday thing by the way? Just a status update from a concerned citizen."

"You first. I'm not good at this."

"As we all know. Honesty, right? From this team member here, you asked, it sucks."

For no reason that Miller could fathom, her eyes brimmed over with tears. "I don't know what's wrong with me," she said. "I was fine five seconds ago."

"We'll talk, tell me everything," he said. "But I'm not a fan."

"Truthfully, me neither. So where are we now?"

"Say the word."

She snapped out of whatever it was. This was Eli. She ran her gaze down along the line of patrons at the bar. "If I said it, I might get thrown out," she said.

"Holy hell," he said. "What word is that?"

She held her finger to her lips.

"Back on then?" he said.

"Back on."

Miller was standing in her sweats staring at the inside of the refrigerator, craving something but she didn't know what, when she heard the front door open. She closed the refrigerator and Eli was there. This person with the more-than-faint aroma of cocktail onions and stale beer, she thought, this was what she wanted. She tried but already knew that she had failed to keep her face from showing what was on her mind. He wrestled his way out of his jacket and dropped it on the floor as she came toward him and they were instantly mouth on mouth, wild and crazy with wanting as they reached out for the nearest horizontal surface, pulling each other down. He grabbed the jacket and slid it under her as she kicked off her sweats, finding him with her hands, and he didn't have time to kick off anything before they were tangled up in a fierce embrace that brought them both quickly to a fever pitch. The floor was hard, the room was cold but it didn't matter as they met with a purpose, bent on where they were going, holding back nothing, riding out the explosion. After a few stunned moments of silence, they collapsed on top of each other and then fell back gasping for breath and laughing.

"Jesus," Eli said, and then, "Honey, I'm home."

"I thought that was you."

"Sorry. It was the look on your face."

"You weren't supposed to see that. Were you afraid? You probably should have been."

"Afraid? Other direction, lady. But now that we've got the meet and greet out of the way, I heard there's actually a bed somewhere that's a whole lot warmer."

"And softer. The floor's not bad though," she said.

"Pretty much as good as it gets," he said.

chapter 32

A BREAK BETWEEN storms produced a day of only light rain and small showers of hail. In a sodden driftwood pile near the access road, Miller came upon a sad sight, the body of a loon. She hoped it wasn't one of the pair from the river.

The wet beach offered up a small number of sea-crud-covered glass bottles in unusual shapes and exotic colors. One was hot pink and emerald green, squat and eight-sided, perfect for a genie. An inordinate amount of Japanese fluorescent light tubes had also washed in. Miller picked one up, confidently recognizing it in the endless parade of similar Japanese objects, only to read the writing on the end which said inexplicably: Made in Hungary.

Wandering along the tide line in her rubber boots, thinking nothing, she glanced up toward the dunes and suddenly stood awestruck, in denial, her eyes on an object that couldn't possibly be real. She shouted then clapped her hand over her mouth, though no one was there to hear. The beach was empty from one end to the other. Slowly, she began to walk in that direction, one step at a time, hardly daring to breathe.

She was still stunned as she bent down and picked up the green globe of a Japanese glass fishing float the size of a soccer ball. It was without question the most fantastic, outrageous thing she'd ever expected to see, obviously old, hand blown, sand-scratched, but unbelievable and perfect and all hers. Luca had said those were the beach rules. Salvage rights. Finders, keepers. Miller held the globe up to the light. The inch of water inside made it even more rare and wonderful.

She'd been reading about glass floats ever since she first opened her beachcombing books. The lore ran deep and wide. Everyone's favorite tale concerned a woman who rose on a sleepless moonlit night and went out to the beach. There she saw something in the waves and waded in to pick it up. It was a glass fishing float that she carried back to shore wrapped in the folds of her nightgown. Then she turned around and the moonlight caught a second round object floating on the surface. By the time she'd finished going back and forth, there were seventy-five floats piled up on the beach. And after that, in all her life, so the story went, she never saw another.

Miller considered that if she went mad from the storms, if all the rain in the western hemisphere poured down in the next week, if the wind never stopped again, it would all be worth it because she had found a Japanese green glass fishing float.

Blinking in the rain and holding the precious object wrapped in one arm, she pulled out her phone with the other hand, praying that Eli wouldn't be at the garage. He answered instantly, before Janis Joplin's epic screech.

"What's up?" he said.

"Are you free?"

"For you, I'm always free."

"I mean are you working? You know how I feel about that."

"Not working, promise."

"Can you come down to the beach? I'm about half way down, the only one here, hard to miss."

"Be there in a second."

"Wow, that's crazy," he said when he reached her. "You did it, you found one. That's incredible. Now I'm a believer, anything can happen out here. It just did."

"Please, would you take a picture?" Miller said. "Just my hands and the float." Who wanted to see her in her baseball hat and iridescent green vinyl raincoat?

Eli snapped several pictures of the float, moving quietly back to get her smiling face, farther back to take in all of her against the wide expanse of beach, the rain coming down. He checked to make sure it was what he wanted. It was.

chapter 33

BEFORE LEAVING ELI'S HOUSE, Miller made the bed and understood why he never even tried. At about an acre across, it required going constantly back and forth from one side to the other dragging sheets, blankets, quilts, then replacing all the hundred pillows. In that other life she'd once lived, she resisted ever getting a king-size bed, holding firm to the opinion that it was important to sleep next to the person you were sleeping with. That opinion came naturally to Eli, however, no matter the size of the bed.

Miller spent the morning in her grandfather's study. In the afternoon the rain came up and the wind was fierce, but she needed to get out. In the parking lot of the Oceanview supermarket, with her hood pulled over her head, she rushed to hold up a frail elderly woman whose umbrella had blown inside out and who was staggering as a result, close to being blown over herself. Horizontal rain. The garden lady's description had been more than accurate.

Then down to Pine Ridge for more postcards, a gardenia scented candle that she'd passed up before, and without Eli, just to finger the soft cashmere sweaters in the high-end clothing store before passing them up, too. She didn't need a cashmere sweater. She didn't need anything. If JC had to spend time out here though, Miller conceded, she would have lived in this store.

Returning to her car in the onslaught, Miller found a parking ticket as wet as she was clinging to the windshield. She peeled off the drenched piece of paper and read the blurred print. She'd violated the law by parking her car more than twelve inches from the curb. But the reason, she wanted to explain to someone, was that next to the curb was a ten-inch deep pool of water. No matter. Somehow she would dry this poor document out and pay it. Though she envied the local police their big black Mackintosh raincoats, still she wasn't the one who had to care about who parked where in the pouring rain.

The drive back up the hill reminded Miller of the Trinity, all those dark pines, made even darker in the rain and dim gray light. She turned toward Oceanview on the two-lane highway that curved gently past emerald green fields, some thick with brush, others no more than damp, grassy pasture. Then everything happened at once. She saw the elk standing huge in the road, saw the pickup in the oncoming lane swerve and skid on the wet pavement, swerved herself, the pickup heading straight for her, the elk bellowing, the Prius sliding uncontrollably, hitting the hard edge of the water-filled ditch and rolling. The airbags exploding. The wind howling through broken glass. And then there was nothing.

Miller came to consciousness slowly, swimming up out of a drug-induced haze. She could feel before she could see, bare legs, tubes, tape, sheets, bindings, pain. There was something else, a hand on hers. Slowly, she opened her eyes. Eli was sitting in a chair next to the side of the bed, his feet up on a second chair, sound asleep, still holding onto her hand. She allowed herself a moment to take him in. This person. Of course he would be there and not anywhere else, ever. She had to catch her breath, trying to hold back the wave of emotion that threatened to overwhelm her.

She traced her thumb along his, the gesture he owned, the one that worked every time. He was instantly awake, blinking against the light before he realized where he was and that she was looking at him.

"Thank you God a thousand times," he said. "Miller, holy Christ, welcome back to the world but I'll tell you what, don't ever do that again, okay?"

Something in her was still so tired. She didn't want to talk, didn't have the energy. She only wanted to keep him in sight.

"But we should make sure of some things," he said. "Do you know your name?" She nodded. "Are you Eleanor Roosevelt?" She motioned just slightly no and wanted to smile, but it hurt too much. "Tina Turner?" No. "Then I think you're all right, though a doctor should probably have some say in that. Is it okay if I call them?" She shook her head no again. Not yet. "What then? Do you want me to tell you what happened? I can just keep talking here if that's what you need." Yes, she wanted him to keep talking. "She was drunk," Eli said. "The pickup driver, not the elk." Please don't ever change. And now she remembered about the elk, that huge dumb thing just standing there in the middle of the road. And the pickup coming at her. "She also had bad brakes, no tread, she just sailed clear across the road and slammed into you."

Miller wanted to concentrate only on breathing and being, but for a fraction of a second she looked at him hard and he understood immediately.

"She's down the hall," he said. "Broken leg, nasty DUI, but other than that, okay." Miller let her chest sink with relief. Then she looked at him hard again.

"You?" No, she didn't want to know about that yet.

"The car? Totaled, had to be." She closed her eyes. When she opened them again, she was asking what else.

"Uh, yes," he said. "Your phone lists both your daughter and me as emergency numbers, thank you for doing that Miller or I'd have been insane till I found out where you were, what happened, why you didn't come home. However, what that means is the hospital called JC and JC called me. Actually, I ended up talking to both your daughters, as it turns out they're together in London."

Oh God, Miller thought. She couldn't even imagine how that had gone. If it wasn't good, too late now.

"I should maybe get the doctor in here," Eli said. "I shouldn't be putting all of this on you till they see how you are."

She touched his hand. She wanted him to keep going. And the longer she listened to him, the more her head cleared.

"They were completely frantic and there wasn't much I could tell them until you woke up, but I did what I could. JC asked me to take a picture of you and send it so I did. Hope you don't mind. So hard when I'm just used to having you there."

Miller watched him. There was more, she could feel it.

"Dell was quiet," he said, "but after we got through everything there was to say about you, JC had a lot of questions concerning yours truly." As Miller knew she would. "I answered as best I could, tried to keep things to a minimum, I'm just here, that's all, I'm your friend. But then she asked me to do what she called Face Time and that caught me completely off guard. I feel like I know what's going on, but fuck, I didn't have any idea what she was talking about. Turns out it's right on your phone, this thing you press while you're talking and then you can see each other. So she got me there. Miller, I love you and I hope I didn't screw anything up, but she's a handful. Honestly, I can usually deal with anyone, but I couldn't quite talk her down off her ledge and I couldn't give in to what she wanted. Dell took the phone away from her and asked a couple more questions, said thanks and that was it. Took me a while before I could think straight again."

Miller nodded, sympathetic and grateful. JC *was* a handful.

"One other thing I forgot. She asked if her dad was here. When I said no, she asked if he'd called and I had to tell her no to that, too."

Miller closed her eyes again. JC would always hurt more than the rest of them, almost more than Miller.

"They said Sam's in some weird time zone, but he'll call as soon as he can and I'm supposed to tell you that he loves you."

Now the circle was complete, Miller thought, the tears rising.

"And to finish it up," Eli said, "the mail ladies came by with flowers, the people from the bar that you don't think know you but they do signed a card for you though some of it's not legible, the clerk at the market sent a roast chicken and the garden store lady gave you a plant. Now I'm getting the doctor." He didn't release her hand, only stood up and reached over her for the call button. "We've got to get you out of here, the food's terrible and I can vouch for that because I've been eating all of yours."

When Miller was released, Eli brought an unfamiliar car to the hospital, a large sedan.

"What happened to the Jeep?" she said.

"With cracked ribs and a broken collarbone, think about how it might feel trying to climb into that thing." There were also bruises all the way down her right side and she still had a headache. "I traded with a guy at the bar. He was thrilled, hadn't been in a Jeep in thirty years. I was thrilled, too. I've never been in a Lincoln in my life."

She considered it just more proof that he got back a thousand times what he gave to people in the way of simply being who he was.

"So this is how the other half lives," he said. The cushioned and perfectly contoured leather seats were heated. The radio sounded like a live performance. The dashboard was carved out of some exotic wood. The engine purred.

"Zero to sixty, what do you think?" But he drove slowly, as if he had fragile cargo. "Don't want to hit another damn elk."

"I never asked about that part."

"She's the only one who made out in the whole deal. They told me she was stunned but then walked away without a scratch."

"On the road when I drove up here that first time there were elk crossing signs everywhere and I wondered about them."

"Now you know."

"Yes, I do."

"Your call," he said. "Your house or mine. But I'll tell you, I think mine's the better way to go. Stairs wouldn't be helpful right now."

"But I don't need to be taken care of," she said.

"Definitely not. You're in a sling and a brace and wrapped up in about eight miles of tape and every time you try and move it makes me want to cry, but other than that, you're fine."

Standing just inside the hallway, with the wall of glass and the ocean in front of her, Miller suddenly felt the shock of what had happened. How many days ago did she make the bed and walk out of here with nothing important on her mind at all? She tried to take a deep breath, but it hurt.

"For my next trick…" she said.

"No way. When it comes around again, it's my turn."

"Don't even say that. No more medical emergencies of any kind, yours or mine."

"Works for me." He went into the bedroom, came back with an armful of pillows and threw them onto the sectional. "This won't be a walk in the park," he said. He winced as she eased herself down. "I'm not going to treat you like china. I've been there and the more you get up and around and do things for yourself, the better off you'll be."

"What did you break?"

"My collarbone just like you, football, my leg when I went over the handlebars of a bike. Never had a concussion, but I did get my four front teeth knocked out."

"Those aren't yours?"

"Well, they're mine, I do own them, they just aren't exactly what I was born with. Are you disillusioned?"

"Totally. The whole thing's off."

"Sorry. If you think it's that easy, you are so sadly mistaken. Are we going back to *The Wire*?"

"Sure, I'll just have to go online and see if I can figure out what's going on. That was hard when they killed that guy in jail."

"What guy? I have trouble watching TV with you. And then, for future reference since maybe you'll want it to pass the time, I'll show you where to find the Food Network."

Maybe things happened for a reason, she thought. As if everything else wasn't enough, now she'd been slammed so hard that she *had* to slow down. Any more and she'd be dead.

chapter 34

ELI WOULDN'T GO to the gym without her, but he still ran on the beach and spent a very disciplined number of hours every day at the garage. She'd watched his work grow over time into the actual pieces. When they were finished, they inhabited the grimy space like exotic gleaming metal birds about to take flight. One touch and they did take flight, opening out like the petals on a flower and soaring off in different directions. Garage employees and customers alike stood and watched, mesmerized. The process was enthralling, seeing the individual segments come slowly into existence, rough and flat at first, then gracefully bent, then polished until they reflected the light. She considered it astounding, how such elegance and beauty could come from one person's mind, one person's hands.

Every night they lay quietly together in the dark, taking up a fraction of the large bed's space, Miller trying not to move, Eli with his hand resting on her somewhere, a constant, always there.

Every morning he made breakfast and she decided that if he hadn't gone into the arts he would have turned somehow to cooking. She couldn't watch the Food Network for more than ten minutes at a time, but he could absorb hours' worth of chatty celebrity chefs in fake kitchens and sweating contestants in anxiety-ridden challenges to their skills and general sanity.

Naturally the weather would calm down simply because an elk had walked into the road and marooned her on the sectional. It was still cold, gray and raining, but the ocean sent off rays of dull light instead of towers of spray and the breeze only whistled around softly in the wind-bent pines. Eli built a fire before he left and the crackling logs added another note of serenity if Miller could only ever get comfortable and sit still long enough to enjoy it.

She reserved her greatest focus for the inane task of assembling an ocean from tiny puzzle pieces, though the endless concentrated search did at times prove meditative, and certainly was useful, along with her lengthy Swedish crime novel, for filling what were now even more acres of time. Scanning once more over the table's worth of odd squiggles, looking hopefully for the edge of one long bill on one of seven gracefully airborne pelicans, her eye was caught by a movement outside.

The sliding glass was open just a fraction to let in some air and there on the railing was a gull, not five feet away, regarding her at the table or himself in the glass or nothing at all, she couldn't tell. There was no reason for him to be there, but he stayed anyway, twisting his head to one side and then the other, nestling down into his snowy white breast as a light rain ricocheted off his waterproof back.

As she watched, a second gull arrived, leaner than the first, with a small head and stringy neck, its same pale eye and soft gray wings saying herring gull, but not the same. The first, perhaps older, was silent. The second kept up a constant dialogue of murmured gull noises. One spoke. One didn't. She had no idea what either of them was doing there, but having them stay for the morning made sense of everything, the gray light, the rain, the ocean puzzle, this quiet life.

After a week, gulls or not, Miller couldn't stand it anymore. She had been instructed to take the sling off a certain number of times every day to perform small range of motion exercises. She used one of those range of motion times to do a load of laundry. Her clothes and Eli's were thoroughly combined, the basket separation had never worked, and in addition were spread out over two households, so that they'd given up and gone to the much more rational approach of dark and light no matter where or whose. In fact, though it was a chore she was long used to accomplishing, mixed apparel a given, a husband's and wife's, still it always shocked and thrilled her a little to see Eli's t-shirts, socks, black boxers, his gray sweats which he washed with the light and she kept throwing back in the dark, his running clothes, all tossed in together with her own underwear, shirts, jeans.

Then she would stand back and breathe, trying to do what he always asked of her and Janelle had as well for different reasons, stay in the moment, right here, right now, where tomorrow didn't exist.

Miller used her second range of motion session to remove the clothes from the dryer and ended up folding each item so tenderly that when she was finished, she had to get out of the house. It was still raining lightly, nothing new there. She pulled up the hood on the sweatshirt jacket she'd managed to zip over the sling with only one hand and walked the two blocks to her own front door. Eli's work was important to him, it was everything, and so it should be, she believed in him, but her grandfather's study had become such a place for her as well.

The professor had been so meticulous and thorough in cataloguing information and materials that it was obvious he planned to write a book. Miller had never known him as well as she'd known her grandmother. He was more reserved than the rest of them, more removed, gave a lot of time over, as she remembered it anyway, to musing, reflecting, standing absently in the kitchen with a cup of coffee, walking down the road with his hands behind his back, staring out over the dunes. What was he thinking, she wondered now? How much time did he spend dwelling on the project that would never come to be?

Miller kept reading back over his notes again and again, reaching farther into the past every time she did. She kept seeing the dedication in that oldest book. Miller felt that's what her grandfather had been searching for, though the path seemed clouded, the relevant documents not there, likely not in existence at all. This whole process stirred Miller, brought back the dimmest recollections of the time when she had actually been a journalism major, learning to write, craft reportage, hone interviewing skills, construct compelling narratives. The fact of that life coming to a close so abruptly didn't faze her at all, because the end of those days had brought that first glowing, magical, euphoric year, Thanksgiving and everything that followed from it, the center of her being.

Now she wanted to continue her grandfather's work, just on her own. If it came to nothing, it was still a journey worth taking, a story so personal that it had to be worth pursuing. In this room, she felt whole, connected, and after all that had happened, all the loss and pain, she was glad to be reminded again of who she was.

The door opened and she belatedly considered that it would have been nice to have texted him.

"How did I know that when I came home you wouldn't be there?" Eli said.

"You're clairvoyant?"

"No, just used to it. Anything you assume about Miller, you'll be wrong, so don't even try it."

"Casting aspersions."

"Speaking the truth. At least you stayed off the beach, so I didn't have to come very far to find you."

"I'm sorry," she said. "I could have texted you. That did occur to me, but only right as you walked in the door."

"It's okay. So how are you?" He leaned on the edge of the desk and briefly took her hand.

"I'm good. Everything works again."

"I wanted to stay around and watch you get dressed this morning."

"Thank you for not doing that." One-handedness was tricky. She was gradually getting the hang of it, but spectators were the last thing she needed.

Eli turned to all the notes and files. "Have you figured out anything?"

"Seems like you can get back to around the mid-eighteen hundreds, but I don't know yet if that's far enough."

"Still, that's impressive, that's your family. You know what it makes me want to do? Call up my grandmother and ask her a million questions."

"You should."

"Maybe I will." He got up and went over to the bookshelves, reading along the titles, then looked at all the boxes of papers in the open drawers. He stopped at the photo album.

"What's this?"

"It was my grandmother's, mostly from the summers here."

"Do you mind?"

"No, not at all. Go ahead."

Eli took the album and sat down on the loveseat with the faded afternoon light pouring in over his shoulder. "Your mother was a big fan of lavender," he said, moving the throw.

"She was. Talk about assumptions. I was sure she was doing this whole entire remodel because she was involved with Hugh Donaldson, when if I'd stopped for even a minute, she was obviously doing it for herself. I knew every inch of it was her, so what was I thinking?"

"What made you decide there was something going on in the first place?" he said, turning over the pages.

"She was so happy about coming up here. Even just making plane reservations she couldn't stop smiling. Maybe since my dad was away practically all the time, she was only thrilled to have a project, something she could put her heart into. And she was always good at this kind of thing."

Eli was quiet for a minute. Then he got up and left the room.

"Where are you going?"

"Just to check on something." Miller frowned. He came back carrying a book.

"What's that?"

"Hugh Donaldson. I needed to see what he looked like."

"Why?" She wondered if she wanted to know.

"Well..." he said. He brought the photo album over to the desk. "Maybe this isn't your mother, but she's everywhere in here." He showed her one of the photos. The picture was taken from the dunes of a group standing on the old deck, the one that leaned, with the plain house behind them before the addition of the French doors. The group included several couples, all teenagers. One of them certainly resembled a leaner, obviously much younger, Hugh Donaldson.

"No, that's her," Miller said slowly. The girl was Jane, tan, leggy, sun-streaked hair flowing down her back. The boy with his arm around her was equally tan, wearing nothing but a pair of rolled up khaki shorts. His feet were bare. She had her arm around his waist. They looked happy, but who could say with just one photo. Maybe someone told a joke, or said, say cheese for the camera. All the relief she'd felt evaporated and the dull ache was back in her chest.

"Eli, if I believe what Luca told me, Hugh Donaldson was long gone by the time this photo was taken."

"I'm afraid to say this, but if that's not Hugh Donaldson, then it's got to be Luca."

"It can't be."

"Everybody's a teenager once, these things happen. It was a long time ago."

Miller looked at him. Slowly he came around. "Or not that long ago."

"What am I supposed to do now?" she said. She was right back in that hard place where she suddenly knew far more about her parents than she'd ever wanted to know. "Is he the one she came up here to see? And what does that even mean? Why did she do that?"

"You could ask him. I imagine that would be an interesting conversation."

"I hate this."

"No wonder he looks at you like that. You're probably the last thing he ever expected."

"Crap," Miller said. "This day's shot."

"Let's go out and get something to eat," he said. "It'll do us both good."

Miller laughed at herself, in bed in the dark wearing track pants and a sweatshirt, her arm in a sling, broken collarbone, cracked ribs, a mother with a past, her mind going where it was going.

"It's been nine days," she said.

"Nine days?" Eli said, and then, "Oh, no. I don't care how good a shape you think you're in. You were in a car that rolled, your arm's still in a sling, all that tape, no way. And it's eleven days."

"I don't have the tape anymore, I cut it off. I wanted to take a real shower."

"You are the worst patient on earth. I thought we agreed that when you wanted to do that, I'd help."

"How much help do you think you'd be in the shower?"

"None, but that doesn't have anything to do with it."

"Where do you get eleven?"

"You're not counting the two days you were checked out."

"Right, forgot about that. But you aren't up for it?"

There was quiet in the dark. "Wrong question," Eli said. Miller closed her eyes. "Every time, you do that to me."

"That's because it's so easy. Let me think about it."

"Think hard."

"Miller, you've got to stop, you're just handing me these lines."

She made a noise. "What is *wrong* with you?" she said.

"One-track mind like every other guy who's a moron, fatal flaw in the species, that's why it won't ever work out."

"Have you thought about it yet? I want to hear a plan, I have expectations. It's that one-to-twelve thing someone told me about."

"Which speaker regrets, obviously." There was more quiet. He found her hand and traced her fingers. "I think all of this was good in your other life," he said.

"Maybe you're right, but so what? In the end, all it showed me was that you can't ever really know someone." Miller paused, gone for a minute. "That car?" she said. "The one I traded to Sam? It was a BMW. An X3. SUV. Manual transmission."

"Which they don't sell in the States."

"Exactly. Not the manual. It was imported, my Christmas gift last year because I'd always driven a stick. So over the top and completely extravagant. We never did things like that. But what was that all about? What was that for? When I found out, in my heart I knew what that car had been for and that's why I would never touch it again."

"I'm sorry, Miller."

"I'm the one who's sorry. You'd think I'd have learned by now to just walk away from it." She shook it all off. "But on that subject," she said, remembering, "I bought a car."

"You did? How? When?"

"Online. This morning."

"You bought a car online. Where is it?"

"At a dealership just over the bridge. Not far. Do you think you could take me there? They won't have it for four days."

"Driving in four days? Really? We'll talk. What did you get? Another drug dealer Prius?"

"No, this one's silver so it looks like every other silver Prius and I won't have CSI guys hunting me down in hotel parking lots."

"A CSI guy can read license plates, you know."

"But will a CSI guy do a woman with hardly anything broken anymore?"

"Here's what, Miller. Talk to me like that and it's on."

"Plan, please."

"Here's the plan." Leaning on one elbow, he bent over her, kissing her just once, but deeply. Then he was up on his knees, carefully removing the pillows, the quilts, her track pants and anything else that got in his way. "Quick," he said. "Like this. But if you move even a fraction of an inch, I stop."

"Don't stop," she said, already making involuntary sounds.

"Then don't move. I understand it's not your nature, but listen to me for once and I'll take you anywhere you want to go."

"I know you will, that's why I asked," she said, suddenly gasping for breath. "Come with me."

"You're doing it again."

"No, I meant it."

"I will," he said. "I do. And by the way, I love you."

She reached out for his hand. "Now I want you to stop, for just one second." He was above her in the dark. She closed her hand tightly over his. "I love you, too."

He took her face that he could barely see in his hands and kissed her again. "Please stay still," he said, his voice gone.

She didn't move, except to clench her jaw and dig her heels into the sheets, trembling, the tears running down her face because being with him was in every way better than anything he ever promised.

They lay close together afterwards, touching down their length, lost in each other.

"Look what you've done to me," she said. She felt as if she'd been turned inside out.

He stroked her hair. "Look what you've done to me," he said.

chapter 35

THE WIND ROARED BACK, clocking in at eighty miles an hour. The bridge to the north, a major artery, closed down after a trailer truck flipped and burst into flames, a conflagration saved only by the accompanying biblical deluge. Beachfront homes in Oceanview were evacuated. An eight-foot log crashed into one of the rooms of the expensive inn in Pine Ridge. So far, the coast had recorded ninety-eight inches of rain. That was over eight feet and when Miller considered it that way, it sounded just about right. No wonder people were scowling at each other in the grocery store.

When this latest storm had blown itself out, she was glad to abandon the rain gear she was thinking of burning and put on her down coat instead. Out on the beach, the rusted six-foot long lid to a ship's locker, a bulbous two-foot-high sake bottle and thirty feet of rope thick enough for docking an ocean liner announced it as a junk day. As always, after the junk came the birds, six half-eaten rhinoceros auklets, a lifeless Cassin's auklet, two dead northern fulmars. In between the bodies, a wooly bear caterpillar humped its way across the sand, awakened into the wrong season and headed toward its demise in the ocean.

Miller frowned at the sight in front of her. Yet another common murre had settled himself resolutely on the damp flats facing out to sea. Having seen the vacationer so easily, albeit with heavy gloves, pick up the other murre, she'd begun to question whether it was the right thing to do, not to carry the frightened bird away but to give him one more chance, place him gently back in the waves.

She moved on, thought about it, overcame her doubts and turned back meaning to locate the small bird again on the broad, shimmering tidal flats. What could it hurt? Immersed in mapping out her strategy, where to put her hands, how to keep both of them from harm, she looked up, shading her eyes to watch as a dark shape swooped down to the beach then sailed low through the sky over her head, broad of wing and graceful, with something struggling underneath. Her mind could barely acknowledge what her eyes assured her was happening. The shape swept in an arc across the beach, gliding up over the high dunes, the white head and seven-foot wingspan marking it indelibly as a bald eagle.

But no, she told herself, he'd been clutching a squirrel, a land animal, a digger, a burrower, something he'd found in the dunes. There were no squirrels in the dunes and the tidal flats were a mirror of the sky without the telltale black and white speck that from a distance had signaled the presence of the murre.

She stood in awe, her senses reeling with what she'd just witnessed. A bald eagle had passed no more than fifteen feet above her. A bald eagle had just snatched the bird she was moving toward. How much closer could she have come and still had the eagle take the murre? How much closer before the eagle challenged her for it? Her hands were shaking.

Miller wanted to understand. An eagle at the ocean, on the beach? She'd never heard of such a thing, certainly not on her own beaches. A shocked couple said they'd just encountered the eagle themselves when their foolish little terrier zeroed in on the arresting form perched erect on the tidal flats and rushed it, yipping.

"I've never seen anything like it," the husband said. "That bird was *huge*."

"I screamed," his wife added.

Miller told them what she'd seen, the common murre disappearing right before her eyes. They shuddered, casting anxious glances at their tiny dog.

An elderly woman striding along purposefully in her long coat and black walking shoes, a beach vision from some other time, some other century, stopped to shake her finger angrily in Miller's face.

"Look at those cliffs. Our dunes are ruined," the woman said. Miller was completely taken aback. "Terrible, awful people who put that grass there. The dunes used to leave in winter, come back in the spring, and that's how it's supposed to be. It's a disgrace, I tell you."

"Are you a birder?" she said, fixing Miller with a steely eye. Before Miller could answer, the old woman decided for herself. "Then you must be pretty familiar by now with that northern harrier. And start looking out for the meadowlarks when they pass through. Gorgeous birds."

"But a bald eagle?" Miller said, finding her voice. "I just saw one."

"Bald eagle? Been his territory forever."

Miller realized that although she'd never seen the eagle, she'd been observing the remains of his dining habits for a very long time.

At the river, she walked carefully along the path of wet rocks, scattering the flock of ruddy turnstones, and climbed up into the island. Once more a presence announced itself, this time in the form of a plastic Ocean Spray Cranberry Juice carafe placed at the base of the driftwood cross. Held up to the light, the carafe revealed its contents, an inch of water and eighty-three cents. Miller went through her pockets, found three dimes and a nickel, dropped them into the carafe and set it back where it had been, her offering to whatever was going on there.

Coming back down the beach, her mind still filled with thoughts of eagles, she looked up and halted. The turquoise van jolted along the sand heading in her direction. She held her ground. There was nothing else to do. She stood staring at Luca as he slowed the van and then brought it to a stop, one arm resting on the open window, watching her. The import of her stare wasn't lost on him.

"Miller," he said, not flinching or looking away, only waiting for what came next. She got the sense that he was not a stranger to confrontation, that he might almost expect it. All she could see, however, was him standing on the porch with Jane. Unable to shake that image, she could find no words.

"Okay," he said. He put the truck in gear and started to drive away, rethought that move, shifted into reverse and backed up to where she was still standing with the same expression, the same hard stare. "I've got a bottle of bourbon in the glove compartment," he said. "Want some?"

"No, thank you." She watched him for a moment. "Are you an alcoholic?"

The blue eyes rested on her, only the hint of a smile in them. Damn you, she thought. "Recovering," he said.

"How's that going?"

"Pretty good, thanks. You have something on your mind?"

"I might," she said.

"I told you I don't do much presuming so you let me know if you feel like saying what it is."

"How much are you willing to tell me?"

"Depends on the subject."

"You're aware of the subject."

"Actually, right at the moment, I'm not. I could guess, but I don't do much of that either. And also, with the telling, I believe it'd mostly be a matter of how much you'd want to hear."

"That's the problem I'm having."

"Understood."

She didn't want the answer to any of these questions.

"Is there that much to say?"

"I could go on for years," he said, and something in his voice almost broke her heart.

"Do you need the bourbon?" she said.

"Not necessarily. I've got my preferences but only up to a point. Could be scotch."

"That's not what I meant."

"Do I need it? No, not strictly speaking. Will I be in pain without it? Yes. Psychic and otherwise."

She made up her mind.

"Will you come up to the house and talk to me?" She held him with her eyes. "I really need you to."

Luca let his gaze drift out toward the water. She saw the slow rise and fall of his chest. He turned back to her.

"Can't do that," he said and then he was looking directly at her, in his eyes everything she hadn't wanted to see. "And I'm not even going to apologize for what I'm saying. I don't want to know what a great life she had, how much money, all the things she could do with it, what the best she had might look like. It got her here and that's all I care about. I don't want to know the rest of it at all."

Miller pressed her hands against her eyes. It was all piling up on her, layers of grief.

"Miller," he said. "Get in."

She wiped her face on her sleeve. "What?"

"Get in. We're going someplace."

"You aren't serious." She had to dig a wad of tissues out of her pocket. Getting in that van was the last thing she ever saw herself doing.

"I am serious. We won't go very far. There are things you don't know, never would, about the beach unless I show you."

"If you're trying to convince me, you're not doing a great job."

"You want to talk? We'll talk."

Miller glanced up and down the beach. The old woman in the long coat and the couple with the dog were gone. There was no one to remember her getting in a battered old van and disappearing forever. She reminded herself that her mother had, it seemed, chosen this person not once but twice, and she would have to go with that.

"All right." She felt in her pockets to make sure she had her phone and then went around to the passenger side. She had to pull hard on the salt-pitted handle till the door opened with a horrible creaking sound. She climbed up onto the stiff cracked leather seat and yanked the door closed again. The van was ancient, the scarred dashboard littered with papers, shells, feathers, tiny knobs and whorls of driftwood. The smell of sweat and sawdust hung in the air. And there was Luca, his hands on the steering wheel, his eyes resting on her.

He started to put the van in gear, but Miller held up her hand.

"Don't go anywhere yet." She pulled out her phone. "I'm texting Eli where I am, just in case."

"Just in case what?" he said. He waited till she was done.

"I don't want your opinion," she said.

"I don't have an opinion."

He turned the van in a wide circle, almost reaching the tidal flats, then headed back in the other direction. Miller experienced a small amount of alarm as he went past the access road and onto the north beach.

"I've never been up this far," she said.

"Didn't think you would be."

"It's so desolate, there's nothing. Perfect for serial killers."

"The next time you find a serial killer out here, let me know."

Miller's eyes were wide as they kept going for what seemed like miles. Luca finally turned the van, backed it up into the dunes and shut off the engine. "Best place on earth, loneliest place on earth," he said. He reached across Miller, opened the glove compartment and took out the bottle of bourbon. Then he felt around under the seat until he came up with two glasses. He handed one of them to her.

"Wipe it off first," he said. "But nobody's been drinking from it for a while."

Two years? Three?

"I don't drink bourbon," she said, though, strange, her mother did.

"Once won't kill you," he said, and poured two fingers into her glass. "Does what's needed, most of the time anyway. You can spit it out if you have to."

Miller closed her eyes. She was holding a glass of bourbon on a deserted beach in a rusted out van with a sixty-something-year-old man who had been her mother's...what? That was the question. She opened her eyes and the whole of the Pacific Ocean lay before her, stretched out to the horizon, endlessly stark and beautiful. She took a sip of the bourbon and choked.

"It'll get better," Luca said. "Give it some time." He had poured himself more than two fingers. He put the bottle down between his feet. "Can't beat the view."

"You come out here and do this a lot?"

"I'm at least a little more industrious than what you're saying, but now and then, yes, I do."

"Alone?"

"Always."

Miller took another sip of the bourbon. She was ready for it and didn't choke this time. It was warm like the brandy. She held the glass in both hands, searching for a way in, the right words.

"I saw a photo," she said. "I thought it was of your brother, but it couldn't be. It was you, with her."

"A long time ago then."

"Yes."

"She was a summer girl," he said. "Came every year. We got together. We got serious. Your grandmother liked me a lot, but she could see the problems. I was a cowboy, a renegade, something like that, just not the best choice for anything ever, and when she began to get stern, lay down the law, we got even more serious."

"You knew my grandmother. You were in that house."

"All the time. Your grandmother was fun. I loved being there. And I loved your mother more than I've ever loved anything in this world."

"Shit," Miller said. She wiped her eyes again. "What happened?"

"The third summer, we were nineteen, she was in college and she didn't come back. She'd said she would, we wrote letters that whole year, talked on the phone when we could, but she didn't come. So I went to see your grandmother and she told me Jane wasn't allowed to come, it was over, there was someone else, all of this stuff to get rid of me. Not in a bad way, your grandmother wasn't like that, in a gentle way, she cared about me. It's just it was clear that none of that was going to happen. What do you do? I got in the car, drove to that college in southern California and your grandmother was right. There was someone, he was older and his name was Whitman Fucking Miller, which is why your name still throws me. Can't tell you how much I hated that guy. He was everything I wasn't, had everything I wouldn't ever have."

Luca stopped and took a long swallow of the bourbon. "After that it took no brains at all. There was a war going on, everyone invited. Hugh went too soon, joined the Army and ended up in Kentucky, where the hell is that? I said fuck all of you, just me and a few good men, don't know why the Marines took me but they did. In six months I was right where I wanted to be, getting shot at in Vietnam. She told me she cried, and I cried too, but then I didn't. What's taken from you, too bad, that's just the way life is, get over it."

Miller couldn't even begin to comprehend that this was happening.

"Did you ever get married after that?" she said.

"Twice. First one was sort of a misunderstanding in Vegas. Second one was to someone here. She still lives in town, hates me, turns around and goes the other way every time she sees me. Why one of us doesn't move, I don't know."

"Children?"

"Not that anybody's told me about."

Miller still held the glass between her hands. She was sipping the drink slowly, though the temptation was there to gulp it down, take the heat and go to some other place far away.

"Were you ever in jail?"

"Once for hitting a cop, that could've been a lot worse. Once with that Vegas thing."

"Drugs?"

"In Vietnam, believe it. After that, no."

"You live alone?"

"Yep."

"And that's okay, too?"

"Do I get the job? Where are you going with all of this?"

"I'm trying to figure out who you are."

"And why she came back."

"That most of all."

"They put me in long range reconnaissance," he said. "Do enough of that and it makes you a total freak-out, jumpy, that's why the drugs. After the service, I moved into a certain kind of security where total freak-outs go, the place where jumpy is good. Nowadays, I live on pension, disability, what's out here and life's a lot calmer than it used to be. I drink, but not just to get through the day, I'm not there yet. She came back because Hugh asked her to."

"To do the house."

"He wanted it to work that way, like I told you, as a favor to me, trying to save me from myself."

"He knew about her."

"He did."

"From the beginning?"

"He was my brother."

"Did you see her right away?"

"We had dinner at the house, the three of us. The house the old way, almost exactly how I remembered it. Hugh had to be there or she wouldn't have agreed. An affair wasn't what she was looking for."

An affair. Miller thought about her father. He was in so many ways like her grandfather, smart, successful, but always somewhere else. She tried to picture the wallpapered dining room, the antler chandelier, Jane with the two brothers around the table, the local wild boys, white-haired now. She could see Hugh outfitting the occasion with candlelight, linen napkins, a vase of peonies, a rack of lamb. How would that be, she wondered, traveling back forty-some years in time? Would the face you thought you loved still be the same?

She took another sip of bourbon, suddenly grasping the concept of people using alcohol for false courage, to face what was hard.

"Where did she stay when she was here?"

"A hotel."

"Which one?"

He named a hotel. He knew where Jane was, which hotel.

One more warm, knife-edged sip of bourbon. Miller let it travel all the way down.

"Did you sleep with her?"

Luca was doing his own job on the bourbon, though seemingly not to any ill effect. "I'm old," he said. "My come-on is I can take off my pants and show you the bullet holes and shrapnel in my leg."

"Has it ever worked?"

"Some women are smarter than others."

"Is it the smart ones it works on?"

"No."

"Did you sleep with her?"

"She was married."

"You're not going to say."

"Doesn't look like it."

"Does that tell me anyway?"

"She was everything to me," he said, "but she's your mother and some things are just better left out there where it's safe for them to be. I hope she had a good life. She and I never talked about all of that, we stayed away from it."

"That's what you did? Talk?"

"We talked for all the time we had and it still wasn't enough."

Miller wondered how many tears there could be.

"Out here? In this van?"

"Sometimes here. Lots of places. This was us, who we'd been all that long time ago. It came back easy."

The tissues were gone, a soggy mess. Miller had to just keep using her sleeve. She had one step left to go and hoped she could get through it. "She died. You knew that."

Now it was Luca staring out at the ocean. "The last time, she told me. And then her brother called. I said I had to know so she'd asked him to."

"Ted?" Miller said, shocked. "My uncle?"

"Don't forget, I would have known him, too. It was all of us all mixed up together. But I got to see her again. That was the only thing I ever asked. And my brother who had such a shitty life for so long gave that to me when I didn't deserve it, didn't ever give him anything. From now on, whatever happens, let it. Doesn't matter."

"So seeing me was..."
"A surprise, but fuck, what isn't."

Luca parked the van at the curb. He'd stowed the bourbon bottle back in the glove compartment. The glasses were at her feet.

"Thank you," she said.

"You're welcome, I guess. You look like your grandmother."

"That's what people say." She hesitated. "Could I buy you a drink now and then?"

"No, you couldn't buy me a drink, but I'll have one with you anytime you want."

"I'm going to take you up on that," she said.

"Your call."

She moved over on the bench seat, put her arms around him and hugged him hard, for Jane. He was the kind she thought he'd be, warm like someone else she knew, and he hugged her back.

chapter 36

THE HEADLINES IN the local paper read: *Sand Cliffs Pose Threat, Whale Watcher Alert, Coast Ready For Easter/Spring Break*. Though crocus had begun to appear on lawns in town and the ruined beach grass in the dunes was sending up new green shoots, the weather remained a steadfast litany of wind, rain and hail. And Miller had some doubt as to how ready the coast was for any influx of people at all. More and more bumper stickers appeared in town, all with the same sentiment: *If it's called the Tourist Season, why can't we shoot them?*

"Good Lord, what now?" Eli said, standing at the sliding glass doors as car after truck after car headed down the access road and came back up in reverse.

Coming up over the rise of the dunes, they immediately saw the problem. The weather had been deteriorating all day long and now the ocean at high tide was rough and full of white caps, churning underneath a cold hard sky. The tide had ebbed momentarily, leaving a group of teenaged boys to stand back and watch as their old faded Chevy Suburban settled deeper and deeper into the wet sand and every tenth wave washed over it up to the fenders. One of the four-wheel drive police cars was parked nearby.

A continuing stream of cars, trucks, Jeeps and campers with no idea of the conditions zipped out from the access road onto the beach. Each driver assessed the situation, sandstorm, wild surf, half-buried Suburban and beat a hasty retreat.

"Spring break, here it is," Eli said. "They'll be lucky if they ever get that thing out of there." He glanced back over his shoulder. "But they're going to try."

A second police car arrived followed by a shiny black pickup full of friends of the Suburban owner. The police, local, familiar, sympathetic, stood around offering suggestions. The friends knotted a towrope between the black pickup and the Suburban.

The pickup groaned in reverse. Everyone pushed. Nothing happened. The ocean crashed. The wind blew. The situation appeared hopeless.

"Oh no," Miller said, turning in the other direction. A large college-aged group broke through the crowd and ran down onto the beach. Clad in surfer shorts and small bikinis, they leaped into the foaming cold waves, screamed and ran back out into the gusting, sand-filled winds. One thin dark-haired girl turned, shivering violently, and said to no one in particular, "God, that undertow was *strong*!"

"That just stopped my heart," Miller said.

"What are they doing here anyway?" Eli said. "Hasn't anyone ever heard of Mexico?"

By the time he and Miller turned back, the swimmers had disappeared into the high rise, the police had given up and were off to tackle other problems on what held the promise of a disaster-filled weekend, and the Suburban had sunk up to the door handles.

In the morning, the news confirmed a difficult night, twenty arrests, fourteen windows broken, one U.S. Coast Guard H60 helicopter called in for crowd control. The police report further stated that a vehicle was found stranded on the beach, heavy tides and surf had prevented its recovery and the storms had taken out the sign prohibiting driving on the south beach.

Interrupting their walk, Eli bent down to study something. "What's this little guy?" he said. The bird was so small that it would fit in the palm of a hand. "That odd bill's going to find it right away." He pulled out his phone. "Tufted puffin. A very young one."

He watched Miller write it down in her bedraggled notebook next to his name. "You should put out your own book. *Birds I Saw On The Beach.* You could have photos."

"But unfortunately," she said, "everything in them would be dead."

"True. Maybe not a bestseller."

Five minutes later, he picked up an old sea-rotted barnacle-encrusted aerosol can. The words printed on it were in the Cyrillic alphabet above a depiction of a large black flying insect. "Russian bug spray. I wonder if it only kills Russian bugs." He glanced up toward the dunes. "Hold on, there's some whole other kind of dead thing."

A huge pale bulk lay in the sand, not long deceased, pecked at a little by the gulls, but still fat and smooth with a ruffled head and an innocent face. It had obviously ridden in with the storms to end up so high on the beach. Miller recognized the man standing over it. It was the bearded aquarium manager.

"That's a sea lion, isn't it?" Eli said.

"Think it's a Stellar," the man said. He introduced himself as Keith. "If that's true, I expect there'll be some people down from the university to do a flensing."

"Flensing?" Miller said. Whatever it was, it didn't sound good.

"An autopsy, basically. You don't see these guys very often down here. They're way more common up north. Don't know what he died of, but it doesn't look like old age. That's another reason for the autopsy."

The aquarium manager turned to Miller.

"You were here last time I was around," he said, and Miller was struck again by just how small a town it was. "You remember that woman and her baby?"

Miller did remember. Marie, who drove down to the beach in her maroon Bronco and nursed her baby in the driver's seat while she stared out at the ocean.

"A couple weeks ago her Bronco got caught in a sneaker wave."

"*What?*"

"She had her baby with her and her car was heading out to sea. The county guy was down there moving logs with his front-loader and just pulled right in front her and stopped her cold. Don't think she'll be back."

Good God, that was unbelievable. Marie had seemed as if she knew more about the beach than anyone.

"That's one of the scariest things I ever heard," Eli said.

"I'll go with that," Keith said.

"How close have you come out here?" Eli asked Miller as they moved on.

"Not that close," she said, shuddering again at the thought. "But there have been times. Too bad, but I think that's the only way you learn."

"I had no idea. When I run, I just have to run a little faster sometimes to get out of the way. Now I'll worry."

"I've been worried too, believe me. But the winter storms are over, aren't they?"

In response, hail showered down out of nowhere, turning the ocean black and building up piles of ice on the sand. Then the sun reappeared, bright in a cold wind.

Eli pushed back his hood again. "Jesus. Not yet. Or God forbid, maybe that *is* spring. Look, more new birds in the river. How can that even be? Are you ready?" He took the binoculars. "For the first time I can see where this is unfair."

"What, being VP?"

"No, being female. She's just a dull old bird color, but you should see him. It's like he's got a headdress on, all these green feathers flying out behind. Can you do breast color?"

"Yes."

"Something close to red."

"Red and rust. Only brings up six."

Eli looked at the phone. "That's him, red-breasted merganser. Actually, on second thought, they're still enough alike that they make a pretty good-looking couple."

Miller stared at him. "Now you've been out here too long. But I wanted to show you something." She led him carefully across the rocks and up into the island. "I thought I'd found a secret place, but apparently I was the last one to know about it."

He studied the cross with its trailing fisherman's line and dangling strands of bull kelp. "Good knots. Whoever did them has tied knots before. But why is this island even here?" He turned to face the other shore. "Seems like it was built up as part of that spit over there. Who would have done that? And why?

And how long ago did the river break through? That must have been a sight."

Miller was watching him, frowning.

"What?" he said.

"Not one of those questions would ever have occurred to me in a million years."

"Men and women think differently, remember? We decided that a long time ago."

"It's a guy thing then."

"It's compensation for all those other things they can't figure out."

She thought for a minute. "If there were only women, would there be no ten lane highways or skyscrapers or man-made spits strangely situated in the middle of rivers?"

"Hard to say. The women in design school came up with all kinds of wild ideas. If there were only women, would there be war and tanks and bombs? Would a woman really pull a seat up to the drafting table and sketch out an AK-47?"

"I guess we'll never know."

"Unless," Eli said, "one of the wild ideas that somebody's working on is...."

"...getting rid of the men? Never happen," she said. "Women are too sentimental. They'd get all teary-eyed and say, but I *need* him!"

"Do they?"

"Of course. I gather, you hunt, I cook, you hunt, I raise the kids--what is it you do again? Oh yes, hunt."

"And plow and plant and build the barn, shoe the horses, shovel the snow, fix the toilet, mow the lawn, take out the garbage, it's exhausting."

"How about we switch? I'll hunt and fix the toilet. I'll just have to go online to find out how to do it. You sew the clothes and raise the kids."

"Disaster all the way around."

"Definitely," she said.

"So we've just made another decision. Everything's staying exactly the way it is. It's a relief to get at least that much settled. What are you thinking now?" he said.

"That I like you."

"I like you too, a lot."

"You know what else?" she said. "The carafe isn't here anymore. The last storm must have taken it out, too."

"What carafe?"

"It was an Ocean Spray Cranberry Juice bottle with money in it, so I added what I had, all thirty-five cents worth."

"And that was for?"

"World peace."

"Nice thought, but I don't know if thirty-five cents is going to do it."

chapter 37

TWO BRIGHT RED stop signs appeared on the south beach in place of the no-driving sign that had been taken out by the storms. One stop sign was nailed to a sturdy post dug into the sand. The other was bolted onto what was left of the concrete pillar. It only took a week before storms removed them again. Miller found the first sign lying mangled under a pile of wet logs on the access road. The second one had disappeared entirely.

Staying true to the task at hand, Miller stopped in at city hall to ask if anyone knew when the official no-driving sign would be replaced.

"I called the Park Service yesterday," the woman at the front desk said. "They've ordered a new one. Hard to say when it'll go up, though."

"Have lots of people been asking?" Miller said.

"Nope."

"Has anybody been asking?"

"Nope."

Since it was her turn to cook, Miller went to the market. The man in charge of the wine section told her he'd lived there all his life.

"Do you know anything about the sign on the beach?" she said.

"What sign?"

"The sign that got washed away, the Motor Vehicles Prohibited sign that isn't there anymore?"

He rubbed his forehead, thinking.

"Why are those signs even there?" she asked. "Do you know? Aren't they to protect the beach?"

"Yes, to protect the beach, I'm sure they are. But Lord, I can't tell you how many times cars have gone into the river. Tourists, they don't pay attention or they decide to drive over to Oceanview and hey, here's this little creek, we'll just go across it. Eighty percent of it's got to be keeping fools from driving into the river."

Away from town, the beach offered a silent world of cold mist and empty spaces, a cathedral of peace and stillness. The calendar might have said spring, but out here the northwest wind still carried a hard edge that suggested at least a passing acquaintance with icebergs and permafrost. A gull soared overhead. Like so many of them these days, this one was missing feathers, the light of the sky showing through a gap in his wings.

Out at the river, Miller watched the loons. She had thought they'd be gone by now, away to their breeding grounds on distant lakes. Instead, they flipped and dove as usual, not appearing in any way tense or agitated, stirred up by increases in the temperature or daylight, not preparing frantically for a journey. She wondered if they just took off one by one or waited, gathering out at sea and lifting in a great mass, winging northward. However it happened, she would miss them.

Terns swooped overhead like angry mosquitoes. At first, they flew so high that she had to shield her eyes to even get a glimpse of whatever was making that loud, obnoxious noise. Then they turned and dive-bombed the river, nasty, sharp-tongued birds.

The wind shifted. Fog closed in, obscuring the horizon. The sky darkened to an ominous shade of gray and a sudden driving rain removed the handful of beach-goers to more welcoming environments.

Hood up, protected and as warm as she was ever going to be, Miller kept going in the downpour. This was who she was now, the beach walker, her senses taking in all that was familiar, alerting her constantly to what was different and deserving of inspection. She knew that even in the rain she could spot a tiny silver fish in the tangled mess of tide wrack, a spider no bigger than her thumbnail crawling across the sand. The journey of the caterpillar down to the sea, of the hawk along the dunes, had become her own journey as well. She thanked Janelle every day for all of it.

Inadvertently stepping into the backwash of a wave, she felt her foot go wet and cold. On inspection, she found that one rubber boot was splitting at the sole, and the other was paper thin at the heel. How many beach miles had it actually taken to wear her sturdy boots down to nothing?

Miller climbed up into the dunes to sit on a driftwood log directly above the body of the sea lion. The fine green blades of dune grass all around that had been fragile shoots were now tough, foot high swords. She listened for any presence of the sea lion to make itself felt, but there was only the pale sea creature itself lying in the sand, bulky in a sea-going way and solidly deceased. What did speak, rather loudly, was the huge neon pink X that Keith had sprayed on the animal's back, which she thought must be visible from space.

She watched the northern harrier hunt, gliding silently along on uplifted wings. All at once he broke his pattern, veered over the edge of the dunes and made a series of tentative passes above the body of the sea lion. In the absolute stillness, Miller could almost hear him thinking, calculating. He appeared intensely interested, but then abruptly wheeled up and turned away.

Suddenly the air was split by the whine of engines. Two off-road motorcycles roared by at speed, the helmeted riders leaning forward in the rain, digging deep tracks with their bikes and spraying sand. Miller followed their bullet-like trajectory until they disappeared in the distance, trailing noise. And then there was silence. Either they had jumped the dunes and headed back into town or missed the wide turn and arced gracefully into the river.

chapter 38

"HEY, SORRY," Keith said as he climbed out of his wreck of a station wagon parked out by the river. He'd jumped when Miller and Eli approached him. "Didn't hear you guys, I had my mind on other things. Got a report of a seal that might be in trouble. You haven't seen one, have you?"

"No seals," Miller said. "Not for a long time anyway. But since you're out here, can I ask? What happened to the body of the sea lion? It just disappeared."

"Those marine biology students came like I told you they would, and the local butcher too. He helps out with these things."

Miller winced.

"Was it a Stellar?" Eli said.

"It was, so it was a sad find but also a lucky one. They got to take tissue samples and such. Plus, here's the even more sad part. It was a pregnant female with a pup inside her. When they rolled her over, it wasn't hard at all to tell how she died. A whole line of bullet holes. She was strafed, best guess is an automatic weapon fired from a boat."

"Is that legal?"

"Not at all, especially with an endangered species, but what are you going to do? I'm not saying it was salmon fishermen, but everybody knows sometimes they lose their whole catch to those guys. Don't suppose they spend much time wondering if it's a rare one or not." Keith gave the same shrug Miller had seen him give before. "Happens," he said.

"Then the sea lion's gone? They took all of her?"

"Nope. She's still right there, just down about six feet now. They did a nice pile of driftwood to mark the spot, said a few words, you have to. Okay, got to go, I need to get back to the search. It's all in what you report." He climbed back in his beat-up car.

The heron settled lightly out of the sky and waded one step at a time into the slow-moving current around the island. Within minutes, however, he had developed some sort of irritation with a nearby gull. He took out after the offender, flapping madly and uttering raspy, honking sounds. Dissatisfied still, he rose and circled out over the river, squawking hoarsely.

"Ruins my image of him," Miller said.

"Jeez, what are those?" Eli said as two thin, mostly white birds circled and screeched, diving down from a height where they appeared as pinholes in the sky.

"Some kind of terns, I think."

"You're not going to look them up?"

"No, I'm not. They're nasty."

"Too bad, guys. You didn't make the cut." He looked through the binoculars. "There are the green headdress ducks again, but it's definitely mating season because now they're behaving very weirdly."

"I'm not making comments anymore," Miller said. "Our discussions about that are too traumatic."

"All I'll say is that you know in the end there are going to be new little ducks anyway. Sort of makes you wonder why they have to go through all of that."

"Maybe it's fun."

"And maybe it isn't."

"I worry about you sometimes," she said.

"I'm jaded."

"You are many things but take my word for it, jaded isn't one of them." They had tight-roped across the rocks and climbed up into the center of the island again. "Great, now the whole cross is gone," she said. "What happened to it? Did the storms really do that?"

"If they could take down metal signs..."

"No, you're right."

"But just think, your thirty-five cents is maybe out there somewhere deep in the ocean by now."

"Probably a fish ate it. So much for world peace."

229

"Or it's lost in the sand and someday five hundred years from now aliens will dig it up and say, what the heck are these funny things, what do you think they used them for?"

"Hey, time traveler," she said. "Are you okay?"

"I don't know, maybe we just need a break."

Miller was suddenly cold. "You mean from each other?"

"Jesus, Miller, don't even say that. It's the last thing in the world I'd mean. Look at us, we're standing here in the rain and we hardly even notice it anymore. That's what I'm talking about. It has fucking got to stop raining."

"Well, until it does there are always the tide pools." The receding full moon tide had once again uncovered them, filled to the brim with whelks, crabs, mussels, clams and dozens of thick old moon shells.

"This is where you got your antenna guy," he said.

"At least I check now, and don't have to go running back and dump them somewhere they didn't want to be."

"Even though he was just a snail, I'm sure he was grateful."

They both bent down in the rain and began to gather shells. Out on the tidal flats, a group of gulls carried on far outside their normal range of frenzy, screeching and keening in loud, plaintive calls. An unidentifiable object in their midst seemed to be driving them beyond control.

"Don't look now," Eli said, "but the gulls are moving in on us."

The gulls had for some reason brought their high-pitched battle closer and were now within arm's reach. They tilted their heads back and shrieked, scolding each other forcefully, then flapped their wide wings and hopped around in consternation.

"Goofy birds," Miller said. "So strange, they've got the whole beach."

"Maybe we've both been out here too long." Eli rested on his haunches, creating ripples in the water around a confused hermit crab.

"They think we're gulls?"

"If they do, our next meal should be the french fries dropped in the parking lot at Burger King."

"People would talk," she said.

"They would, so let's just stay out here."

Though it wasn't ever their way, Eli held out his hand. After only a moment's hesitation, she took it. They wandered through the tide wrack, followed the hawk, stalked the terns, investigated the crumbling sand cliffs, then sat on a log, still hand in hand, to watch as the rain let up just long enough for the low-slanting sun to dramatically light up the clouds and turn the silver flats into a flowing river of molten fire.

"Then this happens," Eli said.

"And it makes everything okay."

"Go ahead, rain some more," he said. "We can take it."

chapter 39

THE MAIL LADIES beamed at their favorite bartender, casting suspicious looks at Miller at the same time.

"Happy Birthday!" they said in unison.

"*What?*" Miller said, staring at him. "It's your *birthday?*"

Eli turned away. "Oh, shit," he said, and then turned back to face the mail ladies. "Uh oh, it's out. You guys, how do you do it?"

"Grandma, right? Recognized her handwriting. From back there in New Jersey. Hope she sent you something nice."

"And be sure to have a drink on us," the other one said.

"Will do," he said and hurried Miller back out of the post office.

"Talk about having a thing for someone," she said.

"They're amazing women," he said. "Just a little dangerous."

"But I think there's something you forgot to tell me. And this is a big one."

"That's one of the seven thousand reasons I purposely didn't tell you."

Eli tore open the bulky mailer. "Wow," he said. "Now *she* would survive. She still knits and she can't really even see anymore."

"It's a scarf?" Miller said. She took in the long length of soft gray wool. "It's beautiful. And exactly the color of your eyes."

He reached in, pulled out another length of scarf of the same soft wool in lavender and held it out to her. "I'm pretty sure this one's for you. I wondered. She asked what your favorite color was and all I could think of was your mother's lavender."

Miller closed her eyes for a moment. "I can't believe she did that. You have to give me her address so I can thank her," she said. She hesitated. "Unless it's not okay?"

"I've told her everything about you," he said. "It's more than okay."

What was everything, she wondered.

"Now that we all know, how do you want to celebrate?" she said. "Whatever you want, I'm here to make it happen. That's what birthdays are all about."

"You're going to regret this. I confess I had thought about it, just in case. And you know what I'd like?"

"Now I'm afraid to ask."

They'd crossed the street and were in the wine aisle of the Corner Market. Miller had been thinking expensive champagne, an elaborate candlelight dinner.

"All those vans and campers that have been going out there more and more often on the north beach?" Eli said.

"Yes?" She was suddenly wary. "What about them?"

"That's what I want to do. I want to sleep on the beach. Only once, just one night."

"By yourself, I assume. Because there's nothing but sand out there. And people you don't know. And dark. And I have never gone camping in my life. And there's a reason for that."

"Uh, not by myself." He reached for a bottle. "Here, we'll have some good wine, cook dinner over a fire."

"Do you even know how to cook dinner over a fire?"

"No, but I have a feeling you do."

"Why didn't you just say you couldn't tell me? That would have been so much kinder."

"And do you really think that would've worked?"

"No."

"So there you are."

"Fuck," she said.

He laughed. "I think that was supposed to be Happy Birthday."

"You have to go away for the entire afternoon," she said.

"Like where?"

"Anywhere, I don't care, you just can't stay here. I'm busy."

"This is why I didn't want you to find out."

"We're done with that. Go."
"Let me help."
"You're joking, right? That's not the way it works."
"Please?"
"Eli," she said. "Goodbye."
"Will I regret this?"
"Absolutely, every minute of it. Anything else? Good, then disappear."

When Miller had ever cooked on an open fire on the beach, there'd been a grate. She dug around in the garage until she found one, aware as she did that everything was still in there, all she would need. Cookbooks weren't a premium in Hugh's collection, particularly those concerned with survival, so she had to sit down and think, bring back memories, ideas. From there it was simple. All the food that was required could be found at the market.

"Now you can help me," she said when Eli returned late in the afternoon. "I need to load all of this in the Jeep."

"Even the king-size blankets? The quilts? All those pillows?"

"Everything. Has it not been mentioned that there's no bed out there?"

"Yes, but..."

"All of it."

"Okay, then what?"

"Then nothing. We're ready."

"You're serious," he said.

"I am so serious. We are doing this."

"Willingly? I'm worried. Is your heart really in it?"

Miller regarded him across a mountain of bedding. "It's you. So yes, my heart is in it, and if there are serial killers out there, I'm expecting you to have a plan."

"Oh my God. But you know what I'll bet you forgot?"

"If you say the wrong thing, you are in for a world of hurt."

"The brandy. When someone's gone to this much trouble, they deserve the best."

"You're right, I do. Bring it."

On the weekdays, the north beach still held only a reasonable amount of campers and vans, canopies already set up, chairs out, fires started.

"How far do you want to go?" Eli said.

"Do you think we can call 911 from out here? Far enough so that we can still see those people, but we can't hear them. Here's good," she said finally.

"Backed up into the dunes? Or on the flats?"

"Only backed up a little way." Miller had it all pictured in her mind, just not with any of it working out particularly well.

"You have misgivings," he said.

"Misgivings doesn't begin to describe it. We'll just see how it goes."

"What should I do?"

"Find a sheltered place up in the dunes and lay out all the bedding. Just leave one quilt here. Then open the wine?"

"Jesus Christ, you have a trench shovel?" he said. "Give me that. No way I'm letting you dig a fire pit. It never even occurred to me that's what you'd want to do."

"Vacations, summer house, it all came back to me."

"I picked the right woman to sleep on the beach with."

Miller looked up. "Don't get ahead of yourself," she said.

When the hole was dug, Eli stood back. "What keeps the sand from collapsing? You have rocks, too?"

"To keep the sand from collapsing. Then we fill in with the wood."

"And I suppose you have kindling and matches and all the rest of it."

"I suppose I do."

"And beach chairs and a table in a bag and what are these, actual plates?"

"I hadn't looked in that garage for years. Obviously, neither had anyone else."

"You've got hors d'oeuvres," he said. He poured the wine. The sun was edging down the sky. They let the fire bank down to

235

glowing coals and sat close, their feet stretched out in the sand, taking in the blue endless ocean.

"Not so bad," she said. She held up her glass. "Here's to you. Happy Birthday."

"Here's to you and me. Thank you."

"You're welcome," she said, and then was silent, sipping her wine. His birthday, but the wine was cold and dry and white. He'd chosen it for her.

"Hungry?" she said.

"Mellow. It's a beautiful night." The sun had slipped out of sight, leaving the sky in fiery hues.

"It is. We're lucky." She retrieved a cooler from the Jeep and laid out the contents on the grate, sliced bread slathered with butter and garlic, long skewers, some filled with shrimp and sausage, others with vegetables. "This will be quick." He only watched as she bent down to tend the fire, keeping a close eye, turning the skewers carefully.

"Girl Scout, my ass. You're Ina Garten and Davy Crockett all wrapped up in one, or Daniel Boone, one of those guys anyway who could survive out in the wilderness."

"Do you know how hard it is to catch a sausage? Or a shrimp that's already on ice at the fish counter?"

"Still. Pretty damn impressive."

They ate with their fingers, grease and napkins everywhere. When they were done, she brought out the tiny chocolate cake with six candles on it.

"Wish five times."

"I only have to wish once," he said, and she knew not to ask.

They wrapped themselves in blankets as night fell and the temperature dropped, keeping warm with brandy while the dying embers continued to glow softly.

"I want to see the stars," Eli said. The ragged clouds along the horizon had fled, leaving a black night sky filled with planets and galaxies.

Miller removed the grate and they kicked sand back into the fire pit, extinguishing the last coals. She turned both of the low beach chairs over so that they could be used as head rests and they lay down side by side, still wrapped in the blankets, the brandy glasses set carefully in the sand.

"It's a test," Eli said. "What constellations do you know?"

"Orion, that's it, and it's gone for the summer."

"The Big Dipper's the only one I know," he said.

"But the rest of it? So beautiful. What is it all?" she said.

"Places far, far away."

"Makes you feel small."

"We are small. Look." He pointed. "Out there? It's moving."

"Not a shooting star. It's going too slow. What is that?"

"There's only one thing it can possibly be."

"A satellite?"

"*Ground control to Major Tom*," he sang. "And we're the only ones here to see it."

"You're crazy," she said.

"*I miss the earth so much, I miss my wife...*"

"And now you're mixing up David Bowie and Elton John, which probably no one should ever do."

"*It's lonely out in space...*"

"It's lonely here with someone who's in dreamland."

"Is it?"

"No."

"I could stay out here with you forever," Eli said. "It's the perfect birthday, exactly what I wanted. Thank you again."

"You're welcome again. Then are you sure we have to sleep out here?"

"That'll be the best part. When was the last time you slept outside?"

"Let me see," she said. "Never."

"And right by the ocean? How can you beat that?"

"How many ways do you want? No, I won't do that to you The problem is the sand, so I've thought it through. We'll wrap up in that last quilt together and that way it won't have any sand in it."

"This I want to see," he said.

"I know it isn't romantic, but before we go through with this, I'm taking off my pants."

She glanced up at the sound of him choking.

"It may not be romantic, but it's a whole lot of other things. In solidarity with you, I'm taking off my pants, too."

Winding the acre of down around them was a trick, and getting both of them to the ground without injury was another trick. Then the task was accomplished and they were lying warm and secure over a thick pile of bedding hidden among the dunes with nothing but the night sky above them and out in the distance, the constant drumroll of the waves.

"Here's what I wanted most of all," Eli said. Turning to her, he took her face in his hands and kissed her. Miller ran her hands over his close-cropped head and strongly down along his back as she returned each kiss, never tiring of the taste of him, of his mouth on hers. They took their time, being careful with each other, wanting every moment to last. She kissed his closed eyes, the curve of his throat, inhaling Calvin amber along with his sweat, the familiar intoxicating smell of him. He pressed his face into her neck, his hands seeking all the hidden places he loved, where her response always moved him. They settled into deeper, longer kisses, giving each other joy that kept building. Cautiously they shifted, finding an equally slow rhythm, coming together only by degrees, tenderly, completely attuned to each other. "Now," she whispered, tightening her hold, meeting him at every turn, both of them trying to muffle the sounds that traveled through the night air as the stars blurred and quietly exploded.

"This," he said softly afterwards, holding her close. Lost in everything about him, she could only nod in wordless agreement.

chapter 40

ELI STOOD IN THE dark beside the silver Prius, waiting.
"Whatever you decide is fine with me," he said. "No pressure."
"I'm giving in," she said. "You drive."
"Good choice. Is the key somewhere so this thing turns on?"
"I've got it."
"When it's already two hours just to the freaking airport, it'll feel like it takes forever to get there," he said. "That's one good thing."
"Out of so many that aren't."
They stowed their bags in the back. As the car rolled through the still sleeping town, a faint light was just beginning to color the eastern sky underneath a bank of storm clouds.
Miller was glad she'd let him drive. She wished just this part of the trip would take forever, remembering coming out on these roads with her mother, the winding two lanes, the small towns, the rain and endless deep green shadows. But they weren't even out of Oceanview yet.
"Coffee," Eli said. "Quick stop." He ran in and came back with a large black for himself, a latte for her.
"How you can do that and not get jittery, I will never understand," she said.
"Not jittery. It gets me psyched, keeps me stoked."
"Just what anyone needs before getting on an airplane."
"That and the men's room."
Miller stared out into the darkness. "You know what that was?" she said, glancing quickly back over her shoulder. "The junction with Route 53."
"Where the garden lady has all those elk on her lawn."
"Right."
"I just hope they stay on her lawn. Looking at what one elk did to you, no one wants to imagine thirty."

"Why don't they spread the word, warn each other not to go out there on the road? I read somewhere that even sand dollars can manage that much."

"I don't think it works that way in elk land. Did you see, they were all on the Little League field the other day. Hope the season doesn't start for a while, they were settling in."

"I'm happy to have missed that. Deer," she said, nodding out the window again. There were four, grazing in a wet field.

"See, there's the difference. They're smarter. You wouldn't ever find a whole herd of deer in a Little League field."

"Wild turkeys," Miller said farther down the road.

"Or wild turkeys either."

They had two hours to do nothing but talk. He had his views, she had hers, and the two were often so wildly opposed that they laughed, and there was the saving grace, Miller thought, always, the ability to laugh. She remembered the women she'd been friends with in college, the ones already looking for Mr. Right. That was the first test, how long you could talk without ever getting bored or running out of things to say. A mere infatuation couldn't hold up, wouldn't make it, wouldn't last. Two hours? Radio on, now.

Instead, she considered that for the two of them it had become the ever more tightly woven fabric of their life together, a shared conversation spanning a divide but also constantly illuminating the odd ways in which they were alike. Which sent her reluctantly back to Jane. Did her mother and Luca have the same intimate ongoing conversation, one that spanned a fifty-year divide? Had her mother ever had that with Miller's father? Miller conceded that maybe Luca was right. The truth should stay where it was, hidden far away.

As they were coming through the outskirts of Portland with the rain pouring down again, Miller's phone went off. It was a text from JC. Since Miller made it a practice to always keep her children informed, JC knew where she was going and why. The text, however, was part of the numbing, unrelenting drumbeat of the last few weeks. Miller knew she couldn't lie to JC about the situation, ever. She just chose not to expand on it for any reason.

Shouldn't she have the same right to privacy as they all did? Even though they might be just as curious, Dell and Sam would never go near such a line of questioning. Miller had been told that with three there was always a difficult one, usually the poor ignored middle child. She had to shake her head. JC couldn't ever be ignored, it was impossible, but if proof were needed of the difficult aspect, it was staring at her from her phone.
Are you there? the text said.
Just getting to the airport, hours to go yet, Miller answered.
Are you alone?
Long pause.
No.
Longer pause on JC's part. They were in the parking garage, retrieving their bags, locking the car.
Time is UP! You HAVE to send a photo!
Miller made a small strangling noise.
"That doesn't sound good," Eli said.
She showed him her phone. He let his eyes rest on her but made no comment.
"I can hear what you're thinking," she said. "Just go ahead and do it. But why should I have to? This is my life, not hers."
"She's been through hell. You've been through hell. She's talked to me on the phone. I'm not some total stranger. She's aware that I was in the hospital with you. Would it hurt? But you know what, just ignore me. I should stay out of it."
"I hate giving in. As a parent, you feel like you're losing something you fought hard for."
"I wish my mom had fought that hard for me, for any reason."
"All right," she said. "This is stupid and I don't want to have to deal with it anymore. Move over, you're in the wrong light."
"I could put on my shades. Or a hat. Or throw my jacket over my head."
"It would help if you could suddenly have gray hair."
"Scare me," he said. There was the smile.
"Never mind. Just do what you're going to do."
"Stand here, that's all I had planned."

Miller took the photo. It was him, being himself. There was nothing else for it. She pressed send and turned off her phone.

The airport was culture shock, loudspeakers, announcements, noise, lines, x-ray machines, security guards, hundreds of people taking off their shoes, stripping off their belts, pulling out their wallets and laptops. No elk or eagles anywhere in sight.

Miller had wondered what would happen when they ventured out of their own small private world and into the real one. Nothing happened. They were the same, observing this chaos from identical perspectives, behaving as they always did toward each other, not changed in the least. The realization took her by surprise.

"It makes you think about your socks," Eli said.

"And jewelry." They both watched the young woman in front of them frantically divesting herself of armfuls of bracelets, a necklace, hair clips, even toe rings. "Or not."

"It's like being in someone's bedroom," Miller said on the other side of the screening when everyone got dressed again.

"It's nuts. But the happy news is, there's a McDonald's. Breakfast?"

"Go for it."

"Come on. Isn't it in all those travel books? For the full experience, eat what the locals eat?"

"I don't think the airport's what they meant."

"Junk food is good, keeps you going."

An hour early for the flight, they ate at McDonald's. Miller admitted that fat and grease and salt did offer a regrettable satisfaction. Then they went to the bookstore.

"Another travel rule," Eli said. "Always have a book good enough that you forget you're on a plane. Trains, you want to be there. Planes, not so much."

Miller opened her backpack. "Agreed. Got it."

"I can't believe you're still reading that. You cry every night."

"It's sad, but really good. I'm almost finished."

"Really good means different things to different people, but if you're almost finished, I'll buy you a new one."

"Then I'll buy you one."

"It's not normal that we do this, you know that, don't you?" he said. "Found mine." He showed it to her, the latest John Sandford paperback in the Virgil Flowers series.

"That was too fast," she said. She came back and showed him the one she'd chosen.

"Rise and fall of the Comanches? Just a little light reading. If it's really a bestseller and as riveting as the book jacket says, maybe I should read it when you're done."

"We'll switch," she said.

"Good. You'll like Virgil Flowers. He's a woman's kind of guy."

On the plane, Eli took the aisle. Miller had the middle. They'd agreed on that because he cared and she didn't. A woman in a business suit wedged herself in next to the window.

"First out and I take you with me," he said to Miller.

"Are you that nervous a flyer?"

"It's not that. I just want it to be over with before it even starts. What do you think, Bloody Marys?"

"It's Monday," she said. "Ten-thirty in the morning."

"And your point is? That's what they're best for, brunch."

"Sorry, I refuse to classify anything at McDonald's as brunch."

They had Bloody Marys. Miller sensed the woman next to her watching them closely. I'd watch us closely too and have a lot of questions, she thought. Which reminded her about JC. She turned her phone back on and handed it to Eli without looking at it.

"Be afraid," she said.

"That's your parenting motto?"

"For this it is."

He read the text, blew out a long breath and handed it back.

"Shit, life's tough sometimes," he said.

Miller prepared herself.

Wow! But thanks for doing that Mom, it was important. We're all okay with him no matter what's going on. We just want to know, is he going to meet Dad?

This was the other JC, tender, vulnerable, the one Miller embraced even when it was the other one who showed up. Because that's what mothers did.

"Goddammit," she said. He could do it to her. That was between a husband and wife. But had he ever taken even one minute's time to consider what he was doing to them?

She had to get the "*wow!*" out of her mind. Eli rested his hand on her thigh. The woman in the suit typed faster on her laptop. Try living my life, Miller wanted to say, and you can't just take the good. She wanted to tell the woman how that hand on her leg was the only thing keeping her from flying out into the void.

They'd managed it, read, skipped the snacks, who needed them after brunch and drinks, and the plane was descending. The window offered a view of nothing even remotely gray, only brilliant blue in every direction, a few white clouds sailing by.

"Sun, such an odd concept," Eli said.

They walked through the terminal, the light pouring in, sandals and shorts a uniform. Outside, it hit them.

"This is insane, it's blinding," Eli said, shades immediately on. "And not only sun but palm trees. I knew paradise had to be somewhere. I want to lie down right here on the sidewalk."

"Maybe reserve that opinion," Miller said. "And if you lie down, I guarantee you someone will walk right over you."

They entered a cab in the line of cabs that were waiting. The sun continued to shine, no threatening storm front moving in, no hail or fog appearing out of nowhere, a miracle. Miller gave the name of a hotel.

"Pacific Coast Highway and turn right, heading north," she said.

"No problem," the driver said.

"The matte black, I see what you mean," Eli said. "And this is me, from New York City, but they drive like maniacs, only in a casual laid-back kind of way."

That about summed it up, Miller thought, loose, one wrist draped over the wheel, but fast-shift those lanes and run those lights anyway. She could feel the knots beginning in her stomach.

They came down the last hill and there was the ocean.

"Spectacular," Eli said. "It's exactly like what you'd think, the same as every dream anyone ever had about this place."

Miller felt that way, too. No matter how aggravating it could be, too many cars and people on one hand, too many earthquakes and wildfires on the other, it was still California.

The hotel was across the highway from the beach, a modest four floors, the top floor providing a view between houses of the ocean, the thrumming all-night noise of PCH providing a soothing background for sleep. Miller had only agreed to all of this if the bill was settled after the fact, the identity of the hotel remaining unknown. Lawyers present at all times. That was the deal. Not that he would come looking for her, try to meet her alone anyway. He wouldn't. Still, she would protect her space and her privacy with everything she had.

"The Harleys kill me," Eli said, standing at the sliding glass and watching the street. He glanced back into the room at the wide bed with its cornered duvet and bank of crisp white pillows.

"We could..."

"The sun's not going to be there forever."

"Half an hour."

"I have to show you everything, that was our bargain, and there's only so much time."

"Miller, I never needed a bargain to come with you. I couldn't have lived with you trying to do this alone. But if you change your mind..."

Out on the corner waiting for the light to turn, Eli was still considering the traffic. "It's the Harleys first, and then all these guys in spandex on bicycles, and then a matte black Lexus, a handful of normal cars, an old VW bus, something with fins from 1957, more Harleys." And then they were on the beach.

"Holy shit," Eli said. Miller had to agree. It was impressive. The beach went on as far as the eye could see, broad, white, clean, huge, backed by an endless row of low-slung expensive houses, all glass fronts, porches and decks, their patios right there on the sand, their view far off in the distance nothing but sky and ocean.

Eli immediately took off his shoes and Miller did the same.

"We can leave them here," she said, dumping hers in the sand. "Beach rules."

"I always wanted to go through an airport barefoot," he said, dropping his next to hers.

The scattering of people on the beach were easily outnumbered by the surfers who came running across the sand with their boards, tugging at the back zippers of their wet suits, wading into the surf, paddling out to the waves.

"Who are these guys on a Monday afternoon?" he said.

"Don't know. The same maybe as the people drinking on a plane at ten-thirty in the morning. Whatever life style suits your tastes."

"This one suits mine."

They walked for hours, in the water, along the flats as the tide ebbed, over the occasional black rock groin, almost to where the shops began then back again, the sun in their face, the waves turning over, the surfers in black sitting on their boards out beyond the break.

"And here's volleyball," he said. It was teenagers with a cooler set up to one side. "Who *are* these people?"

In the alleyway behind the beachfront homes, instead of going across the street to the hotel, Miller turned left. She stopped in front of a low dark cedar shake cottage.

"How are you doing?" she said.

"Me? I'm in heaven. Why?"

"Since there really is so little time, if you're game, we should cram it all in."

"Take me to it."

She slid open the cover on a keypad, entered a code and the garage door silently raised.

"I guess I need a little more than take me to it," he said.

"This is my friend Rudy's house. He's not here, he lives in the city and only comes down on weekends. My friend Rudy from forever. Captain of the volleyball team. The one who told them to let me play."

"A stand-up guy then."

"The best. And no, I didn't sleep with him."

"I promise I wasn't going to ask. Though I am still wondering about who the half was in three and a half."

"Will you please forget about that? So for starters, here's a way to get to dinner. That's what I meant by being game. But we can also take the car." A gray Audi occupied the narrow alley space next to the front door.

"No need for the car, this is great," he said, taking in the assortment of fat-tired, wide-handled bikes.

"Beach cruisers. But first, there's something else." She went through the door that led from the garage into the house. "We could have stayed here but I'm not good at taking people up on offers like that. Rudy's aware of you, though, and he wanted me to give you this."

She crossed the small living room to the kitchen breakfast bar while Eli looked around. Art of every kind filled all the walls and every available extra space, all of it strikingly contemporary and highly unusual.

"Wow," he said. "This is some amazing stuff."

"Yes. I know." Miller took a business card off the refrigerator and handed it to him.

"What's this?" In a handwritten scrawl along the edge it read: *To Eli. Call me.*

"Rudy's wife. Talia Sherman. She owns what Rudy says is one of the hottest galleries in L.A. I'm not very familiar with that world, but I do know that every time you turn around somebody's writing something great about her. She's there. It's a contact, an introduction. What you feel like doing with it is totally up to you."

He ran his fingers over the card. "Miller, thanks," he said, his voice gone soft.

She let her eyes rest on him. "Anytime," she said.

"Pick your ride," she said in the garage. "You won't have a problem, but the first time I tried this outside of being a twelve-year-old, I ran into a parked car and almost took out a woman on roller blades. For me it was getting used to those handle bars, like steering a boat or something."

She closed the garage door behind them. "Can you just hold on a minute till I go back to the hotel and get my bag?"

"That huge thing with everything in it needed for a nuclear winter? Credit card in back pocket, right here," he said. "No I can't, sorry."

"We're going to fight all the way through this, aren't we?"

"Yes, we are. If it came easy, what fun would that be?"

The bike lanes paralleled the one-way street that ran along the houses facing PCH. It was better to introduce him to this at a quieter time of day, before the late afternoon rush started. Naturally, Eli had no trouble. She considered that guys held onto the twelve-year-old forever while women were already hurrying up, on the fast track to whatever completely important adult things came next.

"It's not bad," she said, "twenty minutes maybe, down to the end of this, then out into the streets, through a couple of intersections that are a little scary, and that's it."

They could ride side by side until a bike or runner came the other way. Eli glanced quickly back to a car parked along the curb. Behind it, a half-naked surfer was pulling on his pants underneath the beach towel wrapped around his waist. Farther down, there was another one doing the same thing, and then another.

"Is there a fail rate for that maneuver?" he said.

"Not that I've ever seen. Seems like a talent peculiar to surfers, the first thing they learn. The next thing is to hide their car keys in the wheel well, they all do it exactly the same way."

"Why isn't everybody's car stolen?"

"Good question for which I do not have an answer."

The one-way road became two-way then dumped them out into a maze of streets.

"Stay close," Miller said, rising up off the seat and stepping on the pedals. "We'll do it fast."

In no time they were skidding to a halt in a restaurant lot with car parking and bike parking. Inside, Miller led the way upstairs to a dimly lit cavern filled with cocktail tables and small sofa arrangements.

"Yes," Eli said, taking in the long curved bar with water in changing neon colors pouring down the wall behind it.

"I know your heart's there but while there's still time to grab a table, let's sit by the window."

"Ah, I see." The wide windows showed a sun-lit harbor full of large and very impressive boats. He scanned the bar menu. "Happy hour. Oysters."

They ate their fill and then ordered more food to go for when nine-thirty came around and they were starving. Miller put the containers in her bike basket. On the way back to Rudy's, they stopped to buy wine. They locked the bikes back in the garage, crossed the street, climbed the carpeted stairs, opened the door. A breeze blew through the sliding glass as the light faded away. The night was theirs.

Miller came out of the bathroom in only her bikini underwear, all long legs and tumbling hair.

Eli was sitting on the leather loveseat, his bare feet up on the ottoman, remote in hand, cable-surfing. He looked up. He stood, clicked off the TV and pulled his shirt up over his head as he reached for her.

chapter 41

THEY ROSE WITH the sun and put on their running gear. It was Miller's first time running outside in, she had to think, almost a year. She was energized, alive despite the knots.

"Beach?" Eli said.

"How are you on pavement?"

"Doesn't matter to me." He was stationed in his favorite place, at the sliding glass.

"Then we should go the same way we biked yesterday. It'll be different this morning."

"Why do people keep pulling up into that side street facing the beach?" he said. "What are they doing?"

"Surfers. They're watching to see if the waves are any good."

"The garbage guy? He just got out of his truck and he's standing on top of one of those posts."

"Better vantage point."

"This is a whole different world."

"Yes, it is."

And he hadn't seen the half of it yet, she thought. Mornings before work on a weekday she knew the bike lanes would be filled with joggers, runners, bikers, skaters, dog walkers. Across the way on PCH, the hordes of serious bicyclists had their own much faster lanes.

"Is everyone here a health freak?" he said.

"Just looks like it because it's possible to be outside so much of the time. Go over to the deli sandwich place on the corner, you'll find people who haven't moved off their stool for a week because they can't."

Eli turned around again as a helmeted young woman wearing a suit and heels went by on a motor scooter accessorized with a surfboard hung out on a rack.

"That's you, Miller."

"That'll be the day. Six miles give or take, is that good?"

"It's good. Your pace is better outdoors, not quite so insane."

"I always told you I was a basket case, but I should have warned you about how I dealt with it."

"I'm proud to say that I survived."

They fell into matching strides, the pace loose and comfortable.

"Why did you pick here, this town?" he said.

"Because I was familiar with it from Rudy, and also I used to do training sessions at our gyms up here."

"How far away is it from home?"

"Hour and a half," she said. "Funny, at first I thought this would be the place I'd escape to, the distance seemed like enough. Turned out I was wrong by about a thousand miles."

"Thank God for that."

At the end of the run, with the sun just reaching the rooftops, they purchased breakfast burritos from the corner taqueria. Miller reached down into her t-shirt and pulled out damp money.

"I'll bet that was comfortable," Eli said. In the hotel, he gathered enough single serves from the maid's cart to keep him charged up by means of the coffee machine in the room.

"Actually, pretty good coffee," he said, standing at the sliding glass again. "Now it's the mail guy checking out the waves."

They took a shower together, one of the dangers, Miller had already realized, of a hotel room. Though they weren't on a vacation, furthest thing from it, still the sense of freedom was there, being cut loose from all the normal routines of daily life. And for them, this was immediately part of what it meant. She stretched out luxuriously in the bed, her skin still warm from the steam, her senses full of him.

He stood with one towel wrapped around his waist, rubbing his head with a second towel.

"What's on for today?" he said.

"More beach. Biking down the esplanade. Maybe, if we can make it, all the way down to the best shore break there is."

"It's still early though, right? No need to get going five minutes from now."

"No need at all," she said. "Why? What are you thinking? Is this about Kelly Ripa again?"

"Wounded. Arrow to the heart. Has nothing to do with Kelly Ripa. No, it's this woman who makes me crazy."

"Didn't we just...?"

"Personally, I'm not keeping track. Are you keeping track? I'm dropping the towel. Do you have a problem with that?"

"I do have a problem with that," she said, laughing.

"I don't think you're telling the truth," he said. "So too bad."

They biked down the esplanade, the broad smooth concrete walk that fronted the beach houses closer to town. The decks and patios went by fast with only glimpses of sun-lit living space, white furniture, bars and grills and sleek kitchens.

"You can see right in their houses," Eli said, maneuvering around all the pedestrians and baby strollers.

"They don't seem to care," Miller said. "Maybe they want you to, so you'll understand just how lucky they are."

They continued the journey all the way down through the quiet streets backing the beach till they came to the huge seawall at the end. All afternoon they sat on the beach in a crowd and watched. The break was alive, the waves big and steep, the surfers in their wetsuits shooting down the faces, tipping up over the curls, now and then riding through a long foaming trough.

"The rocks are right there," Eli said.

"When it's like this, only the strongest ones go out. Anyone else would be a fool, you have to know what you're doing."

"The houses behind us," he said. "Has to be big bucks."

"That's the good and bad of a place like this. Down at this end especially it's like they live in a bubble, this perfect world, a beautiful beach, the ocean, all anyone could ever want. Ask them how the other half lives and they have no idea."

"But all you really need is a bike and a board."

"True," she said. "Maybe those guys are the lucky ones."

"And a dog. If I lived here, I'd want to have a dog." He paused, sifting sand through his hands. "Maybe someday we'll have a dog."

Miller looked at him then had to look away.

"One we'd get from the shelter," he said, "and we'd see him right away, we'd both pick the same one. What we'd fight over would be the name. But you know what name we'd end up agreeing on because it's perfect? Winslow. For the nowhere town in Oregon. Yep, that's his name."

Miller concentrated on breathing.

The next day, Miller took out Rudy's blanket and chairs and they spent the whole day on the beach, reading, sleeping in the sun, watching the waves, the gulls, the lines of pelicans winging by, the surfers.

"Why do they run?" Eli said.

"I don't know. They all do it. Maybe they just can't wait to get in the water."

"What are they putting on their boards?"

"Wax. Gives your feet a surface to grip."

"California? This? Right here?" he said. "Perfect."

She put down her book. "I've got something for you. I wanted to give it to you now before everything else goes down and I forget." She pulled a t-shirt out of her beach bag.

"Another friend from school lives here too, has his own surf clothing line," she said. "These shirts are his logo, everyone around here seems to have a whole wardrobe of them. Rudy's a finance guy, but I swear it's all I ever see him wear."

It was a gray t-shirt with a black and white cartoon depiction of a pigeon above the words *Mucho Aloha*.

Eli took off his t-shirt and put on the new one. "Love it. Now I owe you. Because that's the deal, remember?" He let his eyes rest on her. "Do they know, these friends of yours?"

"About what happened? Everyone knows. The trouble is, they were friends of his, too. Good friends."

"What's their take on it?"

"I don't talk about it with them, it's too hard. They've just made it clear that they're always there for me."

"You never say his name."

"For a long time I couldn't. It's Mitch. Mitchell Briggs."

Eli was quiet.

"Are you in touch with his family?" he said.

"I love them and they called, they tried, but I was so humiliated I wanted to die, so there wasn't much anybody could say. Maybe someday we'll be able to talk, but I can't see that far into the future."

"Okay, sorry," he said. "We don't have to go there anymore."

She waited, working through her emotions. "You know what I want to do tonight?" she said. "Since I guarantee you I won't be able to do anything else?"

"I appreciate the heads up, that's important. What?"

"I want to ask about your tattoos."

He rolled up his other t-shirt to put back in her bag. "Why haven't you ever done that before?"

"I think I was afraid to see that part of you."

"Boy with troubled past who inks up instead of doing drugs or starting fires. That's all it is."

"Inks up fairly loud and proud."

"It's like what you said about the gulls. If you're going to be one, then fuck it, go ahead and be one."

They lingered over seafood and local beer at a small restaurant they'd walked to from the hotel.

"We haven't been in a car once," he said. "I like that."

"Tomorrow the car's required."

"What tomorrow? There is no such thing."

They opened a bottle of wine in the room and sat on the small sofa, feet up, the traffic a constant background noise. The tattoos were a complex variety of images, birds, dragons, snakes, orchids, almost obscuring three lines of tiny elaborate script that she hadn't ever wanted to try and decipher before. She read them now with some difficulty, moving her hand down his arm. *In discord, find harmony. In conflict, find peace. In darkness, find light.*

"That's pretty heavy," Miller said. "How old were you?"

"Legally you were supposed to be eighteen, but I started in the black market at sixteen through a friend. In that regard, I'm lucky nothing bad happened."

"It all means a lot to you, it must."

"It did then, definitely. Now I'm just used to it, I don't think about it."

"You never check out the mirror to get inspiration for the day?" she said.

"Uh, no. But you carry it all with you, it's part of who you are and that's as powerful now as when I was a teenager and things were so messed up."

"They still were even by then?"

"Resentments, anger, belligerence. It finally all went away, but I'm always glad I have reminders. You skipped the first question everyone asks."

"Did it hurt?"

"Plain and simple, yes, but not so much like getting stuck with a needle, more like a laser kind of thing. It burns."

"You were a kid," she said. "Did you cry?"

"No, but the first time on the inner arm, I passed out."

"Jesus, Eli. What did your parents say?"

"Honestly, for a long time I managed to keep it from them, I mean my dad and Rebecca, though they wondered about my new bathrobe. And then when they did find out, it was too late. My dad was pissed as hell, but Rebecca's pretty calm about things like that. It's just their other three were watched a little more closely and never had a chance." He started to run his thumb over her palm, but remembered and stopped.

"So that's it, now everything's out there," he said.

"In this life." The knots in her stomach were tightening.

"For now, this life's the only one that counts." He kissed her knuckles and put her hand back down.

They watched one of the Bourne movies on cable then turned out the lights and got into bed.

"Things all right?' he said.

"Not really."

"Turn over." He bent his knees against the back of hers and closed his arms around her. She lay awake, feeling his warmth and the calm steady beating of his heart.

chapter 42

ELI WENT DOWN to the hotel's continental breakfast and brought back six of everything, waffles, pastries, fruit, juice and another mountain of single serves hijacked from the maid's cart, covering the ottoman with food.

The meeting was at eleven. Miller made it through breakfast, through taking a shower, brushing out her hair, packing up. At ten-fifteen, she could feel the bitter taste rising, the color draining from her face.

"Forget it," she said.

Then she was on her knees in the bathroom, everything coming back up, her stomach in full reject mode, the knots like a tourniquet. When it was finished, she sat back against the tub, grateful for the cold washcloth he held out to her.

"Shit," she said. "The last thing I wanted was to go into this looking half-baked."

"Maybe that's the answer. *Be* half-baked. Why didn't I think of that before? I can probably go out on the street and get it taken care of without much trouble. There's time."

Through the tangle of adrenaline and fear still churning, tightening the damn knots, Miller was eternally glad for his presence. "I want to laugh, but I can't," she said. "I'm afraid I'll throw up again."

When she was able to get up, she rinsed out her mouth, brushed her teeth, swallowed some water and felt stronger. The mirror didn't quite confirm that. She considered that she looked exactly like a woman about to come face to face for the first time in almost a year with the loving husband who had left her for Lauren Metcalf.

"Ready, steady, go," Eli said. "No sweat."

"I think I'm still missing the ready and steady. But sure, no sweat."

They checked out of the hotel and walked across the street to Rudy's cottage.

"What are your thoughts on this?" she said. "If you want, you can stay here, or I can drop you off farther in town where there's more to do and pick you up later on."

"None of that's happening," he said. "I'm driving you there. I'll be with the car waiting for when you get out."

"I don't know how long it'll take."

"I don't care how long it takes."

Eli slid the Audi into the fast-moving local traffic. Miller clenched her hands tightly together. Breathe, she kept telling herself. Her heart was pounding.

"Ferraris," he said, "that's another thing there's lots of here."

"The dealership's right down the street."

"I guess that explains it. In a way. We'll go to the bar at the airport. Think about that. We'll have margaritas."

"And hot dogs," she said.

"If you want hot dogs, we'll get hot dogs."

"I'm still trying to get past the idea of being half-baked."

"That would have been a challenge, to see if I could score that fast."

"You're used to doing that?"

"Look at me, Miller. We live together. Do I go out cruising for weed, ever? Again, it's those younger years. And the memories of the lovingly stoned mom."

"But it's useful sometimes?"

"I'm about to pull over the car. Have you never smoked dope?"

"Athlete, hello. Sheltered, stupid, whatever. No, I haven't."

"Grew up in California, went to school in California, a stranger to marijuana. No one would believe it. We could fix that, but it'd be more like corruption at this point, and I wouldn't do that to you. Are you even curious?"

"Actually, I'm not."

"Good. We'll keep it that way."

"But you could find it if you wanted to? Up there?"

"Especially up there. All I'd have to do is turn to the guy standing next to me in the garage."

"Great," she said. "Keep talking to me."

"About that?"

"About anything."

"So he finally kills the buffalo," he said.

"What?"

"The guy in that book I bought way back there. He slogs through the snow and across freezing rivers and gets frostbitten and feverish and lost and then there they are, a line of males, it's in Alaska, remember?, and he's just about at the end of his allotted time and weak and sick and he shoots one. Then he has to skin the damn thing and butcher it and haul it in pieces back across the ice to his campsite and pray the bush pilot remembers to come back for him. And that's how to put food on the table. His version, anyway."

"So it's a guy thing."

"Pretty much. And in the end, sad to say, it's also a dad thing. His dad was one of those tough guys, made him and his brothers hunt as young kids, sit up in trees for hours, stalk game all day, that kind of thing."

"Which translates to, for the hell of it," she said, "or what? the fun of it?, go shoot a loon and leave it in the ditch."

"Shoot a deer and hack off the antlers."

"But what you're saying is, if that had to be dinner, those kinds of guys wouldn't have any idea what to do with it. They'd starve."

"Right. You can't eat the antlers. Well, maybe you could boil them for soup or something."

"Turn in here," Miller said. It was the parking lot of a large hotel with the water and the yachts just beyond. He took one of the spaces at the far end.

"I'm with you when you go in there," he said.

"I know you are," she said and her eyes filled.

"Margaritas, hot dogs." He leaned over and pulled her close. She stayed there as long as she could. Then she had to get out of the car.

When she came back out of the hotel, she was walking straight and tall, dark hair flowing, shoulders squared, face pale, no expression. Eli was leaning against the car, his eyes on her. Behind her, several men exited from the same door. Three continued on. One of them suddenly stopped. He had a cleanly shaved head and was lean and gym-built, deeply tanned, impeccably dressed in a crisp white shirt and expensively draped slacks, a folio case under his arm. As Miller moved across the parking lot, Eli watched the designer sunglasses slowly rise, positioned now on top of the head, the eyes narrowing, staring Eli down.

Miller reached him.

"You okay?" he said.

She nodded. "What are you looking at?" she said. "Is he back there still?'

"White shirt, gray pants?"

"Yes."

"I've got lasers drilling through me."

Miller let out a long breath. Let him, she thought. Who cares. She didn't want to admit to the small brief wave of satisfaction that washed over her. *Fuck you* couldn't help but be a part of it, but that wasn't the purpose. What Eli was to her had nothing to do with any of this and certainly not with him.

"Let's get out of here," she said.

"Consider it done," Eli said, opening the door for her.

Mitchell Briggs was still standing there watching as they drove away.

"Maybe not what he was expecting," Eli said.

"That's his problem."

Eli negotiated through the Ferraris again. "Did it work out the way you wanted it to? Jesus, there's a Maserati."

"It's split into two parts now. The house is separate for six months, the rest moves forward, end date, soon."

"So what happens with the house?"

"He wants the kids to come home and have a chance to think about it. Don't even ask me my opinion on that."

"Think about the house?"

"Think about all of them living there since I refuse."

"All of them meaning her?"

"Don't know, she was never mentioned. If she had been, I would have walked. But it's ridiculous anyway. When Sam comes home, whatever he's going to do, he needs his own place. JC's got another year at least in London. It's only Dell and she's working in Tahoe this summer. So what the hell. He doesn't even get it."

"Six months, though. That's some time."

"I feel like my head's going to explode," she said. "I can't deal with it." She put her face in her hands. "Shit."

"At least this much is over. Miller, what do you say? I could spend the rest of my life here, but for now, let's you and me go back to, where was that place again? Oh yeah, Oregon."

"Back to the rain."

"Maybe the worst part of that's over, too. It has to stop raining sometime, doesn't it? And there's this." He handed her his phone. "Go to photos, choose the last one."

"You are a crazy person," she said. "It's a bird."

"But what bird?"

"I have no idea. A shorebird of some sort, but an odd one. You took that here?"

"While we were out on the beach. For entertainment value later on."

"I can't believe I didn't even see it. That's how screwed up I've been. We'll wait for the margaritas. I don't want to look it up till we can do it together."

He reached out and closed his hand over hers, the pressure warm and strong, welcome. "I love you, Miller," he said.

"I love you, too," she said. She didn't even have to think about it. It was the truth coming from some better place inside her, complicated, yes, but also very real. She allowed herself to exhale, come back to what was good in the world.

chapter 43

IT WAS BRIGHT at the beach, almost balmy. The steady northwest wind had given up its freezing edge and turned merely cool and refreshing. Sun made all the difference.

The sea was stirred and choppy but far from wild, brilliant white on the crests, emerald green in the troughs, staying within its boundaries, behaving. The tide was out so far that it had left sandbars behind, but the tide pools contained no debris, no black wood slivers, no channeled basket shells, no tiny blue and green crabs. The ocean kept its treasures now, hording them in hidden currents and deep cold places, saving them till winter came again.

"Just an old surfboard," Eli said, moving the broken pieces with his foot. "And not even from Japan. There are your favorite birds."

The three terns stood quietly in a row far out on the empty tidal flats.

"Watch," Miller said. She walked toward them, setting off a cascade of raucous, shrill calls. She stepped back and the noise stopped instantly.

"Smartass little guys, not afraid to let you know how they feel."

The northern harrier floated along the dunes. The sanderlings rose in a whirling cloud. A gull stood alone, caught in its change of plumage, half snowy white adult, half mottled brown juvenile. A golden retriever chased a stick. The stick landed and broke in half, offering an unsolvable dilemma. The dog lay down in the sand, guarding both pieces. Two young surfers waited patiently for the right wave, or any wave, in the calmer seas.

"Now that's amazing," Eli said. "With the whole damn beach to choose from, she decides on right there?"

A large blond woman in a black bathing suit bent to rearrange a pile of driftwood as a windbreak. Satisfied with her work, she

carefully laid her towel down and placed herself on the still cold sand directly over the slumbering remains of the sea lion.
She has no idea, Miller thought. But how could she? All this time and even they were still just beginners at learning the ocean's secrets.

In the early evening, the temperature dropped, but the light remained, slanting into the high-ceilinged room, casting shadows along the sectional and reflecting off the slick surface of the breakfast bar.

"We should talk," Eli said.

"I know," Miller said. "Summer's coming up."

"My plans? Move to the Friday/Saturday shift at the bar, it's more money and they're offering. How do you feel about that?" he said. "Sell my motorcycle and buy more of the equipment I need."

"Anything you want to do is fine with me. You'd really sell the bike?"

"That one trip was so much more than I expected in every way you could possibly think of. My motorcycle days are now officially over. Especially since I just don't ever see you going for the role of biker chick, Miller. Correct me if I'm wrong."

"Biker chick. That's all I'd need. And I've already tried to do myself in two other ways, so why go for a third?"

"End of that discussion. You?"

"I'd like to spend time in my grandmother's garden."

"Planting some cactus, right? Excellent idea."

"Try rice or watermelon. No, it's the climbing roses. They're still so beautiful, but now they're everywhere, threatening to take over the back of the house. And the calla lilies need work, too. But there are more serious things."

"I'm not unaware of that," he said. "Go for it."

Miller sighed. There was only one way to do this. "The three of them are planning on driving up here," she said. "I don't know how or when, I haven't asked any questions, neither have they, so far, but I'd expect sooner rather than later since they all have other places to be later on."

"This is where I'd be headed if I were them," he said. "So you're wondering how to handle that. Here's how. Any way you want."

"You don't have thoughts?"

"No thoughts. You're what's important to me so whatever you're comfortable with is the way we'll go. If you need me to disappear, I can do that. No problem."

"I wouldn't ever want you to disappear, and I hate to tell you this, but if JC's involved you won't have that option anyway. She'd hunt you down. Scared?"

"Only a little. But if we lived differently while they were here, or anything, I'd be okay with that. Which brings us full circle." He reached out for her hand.

"Wait a minute, you're making me nervous."

"Just please keep breathing. My dad and Rebecca want to come out, too."

"Yikes," Miller said. She'd forgotten all about that side of things.

"Summer at the beach. We've done the hard part, now all the rest of them can have the good weather, assuming there is such a thing. But just sometime. We'll see how it goes."

"Too much. We can't talk about this anymore."

"Got it," Eli said. He turned on the game.

"Thank you. Who were we going to watch again? And is it really better than *Breaking Bad*?"

"We've been bingeing on *Breaking Bad* and this is one of the Yankees' best season starts, plus Giancarlo Stanton is incredible. It won't be easy, but I promise you will come to appreciate the Yankees. There's so much to love and hate at the same time."

"I kind of fell for Mark Sanchez, so who's this Giancarlo guy?"

"That's not quite what I meant."

Miller glanced down. His phone was lying in the cushions and an odd image caught her eye. "Eli, someone's texting you."

"Maybe it's my drug dealer. It can wait."

"Maybe it's your grandmother."

"That'll be the day. Thank God she doesn't have a cell phone. Makes the world seem a little less crazy."

"I won't say anything else."

"What?" he said. "Okay, if you want, I'll answer it." He picked up his phone. Frowning, he stared at what was on it. Miller closed her eyes. Her reaction had been immediate, searing and intense.

"From bad experience, I know what this is," he said. "I just don't know why."

Miller had to control her voice. "Who's it from?"

"That's the other odd thing. It's from Monica and I haven't heard from her in ..." There it was. "What the fuck."

"Do you mind?" Miller said.

He passed her the phone. She studied the grainy image carefully, though she'd realized from the very first exactly what it was. When the text started coming in behind it, Miller quickly handed back the phone and tried to get up. Eli put his arm out to stop her.

"Whatever this is, it's nothing," he said. "And there are no secrets, remember?"

She removed his hand and walked back to the breakfast bar, holding on tightly to stay calm. There was the baseball game on the widescreen TV, but she couldn't focus on it. Eli spent several long minutes reading the text. Then suddenly he reached back and threw the phone across the room with so much force that the glass screen broke against the shelves with a loud crack. Miller jumped. Her hands were shaking

"That's breech and has to mean Caesarean," she said. "Soon."

"Sunday. Three days from now." Miller felt the cold reaching far down inside her. "But it's not mine. I told you what she's like."

"Everything I heard you say was about someone smart and sure of herself, someone who doesn't need to deal in deceit."

"She says she thought she could handle it on her own, but she can't."

"Who on God's earth would if they had any kind of choice?" Miller slowly removed herself from the breakfast bar. Walking carefully around it, she picked up her coat from one of the dining room chairs.

Eli heard the movement and turned. "What are you doing?" he said.

"Going home."

He was up off the couch and coming toward her. She held up her hand to stop him.

"This is you and me and we are home," he said.

"My real home, wherever that is." Her voice was flat.

"You can't."

"I can and I am." Coat on, she reached under the sink for a garbage bag.

"I know you," he said. "I know how fast you can bail. Don't do this to me."

"I need to get my things."

"Miller, Jesus fucking Christ, nobody even understands for sure what's going on."

"I understand. And in your heart, you understand. And you'll be there for her. That's you, Eli. Forget Rudy, you're as much of a stand-up guy as anyone I've ever known, caring, decent, honest, always, and even with everything that comes after, you won't hesitate, you'll do what's needed. And that's exactly the reason why I have to go, right now."

She went into the bedroom, opened drawers and shoved random clothing into the bag. He followed her into the bathroom, seemingly in a daze. At the sink, suddenly coherent, he reached around her and grabbed the bar of coconut soap. "You're not taking this," he said. "This is mine." The scent of her at least would stay with him forever.

She was done. "When you're ready, take anything you want from my place. I don't care what you do with the key."

"Too fast, it's all too fast. I can't even think." But when he went to touch her, she held up her hand again. "Sit down with me," he said, "I'll open a bottle of wine. We'll talk it out. Tomorrow maybe everything will be different."

"There won't be any bottle of wine," she said, "and no talking it out. That time's past, or it never was. Tomorrow, sometime early, you'll have to buy a new phone."

"I love you," he said. "Does that suddenly mean nothing?"

She closed her eyes, asking for strength. "Yes, nothing. How you feel about me, how I feel about you? None of that matters anymore." She had to make it hard, leave no hope. Otherwise she'd be his Lauren Metcalf and the thought made her sick.

"Just like that. No questions asked, no attempt to find out the truth?"

"I've been there and here's my truth. I want this so badly for you and I believe her. Maybe it isn't how you ever saw it happening, welcome to this new part of the world. Now we say goodbye and move on with our lives. That's the way it is."

"You don't even know where you're going."

"That doesn't feel like anything new. I'll find my way. And you already have your way. I wish you well with all my heart, with everything in me," she said. "You can't ever doubt that."

"Stop," Eli said. "If you say one more word, I swear I'll put my fist through one of these walls, just in case you were wondering how I'm feeling right about now."

Miller saw herself in this very same place, the surprises in life, when she found out about Sam, about Lauren Metcalf. When she stood in Janelle's office and had to ask for help. Something overtakes you, she thought, makes you numb so that you can still function in a world where you can't see or hear or feel. She covered her mouth with her hand, willing herself silent.

"Stay the night at least," he said. "One last night?"

And how hard would that be? She was aware that he already knew how hard. They could both see it.

"What am I supposed to do?" he said. "How will I know where you are, if you're okay, if you're safe?" His voice rose and now he was shouting. "*How will I fucking know?*" She couldn't bear the look on his face. She turned to the door.

"Wait," he said. "I'm asking one thing of you, one thing only, and I'll tell you what, you've got no goddamn choice, you have to do this for me."

She couldn't cry. If she did, she'd never stop. Sometime much later, she wouldn't feel the need to cry, she'd be glad for him. Now was another question. She dug her fingernails into her palms.

"Don't ever change your number," he said. "I'm not asking you, I'm telling you. And if telling you doesn't work, then I'm begging you. I won't come looking for you, but I have to know that if I did, I'd be able to find you. I have to know that even if you didn't pick up, you were still out there somewhere hearing me call."

She had to get out fast. Yes, she would do that. For him, but also for herself. Could such a small thing sustain someone? It would have to.

She opened the door and closed it behind her. He was where he belonged again, back with the blondes and the redheads, his whole life ahead of him. Thanksgiving came to mind, the tears, the promises, everything that was good. She hoped somehow he would have that, too.

The process in the house was simple in reverse, heedlessly dumping belongings into bags and suitcases. It took no time at all. The flutes and dessert plates, the DVDs, the sweaters and long underwear, the green worn out boots and metallic raincoat, all of that, leave it. The enormous shell collection, leave it. The falling apart notebook with his name on every page? Take it, she had to. In addition, she took the box with her grandfather's notes and that oldest book, the one with the dedication.

How far was the Trinity? Or the ocean view motel with no ocean view? She could get that far, she had all night. After the Trinity and the 5 and L.A., then there would be questions. But she didn't need to be asking any of them right now. She only needed to get away, *far away, an easy thousand miles away*, to some quiet private place where no one could see her cry. Then she would pull herself together. Again.

In the dark, with the car loaded, she knocked on the door. This was not a good idea, she kept telling herself. He was probably deep into his Jack, likely wouldn't even answer. But he did and stood frowning at her in the moonlight.

"What are you doing here?" he said. "Is everything all right?"

"No, it isn't. But it will be."

"Do you want to come in?" Luca said. She was grateful. He was himself, only looking concerned about this woman standing on his porch.

"No. I'm on my way out of here."

"How you're putting that, is it for good?"

"Yes, but it's different than you might think. Better. And I have to let the rest of it stay unsaid."

"Remember who you're talking to," he said.

"I wanted to give you this," she said. She held out her hand. "It's a key to the house."

"I don't want it."

"I know you don't, but I'm giving it to you anyway. Eli will be in there just for a little while in the next day or so, but after that it's yours for as long as it takes you to open that door."

"You're more like your mother than you know," he said.

"Lord, I hope not, but I'll be grateful to you forever that we talked, that I found out about you and how much she meant to you." And how much you must have meant to her, she thought.

"Enough," he said, stepping out onto the porch. "You're starting out now?"

"I have to. And don't be shocked if you pick up the phone someday and it's me."

"Call the bar," he said. "I don't have a phone."

Call the bar. How would she ever manage that? "Of course you don't have a phone," she said, and then she held onto him tight, the only other person, the only other connection to this place that had given her stillness, peace, and for that one precious moment in time, Eli Greer.

chapter 44

MILLER GOT OUT of the cab on a late fall afternoon in an unfamiliar part of downtown L.A. She wore good black jeans, black ankle boots, a scarf, a velvet coat, a better chopstick in her hair though it didn't matter. She didn't anticipate meeting anybody. This would be quick, hold her breath, in and out. Nervous? No, she told herself, just emotional, and how could she not be?

From the outside, the gallery was blank, a small discreetly placed name plaque, a door, that was all. Was it a secret? She realized she didn't know how these things worked at all. She gathered up her courage, opened the door and found herself in a reception room with no one around, desk empty. Only Talia Sherman's name crawled in digital turquoise along the wall. Talia had told her to come, had said it would be okay. She would have to rely on that information being true.

Miller hardly dared to imagine what she'd find. She'd seen a photograph of just that one piece and it was so spectacular she had to walk around, walk away and then go running for an hour before she could look at it again.

The hallway led through a circular maze to a large space at the back, imposing, all white. She congratulated herself on the accuracy of her instincts. She didn't know anything and she'd come totally unprepared. The new pieces were there, twelve of them, much larger than the first ones. Another difference, these had color, the hard cold blue of the winter ocean, and in each one, a segment done in black. They stood on pedestals, expertly installed and lit from above, silent, still, though she was aware of how mesmerizing each would be when set in motion.

Obviously, a crowd was expected. A set of white tables occupied the entrance, one of them in the process of being assembled as a bar, glassware and bottles set up, coolers open.

Miller glanced around. Though she could hear footsteps, voices, Talia had assured her only the staff would be there. The opening wasn't until six and for this small window of time she could have the place to herself. Suddenly, though, the two end walls came alive with ceiling-high videos. She was startled and then completely taken aback by the presentation. The far wall showed a huge close-up of one of the pieces slowly, beautifully, opening, turning, lifting, spinning, rotating, closing, then slowly opening again in an endless, hypnotic loop. The near wall, however, focused in on a workshop, a piece in progress, the forge, the heat, the bending metal, but most importantly, the artist in profile, wrapped in a heavy apron, his t-shirt stained in sweat, his gloved hands carefully constructing. Her nerve endings registered the sight of him.

A technician came out to inspect the screens. If he was concerned about their impact, Miller wanted to reassure him on that point. He looked in her direction, nodded, but that was all.

She meant to go through the wide space slowly, examining each piece on its own, feeling her way through his thought process, knowing how intricately he designed them before he ever began the actual creation. She was stopped cold right at the beginning, however. First by the price, which was astronomical. Second, and for this she truly had not been prepared at all, the title. He had called it Corinne I. She was afraid to look at the others, but required only Corinne II, III and IV to be certain. They were all Corinnes. What did the name she never used have to do with any of this, but especially those cold colors, the suggestion of endless, almost painful, solitude? Well, she considered, maybe everything.

The videos were still playing. If she turned, she would see him again. She was glad she'd come, it was all beyond her wildest expectations, but she was aware now that she should exit quickly. The bartender was at work behind her. She could hear the clink of glasses.

"Champagne?" a voice said, but it wasn't that bartender, it was the other one, the one whose image filled the room.

She closed her eyes. No. Talia had promised. She turned.

"Damn you," she said.

"I don't think that answers my question," he said, coming toward her. "Champagne?"

"No," she said. "I have to leave."

"There's this woman in my life who never stops saying that to me. Why is that?"

"Eli, they told me you wouldn't be here. That's the only way I would come."

"I shouldn't be here. I've been working hard for the last twenty-four hours to get this thing set up. I'm running on fumes. But I had the strongest feeling, the in-your-gut kind of thing that you shouldn't ever ignore. That's why I came back. And here you are."

"I'm stunned by everything," Miller said. "I'm speechless."

"Good, keep it that way for only a couple minutes and then we'll talk. But first, I want you to meet someone. I just never know where she is."

Not the redhead, she prayed silently, please don't do that to me.

Eli put his fingers in his mouth and produced the familiar piercing whistle. What came flying was a small child with short dark curls who never broke speed until he caught her up in his arms. Her dress, which had been a ruffled blue, was now streaked down the front with smears of what was possibly chocolate. Miller couldn't help herself. The tears tracked silently down her face.

Eli reached out to gently wipe them away and had a moment himself. He took a deep breath. "This is Sam," he said. "Now we have kids with the same name. It's actually Samantha, but that doesn't quite suit her, as is maybe evident." He held out one tiny hand and licked the chocolate off, causing a peal of giggly laughter. "Ack, I hate that stuff," he said and made a face, to more laughter. "We brought five changes of clothing just to get through tonight and she's destroyed three already." Miller wiped her face with her hands. She could hardly breathe. Here was what she had wanted for him, a beautiful child who was his exact likeness and whom he obviously loved beyond all reason.

Eli was still holding her with his eyes. "Thank you," he said, "for coming here. It means the world to me. Never mind about the rest of it. I just hoped with everything in me that one day you'd get to see her. Will you say something? Anything?"

Miller was spared from having to trust her voice by someone tousled and athletic-looking, close to Eli's age, who appeared out of nowhere and held out his arms for Sam.

"This is Jeremy," Eli said. "My better half. Miller, I'll only do this to you once. J, this is Corinne."

Jeremy's face softened with so much warm regard that Miller felt herself flush. But then she turned to Eli, the question in her eyes.

"Thanks for thinking that for even one minute, Miller. Makes a hero out of me."

Jeremy laughed. "I am, he's definitely not. Wouldn't have worked out anyway."

"Jeremy's Sam's nanny and the best thing that could possibly have happened to any of us. He got the job when he didn't turn and run in the first five minutes."

"It's been a hard day," Jeremy said. "But I think things just got better. Give her to me. We'll move on to dress number four."

"He loves her," Eli said, watching them leave. "And he's doing this for me because he knows about you. There's a bar right down the street. It's not like I have any idea what's going on in L.A., but I checked this one out yesterday. Please say you'll come and have a drink with me. We'll do champagne. Now it's a big night in more ways than one and you still haven't said anything."

"I thought I'd slip in unnoticed, see your work, be so incredibly glad for you, then go away again."

"Thank God that's not what happened. Just come with me. I promise it'll be okay."

"I can't," Miller said. "You have a wife and more than anybody, you understand how I feel about that."

"No wife. We're both absolutely committed to Sam, we love her, that's never going away. But we agreed in spades, the dearly-beloved-for-all-eternity part? Or even two days? Not for us, not in a million years. Can't do it. Wrong two people."

"Eli," she said. "I'm sorry."

"Trust me, I'm not."

They sat at a quiet table in the corner.

"You were there for everything, you made it, didn't you?" she said.

"I left right after you did, I couldn't stand being there without you. So yes, I was there and it was a mind-blowing experience, particularly with only three days' notice that your life is about to change forever. That was an interesting phone call trying to explain to my dad and Rebecca, a long silence on the other end of the line and then, more power to them, they just accepted it and went crazy."

Miller smiled at the thought. The champagne arrived and he poured for both of them. "And when you saw her," she said, "you knew."

"That, too. Monica got the test done anyway, but you were right about her, about it being true. You were right about everything. I'm sorry I was so angry. I'm sorry we had to part so badly. The whole thing about ripped my heart out, and this time it was for real. I know you always believed it would come to that, but you know what? I never did."

She lifted her glass. "Congratulations," she said. "You deserve all the good that's come to you."

"Thank you. You were the only thing missing. I can't tell you how much I needed to see you walk in that room. So where did you go? Really back home?"

"Two towns away, the whole mayor thing. And inland. Not a very big house but comfortable, on a couple acres of white-fenced pasture where a friend keeps her sweet old horse. Nobody rides him. She said I only had to talk to him so he doesn't get lonely. And six chickens."

"Sounds nice. Are you happy there?"

"It's peaceful. That's all I ask."

"So I don't need any updates on the gym."

"Please tell me you're not doing that again."

"I'd sort of worn out those old videos and then the universe smiled on me and just like that, someone put up new ones."

"They're promos. That's all they are."

"They're you. And Soul Cycling? What the hell is that?"

Miller looked at him, almost forgetting how much time had passed between them. "I'd give anything to have you in one of my classes. You'd love it, it's so intense."

"Careful what you wish for. Looks insane," he said, and then, "Permission to ask."

"Go ahead," she said. "You know you're going to anyway."

"Is there anyone in your life?"

"Same three people as always, my kids."

"So you're not engaged, married, seeing anyone?"

"No."

"Sleeping with anyone?"

"Eli, no."

"Were you?"

"Not that it matters, but, no. Not interested. At all. Change of subject. How do you work things out between the two of you?"

"We share a big old house with Sam in the middle, and Monica has an apartment in town for when she's got something going on. That's who she is, a great mom, Sam's everything to her, but for the rest of it, she wants her space and her freedom."

"Permission to ask," Miller said, hating herself.

"I've been waiting for you to. No, I don't sleep with anyone and since that's got to be the next question, not even with her. Especially not with her. She never takes that seriously, and she could tell anyway that something had happened. That I'd changed."

"Next subject," Miller said quickly. "This show's so huge, it can't be your first. Is it?"

"I had a small one in Portland with those pieces from the garage. They all sold, I got some press, a pretty big commission on top of it, and actually, before I could work up to calling Talia, she called me.

"Did I say thank you enough yet?" he said. "I owe you so much for everything. And you know, Miller, those conversations we had about God knows what, all over the map, you and me? Instead, I should have been asking you why they never sleep, and what gets the vomit smell out of a car seat, and how there can be so much shit that it oozes out of the diaper and down their legs and it's so disgusting that it's you vomiting in the car seat. Or that they don't eat the stuff that comes in those jars, and you can't have just one special animal you have to have seventy-five, and the bathtub crayons they say wash off, that's bullshit, no they don't. I've never appreciated you more than in the middle of the night when I was walking and rocking and singing and nothing helped and you did that for three kids almost at the same time and you're still sane."

Miller could only keep smiling. This was Eli. "You don't owe me anything," she said. "We're even in every way. Now I do have to leave."

"One more glass of champagne." He poured again. "Have you been back?" he said.

"Not yet. I know, I have to do that. And soon." She didn't even want to think about the way she'd left the house.

"Good," he said, "because I need my pants."

She stared at him. "Your pants? I thought you went and got everything. Didn't we talk about that?"

"Who knows what we talked about. It's all a bad dream to me. I only know I'm missing pants, sweats, my favorite Nikes, half my socks, actually, everything in that last load of laundry if it's still sitting there. And my Mucho Aloha t-shirt. That was what hurt the most."

"You had a million other things on your mind."

"That's the truth, but when I woke up from the shock with a six-week-old baby screaming at three in the morning, the first thing I thought was where the fuck is that t-shirt?"

"No, you didn't."

"No, I didn't. I thought something else entirely. Want to know?"

"No," she said quickly.

He kept his eyes on her. "I want to go out there with you when you go."

She waited. "It's almost eighteen months," she said. "That's a long time and we're both fine. Isn't that what anyone hopes for? You survive and you put it away. Like my mother did."

"I hate to tell you, but if you decide to come looking for me in forty years, don't expect too much."

"I won't expect anything. I'll be dead."

"Do you feel like we've had this conversation before? I do, and I know exactly where and when and why."

Miller wrapped the scarf around her neck and reached for her coat. "Eli, this is my fault and I apologize," she said. "Goodbye is still the only option. When you're ready, the right person will be out there waiting for you and nothing can be allowed to get in the way of that."

"And will the right person be waiting for you? The one who leans on your fence and says, hey, I like your horse...and your videos, and by the way, who's that guy who keeps texting you?"

"This is about you, not me," she said. "I've got an attitude these days where I torch anyone who even thinks about it."

"That's hopeful, keep going with that. But if we go with what you want, if saying goodbye is what has to be done, then we've got to do it right. That last time almost killed me." He pulled out his phone and scrolled through it. Then he held it up to her. "If you make me stay in a hotel, it'd be this one. That woman in my life? She recommends it and I do have some familiarity with the parking lot. But hold on." He scrolled to another photo.

"Eli," she said.

"Here. Way better. A condo in the high rise. We'd be on neutral ground, not your place or mine. I went through all of them and this one's the best, for the view alone, but everything else looks good, too."

"You've been thinking about this."

"Possibly now and then. Or twenty-four seven."

"This would be your idea of goodbye?"

"Off the charts. A spectacular goodbye."

"This is just crazy. And now I'm late and I really do have to leave."

"Let me signal the bartender. He can get you a cab. Where're you going?"

"To have dinner with Rudy."

"Who's still a stand-up guy?"

"Absolutely. While you get to be with all the fans of your incredible work and your beautiful twenty-foot-high self."

"Embarrassing," he said. "Not my idea, but not my call either. I'll tell you what, since I've found out what it means to have a kid, I've been afraid every day of everything, but I'm not afraid of this. Let me see your phone."

"Why?" she said. "Never mind, I know why."

"Do you? And you're giving it to me anyway? Pretty confident, woman."

She watched as he started to page rapidly back through a blur of photos, but suddenly pressed with his thumb to stop them.

He held up the phone to her. "You have pictures of the horse?"

"I have pictures of everything that means something to me."

"That just upped the ante."

He began scrolling again and then slowed till he found what he wanted. He looked at her.

"This is why I'm not afraid," he said, holding up the photo of himself that he'd sent to her at Christmas.

"I saved it for the cat."

"If I were to be completely honest, which you're not being, that cat's worthless." He studied the photo again. "The guy's pretty good-looking though. And I hear he's Boy Scout material, brave, clean, reverent, does the dishes, doesn't hog the blankets, shares the remote, has changed a million diapers. Come on, what's not to like?"

"Give me some time. I'll come up with something."

"You can't think of anything right now, though?"

"Unfortunately, I can't."

He took out his own phone and didn't have to page very far back before he held it up. She was standing on a beach in front of the dunes, wearing a baseball hat, grinning in the rain and holding up a green glass Japanese fishing float.

"I can't think of what's not to like here, either," he said. "Among so many other things, the way you left, no holds barred, take no prisoners, you did that for me so I would get to see my daughter being born. Do you think I'll ever forget that?" He glanced over his shoulder. "The bartender says the cab's waiting. I'm not going to touch you, or the cab would be waiting a whole lot longer. I'm only asking that you trust me. Give me your word that you'll let me know a date and a flight you'll be on and we can do this."

The beach, the wind and rain, the wild ocean, the birds, and this person in front of her.

Just for a while.

Just for one more brief moment in time.

"This is not what was supposed to happen," she said.

"It's us, Miller. The heat and joy and comfort and all those thousand other things? It doesn't just go away. We still have it. It's still right here."

There was no one to even talk to anymore. Janelle had gone from therapist to friend. Maybe she could call Luca at the bar.

It didn't matter.

"I give you my word."

"Will it be soon?"

"It'll have to be soon because I'm going to suffer all the way through till then wondering how I screwed up."

"You didn't screw up. You just forgot that it was me."

She didn't mean to laugh, except that it was a ridiculous statement. Who could forget? It was impossible. She hadn't even tried.

"Eli," she said.

"I know," he said, and smiled his smile that lit up the room.

Printed in Great Britain
by Amazon